RRAGP

D0286476

"Lover, cat
Dosha said i

Laughing, she was off and running, taking deep breaths of the cool, predawn air that filled her lungs. She did not look back and didn't stop until his strong arms swept her up from behind. He had caught her. They stood still for a moment, and then he slowly carried her down onto the soft, black sand and crisp green grass of the clearing just beyond the splashing waterfall.

With his face in her hair, Christian held her close and murmured, "Run away from me, will you?"

Dosha now lay breathless and motionless in his embrace.

"In a minute, I will make you pay for making me chase you, my little devil," Christian said as he kissed her lips. "I will make love to you until daylight and I'll never let you get away."

"Then I won't even try," she whispered.

FEB 1 2 2007

FRANCINE CRAFT

is the pen name of a Washington, D.C.–based writer who has enjoyed writing for many years. A native Mississippian, she has been a research assistant for a large psychological organization, an elementary school teacher, a business school instructor and a federal government legal secretary. Francine's hobbies include reading, photography and songwriting. She deeply cherishes time spent with her good friends.

FRANCINE
CRAFT
If Love Is Good to Me

KIMANI

If you purchased this book without a cover you should be aware that this book is stolen property. It was reported as "unsold and destroyed" to the publisher, and neither the author nor the publisher has received any payment for this "stripped book."

To God in all His glory, I want to give thanks for the talent He has given me and His splendid help and blessings in everything I undertake.

I wish to acknowledge the wonderful help I received from Charlie Kanno in putting this manuscript together.

To June M. Bennett who has been a wonderful friend and whose charm, grace, and loveliness enrich all those who are privileged to know her.

To Herschel and Marietta—ah, those lovely lovers.

KIMANI PRESS™

ISBN-13: 978-1-58314-783-2
ISBN-10: 1-58314-783-7

IF LOVE IS GOOD TO ME

Copyright © 2006 by Francine Craft

All rights reserved. The reproduction, transmission or utilization of this work in whole or in part in any form by any electronic, mechanical or other means, now known or hereafter invented, including xerography, photocopying and recording, or in any information storage or retrieval system, is forbidden without written permission. For permission please contact Kimani Press, Editorial Office, 233 Broadway, New York, NY 10279 U.S.A.

All characters in this book have no existence outside the imagination of the author and have no relation whatsoever to anyone bearing the same name or names. They are not even distantly inspired by any individual known or unknown to the author, and all incidents are pure invention. Any resemblance to actual persons, living or dead, is entirely coincidental.

® and TM are trademarks. Trademarks indicated with ® are registered in the United States Patent and Trademark Office, the Canadian Trade Marks Office and/or other countries.

www.kimanipress.com

Printed in U.S.A.

Dear Reader,

I fervently hope you will enjoy reading Dosha and Christian's story as much as I enjoyed researching and writing it. The sagas of the Brown Babies of World War II are some of the most fascinating in history. These are the children of Black-American G.I.s and European women, some of whom were interracial children themselves.

It has been such an inspiration to me to get your letters of praise, criticism and helpful suggestions. You've made my day more often than not, so I look forward to more letters from you all.

And please be sure to check out the contests that go with each book. You'll find the particulars of each contest on my Web site, www.francinecraft.com. Past contest winners have been very enthusiastic about the yummy and lovely prizes!

Francine Craft

Prologue

Dosha Steele glanced at her fiancé, Christian Montero, and smiled. Their glances locked as a small thrill shot through them both. Dosha felt her blood run very warm as he took her hand. His grandmother with her cap of white curly hair, half closed her eyes as she looked at them.

"Ah, watching you two takes me back to my marriage that led to my daughter, as hers led to Christian. But first the cards." She held up a deck of thin ivory Tarot cards.

"They're so beautiful!" Dosha exclaimed.

"A gift from my late husband, Isaac. They come from Egypt. They tell an intricate and wondrous story and their magic has been good to me. They hold hidden occult meanings. The cards have saved me and others much heartache."

The three of them sat at a table in Socorro's, his grandmother's, cozy apartment living room in Christian's large house. Dosha liked the sound of Christian rolling the r's in Socorro's name when he said it—So-ko-ro.

"Bring her luck, my lovelies," the older woman told the cards. "I'll tolerate no less." She shuffled the deck, then held it out to Dosha, saying, "Please shuffle."

Dosha took the cards and shuffled as excitement played through her. Christian had watched and listened to Socorro read fortunes all his life, but he was still entranced by the mystery and romance of a reading. In her long life Socorro had devised a unique system of reading the Tarot. She claimed visions filled her as she read. Socorro was seldom wrong and Christian was very proud of her.

Throughout their island of Puerto de la Cruz in Spain's Canary Island of Tenerife, people sought her as a *reader*, which was what an interpreter of the Tarot is called the world over.

Glancing at the deck, Socorro chose cards that reflected the presence of the woman before her and smiled. She carefully divided the cards into ten packs, with seven cards face down in each pack. She began by drawing a deep breath and they could feel her leaving them, going into the inner place that told her so much.

After a moment she smiled more deeply as she spread the first pack. "This is the beginning of wondrous happiness, the divine pack," she murmured and moved on to the second and third packs which showed splendid parenthood. At the fifth pack she looked up with a brilliant smile. "Success is for you both, but you must work hard and value it. Don't lose sight of your love for one another."

She didn't speak again until she had begun the sixth pack. "I'm not perfect. Don't expect me to be. I don't see clearly here. Only God is perfect. But this is the pack that foretells sacrifice and you need to know," she fretted.

With the seventh pack she closed her eyes. "At least one of you will live to be as old as my eighty-five and you will still know deep love."

She paused again, frowning. "And it's at times like this I don't like being a *cartamantica.*" She looked at Dosha. "That's the Spanish term for fortune tellers. Let's see, Christian, you're thirty-four and Dosha is thirty-four. Your life is there for you to enjoy, as you will, fully. And the cards certainly don't tell me that your way will be hard."

She raised her eyebrows then and drew a deep breath. There were three more packs, and why did she dread going into them? She was too anxious to bring only good news. Move on, she told herself as her hands trembled a little.

Three more packs. The next pack held the Major Arcana card called "The Hanged Man." Had the sign been positive, it would mean only self-sacrifice. But the sign was negative and Socorro knew that foretold treachery and catastrophes…and death.

As she read the eighth pack Socorro had a vision of carnage and destruction. Socorro envisioned dangerous roadways and threats to the female figure. Who or what threatened the woman Socorro could not tell. It was at times like this that she hated her calling. *Why tell me some,* she asked her spirits testily, *and not all? I need to know more.* But the spirits were silent.

Socorro held up her hand. "Wait. I'll try a regular deck. Sometimes they give me a truer prophecy." She took a deck of cards from the casing and shuffled them and passed them to Dosha.

Then she said, "Cut, please."

And Dosha cut, only to find the ace of spades staring up at her. *The death card.* They are only cards, she told herself. And the death card could mean death—or nothing.

Christian sat to Dosha's left and he saw the death card and flinched as he looked at her. Since she had known him, Dosha had studied cards a bit and was fascinated by them although she certainly didn't altogether believe in the magic foretold. They were all cards, she thought, and *only* cards, but she ran her tongue over her suddenly dry bottom lip.

Dosha faced Socorro, so couldn't see what Socorro saw when she went back to the Tarot and read, but she saw a quick, frightened expression cross the old woman's face and she wondered. "What is it?" she asked before she turned. Her eyes met Christian's and she saw dismay in them.

"You'll both need to be very careful," Socorro said. "I'll not make this less than it is. Happiness is yours. You love each other. Everything this earth can offer will be yours, but there is envy and malice around you, more than I dreamed, and there are those who will betray you and seek to destroy you.

"I'll read the cards again and again for you so you will know how close at hand these dangers are, or how far away. *The future is the child of the past and the future is now.* Live with God and be strong. God overcomes evil in one way or another—always."

Socorro passed a hand over her brow. "I must be tired and perhaps I'm losing my gift."

Christian shook his head. "No. You simply need some rest."

But Socorro continued to the tenth pack which went back to joy and happiness and she wondered if it meant they would sail through these stormy seas and land on shore triumphant. When the reading was finished, she gathered the Tarot cards and put them in the ivory case. When she looked up it was as if she had been away on a journey from them and had returned.

"I have something for you," she told Dosha, reaching across the table and taking the younger woman's hand. "It's a special wedding present. Isaac gave it to me on our wedding day. Take it with my love and be happy."

She took a flat package from the table drawer and handed

it to Dosha. The gift was wrapped in cream linen with a golden bow and golden bells. "Please open it now."

Very slowly Dosha undid the wrappings and opened the dark blue leather, cream satin-lined box. She gasped with delight at a large diamond-encrusted pearl pendant on a heavy gold herringbone chain. "It's exquisite!" Dosha exclaimed. "*Abuela*"—grandmother—"it's your pride and joy. Can you bear to part with it?"

"I can and I will. Isaac would want me to. He was a man who believed in love and he wanted the best for you. He would have loved Dosha as I do."

And Socorro was happy as she looked at her grandson and his bride-to-be. Dosha with her cloud of dark curly-kinky hair, silken nutmeg skin and her tall, narrow-shouldered, wide-hipped figure. Christian was her physical mate in every way with his olive skin so like his grandmother's. He was six foot two and fit, with his wide shoulders and narrow hips. She smiled now thinking that he had once set out to be a toreador until he was badly gored by an enraged bull. That had put an end to that dangerous dream.

Later, Christian had married Isabel. She had thrived on danger and edgy excitement. Socorro had not liked her at all. Now Christian would marry Dosha, and Socorro was happy as Christian was with the new woman in his life.

Christian glanced at his watch. "We need to leave," he said. "We're off to Tenerife and then to Washington, D.C."

Socorro nodded. "I always hate to see you go, but I do like your new job, Christian. So much better than bullfighting." She grinned and didn't give him a chance to respond. "So the wedding is July eighteen. You know my heart is with you, and your *padre*—father—will be there."

Then she said with half-closed eyes, "Send pictures, as many as you can. You know I'm quite good at my computer and I'll look forward to receiving them."

They stood up then and Christian hugged his grandmother, pressing her buttersoft medium height frame to him. She smelled of the expensive lavender perfume she favored. Her pale olive skin that reflected her Spanish, Gypsy, quarter-African heritage was blemish-free, with far fewer wrinkles than most women her age.

Dosha came to her and Socorro hugged her fiercely. "You replace the daughter I lost," she said, "Christian's mother, Magdalena. Be happy, *querida*—dearest one—and don't worry about the cards. They are often wrong."

But Socorro felt a cold finger of fear trace along her spine as she spoke. Then she said "Christian, you will be careful?"

"I'm always careful, *Abuela,*" Christian said lightly and hugged her again.

On the way to Tenerife Norte Airport in a taxi, Christian held Dosha's hand. "What do you make of the reading?" he asked. "I hope you're not spooked? They're only cards."

Dosha thought a moment. "I believe in the spirit world," she said slowly, "but not altogether. I'm sure there are simply people who see more than the rest of us. They feel, they divine and they're given special knowledge. But my cutting on the ace of spades—the death card—didn't frighten me. Well, maybe a little. We don't know what's around the corner for us. We can only pray and hope for the best."

He squeezed her hand tightly, laced her fingers through his. He loved her with all his heart and he would give his life to protect her. Like Dosha, Christian only believed in the Tarot and in fortune telling in a limited way, but he did believe in Socorro. She had the gift of sight and was revered and sought as a seer in all Tenerife and beyond. And many of her predictions came true.

She had warned Isabel, his first wife, to slow down, be careful, but Isabel had laughed at "the silly old woman who had nothing better to do with her time." Isabel and her unborn child had died in an automobile accident in a lonely ravine in the hills below El Teide. Fate had little to do with it. He had killed her. That much he had to live with. The pressure of his fingers increased on Dosha's fingers. He couldn't shake the knowledge that Soccoro was seldom wrong. The death card Socorro had turned up was a presence in the taxi with them and he couldn't help but be afraid.

Chapter 1

Minden, Maryland

Christian Montero let himself into the small, elegant apartment building in Minden, Maryland, where his fiancée, Dosha, lived. The building had only three stories and he walked up the stairs to her top floor corner apartment. Before he got to the very top of the stairs, he could hear his beloved playing Beethoven's "Moonlight Sonata" and he continued climbing. But he paused as he got to her door. She was nearing the end of the piece that was one of his favorites. She was good, he thought, and he let the music wash over him as she finished. He knocked softly.

And in a few seconds she was in his arms and he held her firm, lush body against his rock-hard frame and enjoyed the light fragrance of the Tahitian gardenia perfume she wore. For a few moments he nuzzled her neck.

"You smell good enough, you feel good enough and you look good enough for me to just swallow you whole. You had better speak up before I go ahead and do it."

She kissed the corner of his mouth and grinned. "I'll enjoy being a part of you."

He held her tightly. "I missed you this morning and you missed a good breakfast. I wanted to come over sooner but I didn't wake up."

"I don't wonder. You didn't leave here until one. It's a little after ten now."

"We have time..." He started to kiss her again, slowly, deeply and she shuddered with love and pleasure, her body relaxing against his until she felt liquid, totally compliant.

She pulled a little away. "Um-m-m, don't get your engine revved. We don't have that much time. Besides, you ought to be sated after last night."

"Are you?"

"Don't expect me to answer that. I'll only incriminate myself. Chris, if being engaged is this wonderful, what will our marriage be like?"

His index finger caressed her lips lightly. "Well, in a few days, we are going to find out. We have something special, my love, and everything in me tells me it will last forever."

Then she touched the narrow inch-long scar beside his right eye, kissed it a lingering kiss and he pulled her closer. "*Querida,*" he told her. "I cannot begin to tell you how much it moves me when you kiss my scars. All memory of pain leaves me and I am whole again."

He held her away from him and his eyes ravished her tall, lissome body. She wore a cream-colored silk sheath, lined and closely fitted with a boat neckline and cutouts along the three-quarter sleeves that showed off her silken skin.

"We're due at the college at eleven," she said, "and you'll give your wonderful speech about Puerto de la Cruz and being a Spanish Brown Baby descendant brought up there. Oh, Chris, the students are going to love this. I'm so glad I thought of it. Summer school gets boring for most of them. Make-up classes. It's hot and they'd rather be out having a good time."

"Like I'm having right now."

She laughed. "Don't kiss me again or we'll both be having a really good time."

"Like last night? That was heaven itself."

"And more."

"I listened to you play before I came in. I told you Ramon Muñoz wants you to work with me on the Arts and Culture project in the United States, Africa and Europe." He took her hand and frowned. "*Querida,* you are so great a pianist and you enjoy teaching so much. Can you bear to give it up? Are we asking too much of you?"

She shook her head. "No. I like the idea of reaching thousands where I reach far fewer now. It's something I want to try and I'm going to love working with you." She tweaked his nose. "My own personal banker. The love of my life."

Christian was a bank manager with Banc International, a worldwide bank that was focusing more and more on the "people" side of banking. He was being groomed for a top level management post. Looking at his tall form as he took off his suit jacket, she almost salivated at his well-formed biceps, abs and pecs.

He patted her slightly rounded stomach and his eyes were sultry. "In a few months, you will be mostly flat no more. I am going to throw my condoms off a cliff and we are going crazy with bone-melting lovemaking."

At times he could be so funny and so sexy. Then just as suddenly, his eyes would become shuttered and he would be light years away. She shook him lightly. "Honey, where do you go when you're away from me like this?"

He came back to himself and looked at her tenderly, but his expression was somber. "One day I will tell you," he said softly.

She drew up her shoulders. "We're still standing here and I haven't quite finished dressing. No lipstick. No eye makeup. I'm really naked without my makeup."

He half closed his eyes. "Not as naked as you're going to be if you don't get started. I don't want to let you go."

"Me, neither. I guess it's a good sign. Did you talk with Socorro this morning?"

"I did and she wants you to call her later. My grandmother said to assure you that it is only good news she has for you and that she forgot to give you a jade ring she wants you to have for luck. The old girl is really crazy about you."

"The feelings are mutual. Honey, I'm not going to wait to send her wedding pictures. I'm going to take my digital camera when we meet with Roland for a fitting of my wedding gown this morning. She's a woman and she'll enjoy seeing every stage of the process."

"You're so sweet."

"I'm glad you think so. That's surely the way I feel about you." She hesitated for a moment; she shouldn't have asked it, but she was going to. "Christian?"

"Yes, *querida?*"

"Does this wedding remind you of your wedding to Isabel? Does it make you feel sad?"

He thought a long moment and his eyes were far away again as he motioned her to a sofa. "Let us sit for a moment, love." As they sat close to each other, he took her hand in his. "There's no comparison."

"But you two were so in love. I heard about your love for each other all over Puerto. You were the ideal couple, people said. What a horrible end."

He nodded. "Life deals us hands we never expected, but

sometimes there are wonderful things we don't expect, either."

"I want to make it up to you," she said fiercely, but he seemed to listen to some distant drummer and she didn't call him back.

She got up, reluctant to leave him if he needed her, but he didn't seem to need her now. "I'll be back with you in a very little while," she told him.

He roused himself and smiled. "Do not let me have to come after you, then we will never get where we are going today."

She grinned. "But we are insatiable lately. We haven't always been this keyed up."

"We are anxious, eager to be married, afraid the gods are going to separate us and this I know I could not bear."

"I couldn't, either. I…"

She began to ask another question about Isabel, but he stopped her with a question of his own. "You had a deep love once and it hurt you. Do you think you have recovered?"

"Oh, yes, you've erased every other lover from my life."

"Do you think of *him* often?"

"No. I haven't seen him since he went to prison…." She hesitated then. "He got out just before I went to Puerto. I would've told you, but I didn't want to spoil what we were experiencing. He said he was sorry. Well, he damned well ought to be…"

He took her hand again. "Don't talk about it now if you don't want to. We all have our demons to exorcise. We'll help each other to do so."

"Yes. Sweetheart, I better go and finish getting ready. Make yourself comfortable. Fix yourself a drink, or I'll fix you one before I start. At the college Matt wants to meet you again and wish you well and the students want autographs before and after your talk. Oh, Chris, I'm so excited."

He grinned. "So am I, and it is not altogether about the talk today. I do not need a drink. I am a bee surrounded by honey. I feel like dipping in."

She threw back her head, laughing. "You're thirty-four and I'm thirty-four. We're not teenagers. Where's all this lust and passion coming from?"

"Love helps it along. I only know that around you I feel alive, intensely, feverishly alive. I'm at my best and my fervent wish is that I could live with you forever. I didn't feel that way before I met you." He gave her a quick squeeze. "Okay, leave me please before we are a tangle of bodies again."

She got up, still laughing. "Oh, we're a pair, all right. We *need* to be married. We should've married months ago."

"But you wanted a big wedding."

"Uh-uh, my *mother* wants a big wedding. I would've married you a week after we met, but I'm her only daughter and I like pleasing her when I can. She's in heaven."

"And you, my love?"

She was somber then. "Whenever I am with you, I'm in heaven, too."

In her bedroom Dosha couldn't stop smiling. Seated at her dressing table with the triple mirror, she thought love had done wonders for her. She had never considered herself a beautiful woman, but thanks to Christian, she was close to it now. Rispa had always somberly told her, "Don't expect looks to get you what you want, love." But now that she had Christian Dosha knew she was radiant.

She spread her makeup cape around her shoulders, put a towel across her lap. She had already thoroughly washed and creamed her face, now she began to expertly spread on her expensive makeup, using liquid blush foundation, a touch of finespun rose-tinged powder and green eye shadow. Then she brushed mascara onto her long, thick eyelashes. She loosened her springy, curly-kinky earth-brown hair and the healthy, elastic curls sprang free. Christian loved to play with her hair, bury his face in it.

As she worked, her mind went back to the first time she had met him. Marty had asked her to go with him to a friend's house to see one of Marty's best paintings and that painting had turned out to be the stunning portrait of Isabel, Christian's late wife. Dosha had stood with her brother, entranced at the genius of that painting. The spirit of the woman was there with them, her flesh rendered little less perfectly than Michelangelo's *David.* She had turned to compliment her brother and her eyes had locked with Christian's across the room.

She had stood rooted to the spot. Then he had moved toward them. He was ruggedly handsome, yes, but in a natural, unadorned way. He had a rough, masculine edge and he seemed to pose a hint of danger she was drawn to, was half afraid of and did not understand.

She had been faintly aware after a little while at Marty looking at the both of them, bemused before he introduced them. "This is Dosha," Marty had said. "I've told you about her. You've seen her photos."

And Christian's voice had been husky. "They don't do her justice. They do not capture her spirit." He had lifted her hand, kissed it, and that kiss had burned her flesh. Nothing she had ever felt compared with what she felt with Christian from the beginning.

He had asked her to drive with him to the hills below El Teide mountain and she had consented. He had invited Marty, too, but a smiling Marty had declined. So they had gone, had dinner in the early evening under a summer sky on the terrace of a quaint Spanish restaurant and their love had begun.

They had watched a waterfall sparkling by night lights and a full moon and she had been entranced. He had drawn her to him and kissed her throat very lightly. "You smell like the earth after a summer rain," he told her. "Fresh, full of flowers and sun. I'm glad I met you, Dosha, and I'm never going to let you go."

She had never been a bashful woman and she was forthcoming now. "I'm very drawn to you, too."

"You wear no rings. Are you free for me to stake my claim?"

"Yes."

"Then I'm going to court you. Will you let me?" Suddenly, he had sounded unsure of himself.

"Try me," was all she could say and she had moved closer and they were kissing deeply, their tongues exploring the hot hollows of their mouths and both were trembling with long held-back need and desire.

He had stopped abruptly, laughing ruefully. "I am going to take you home before I kidnap you like any pirate. With you, I am not altogether civilized, *querida.*"

Then he had suddenly changed the subject. "Have you never been married? Have you no children?"

"No to both questions."

"But you've been in love. You are a woman who has been loved and deeply. What happened?"

She thought a long moment. "Yes, I've been in love and it turned out badly. My husband-to-be cheated on me and then he went to prison." She did not want to continue. "One day I'll tell you about it, but not now."

"I'm sorry." He lifted her hand and kissed it, then again. "New love heals old pain if we let it."

Here we are, she had mused, talking about love, and we've only known each other a few hours. Could it happen like that? It could happen and it had happened to them just that way.

They had seen each other steadily during the two weeks

she had visited Marty in Puerto de la Cruz and in a month they had become engaged. In the following months Christian had visited her in Minden, Maryland as often as he could and she had gone back to Puerto.

And, ah, his family. Chief of the Homicide Division Rafael Montero fell in love with the woman his son had chosen and his grandmother, Socorro, the noted fortune teller, told her why. "You are incredibly like my son-in-law's wife and my grandson's mother and my daughter, Magdalena. Oh, marry Christian and you will have two slaves for life. They both love you so."

Dosha had laughed, her eyes sparkling. "I'm afraid I'm *his* slave. I love Captain Montero, too, and you know I love you. You're a wonderful family."

"And you will make a wonderful addition. The cards have long told me that you would come to us one day. That knowledge has soothed my spirits. Now you're here and welcome."

Dosha came out of her reverie, rotated her shoulders and her neck. Good thing she had worn no lipstick a few minutes ago when Christian had kissed her so ardently. They both had deep hungers that had gone unfilled for a long time.

She smiled faintly again as she remembered the feel of his lips on her skin and smoothed on cinnamon-coral lipstick with a brush, then the whole stick. There, she was done. She wondered why she had put her dress on before her makeup and it occurred to her that she wanted to show off her form and the dress to Christian while he had time to watch. Now she removed the cape and the towel.

Standing, she stepped into her tan leather, medium-heeled sandals and twirled while looking at herself in the triple mirror in the closet alcove.

In the living room, Christian sat on the sofa with his big hands between his knees. It was quiet with only the sounds of the electrical appliances and a grandfather clock's steady tick. That clock would go with them to their house in Puerto de la Cruz.

The quietness reminded him of the time when he had met Dosha and the wonder he had felt after years of heartbreak. It would help if he could talk about that heartbreak, but he couldn't. He had buried Isabel in his past and she would destroy him again if he ever resurrected her. Yet he ought to talk fully to Dosha about her. He needed to explain to her how much he loved her. She needed to know that she came first, would always come first.

Isabel had been his love, too, he thought bitterly. He had loved her with all the love his youthful, hell-bent-for-danger life could summon up. She had adored his dreams of being a bullfighter, had lured him on.

"Oh, yes," she had breathed. "I would adore being a matador's wife. You are young, handsome, virile and I'm beautiful. Together we could rule the world."

He had laughed. "Or at least Puerto, or maybe even Tenerife."

She had grown somber. "No. The *world, querido.* Or Europe anyway. No less will do."

With his father and his grandmother fearing for his safety, he had haunted Pamplona, Madrid, making friends with matadors and picadors. He sought out anyone who could help make him a bullfighter and worthy of rich, spoiled and beautiful Isabel. And it had almost worked.

In his first big bullfight, the bull had been crazy. Everyone had told him the bull was a bad hombre, had warned against the fight, begged him to take a tamer animal because he was so untried. But Isabel would be watching him in his first triumph and he meant to give her all his glory. They would go home that night and make love as it had never been made before.

But God and the bull had other plans and Isabel had seen him make an awkward thrust. The enraged bull went wild. He had gone down with the beast of hell clawing at his flesh. The pain he knew that day had been enough to last a lifetime and it seemed aeons before the picadors had been able to bring the bull under control. They had killed it. El Diablo, they called the bull when they talked about him after that. *The devil.*

Isabel had wanted him to keep fighting bulls, but he healed very slowly and he no longer had the heart for it.

And Socorro had raged when they told her about it. "They killed the bull," she had spat, "but they should have killed Isabel."

A couple of years later, he and Isabel had married while he was in college. He had graduated with honors and gone to work for Banc International. At first, Isabel had liked the glamour of that life, then complained that it was dull. She had cooled toward him then. She flirted openly with other men and Christian suspected that she had lovers. It was like a dagger in his heart. How could he love someone who hurt him so?

"There are reasons for divorce, my son," his father had sadly told him. "She's not the wife you need. She's sophisticated in ways that are not good. You're making a niche for yourself in banking and you like it. . . ."

"But my wife finds it an occupation for dullards."

"Your wife," his father had said slowly and had not said more.

In all there had been six years of heaven and hell. Throughout that time, their marriage had remained the toast of Puerto; the young, failed, heroic would-be matador and his beautiful, rich wife. Isabel grew clever at hiding her affairs and plunged herself into public service. She worked with children at the Puerto hospital, visited and gave gifts to the elderly and the poor. By then they had separate bedrooms at her request. "Our hours are so different and I'm up late."

It had not mattered by then and it was only a little while later before the whole mess blew up in their faces...

"Christian?"

He looked up quickly and took a deep breath. He was past that heartache now. But he wondered now if he really was.

His wonderful Dosha came to him. "Honey, I'm ready. Matt would like to talk with us a few minutes before your presentation, so we had better go now."

He stood up, his need to hold her overwhelming. "You look like someone I could hug and kiss for the rest of the day."

"In just a little while we'll be doing just that on our honeymoon," she said with a shy smile.

"We could just elope."

She laughed. "But your father's flying over and my twin would kill me. Not to mention my mother."

"Does my opinion matter?"

She touched his face. "You matter to me, my darling, more than anyone in this world. Always know that."

Chapter 2

Minden Community Junior College was one of the show-places of the County. A mile from town, it was nestled on two hundred acres of prime forested land not far from the rolling Chesapeake Bay.

As she turned her burgundy sedan into the big white archway, Dosha laid a hand on Christian's knee. "Nervous about your presentation?" she asked him.

"A little, but I'm looking forward to it."

Inside the building that housed the Music Department and the auditorium, Christian and Dosha went immediately to Matt Darby's office. A ruddy man with a leonine shock of blonde hair, Matt was head of the Music Department. In his office, he greeted them warmly as he and Dosha hugged and he shook Christian's hand.

"The students are really keyed up with anticipation about your presentation on Brown Babies, Chris. It's a subject I'm anxious to know more about, too," Matt said. He glanced at his watch. "Why don't we go on to the auditorium and get you set up?"

Settled onstage, Christian showed no signs of nervousness as he looked out on the earnest faces he would entertain and instruct today. Dosha sat onstage with him to hand him the extra materials he needed. Matt introduced Christian to the crowd.

With his audience seated and eagerly awaiting what he had to offer, Christian began his presentation.

The audience followed him closely as the slide show ran smoothly.

Once the slides were finished, Christian launched into his story of what being the descendant of a World War II Brown Baby was like in Puerto. He talked about Socorro, his part-African, part-Gypsy, part-Spanish grandmother and her American GI husband, Isaac, who had finally decided to settle in Puerto de la Cruz.

He talked lovingly and at fair length about his life growing up in Puerto, his family and his friends. And he told them that once he had trained to be a toreador. Dosha flinched at the remembered pain of his wounding. Then the floor was open for questions and he was flooded with them.

"Did you encounter a lot of prejudice growing up?" one lanky youth asked.

"Not really," Christian answered. "Some, of course, since it is the way of the world. But I had a tight-knit, loving family and believe me that takes away most of the pain."

A young man stood up. "My great-grandfather thinks he may have left a child in Germany, but he isn't sure. He tried to find out, but his love had left the town where he met her. Do you know how many Brown Babies there were in all Europe? And how many in Puerto?"

Christian thought a long moment and bit his bottom lip. "I only know there were thousands of Brown Babies left in Europe, many of whom migrated to Spain because of the liberal, cosmopolitan people there. In Puerto we were simply thought of as Spanish."

"Okay." A short, stocky youth with a scowl on his face was on his feet. "Look, sir, how many European countries and how many countries period let these children become citizens? And was the United States one of the ones that did let them become citizens?"

Again Chris thought a long moment. "There were only thirty-eight countries in the world that allowed these children to become citizens. The United States was one of them."

As the presentation ended a few minutes later, the students got to their feet, clapping and cheering in their appreciation.

Dosha turned to Chris, hugged him briefly and whispered, "You were wonderful, sweetheart."

At the reception that followed the presentation, Matt Darby greeted them. "Well, your man showed his mettle today," Matt said. "Lord, how I'm going to miss you this semester. But you *will* be back next semester?"

"I plan to. Chris has just been promoted, but it's not clear where he'll be stationed—in Europe, Puerto or in the United States. There's some talk that we'll alternate homes."

Just then Christian appeared at her side. It was time to go. As they took their leave through one of the side doors, they practically walked into Daryl Stoner.

Dosha gasped, reeling with shock at her former fiancé's appearance. Christian quickly steadied her. Daryl drew a harsh, deep breath and expelled it. "Dosha!" His voice was hoarse, ragged.

For a moment Dosha couldn't speak. He looked the same, she thought. Light brown skin, handsome features, curly black hair and hazel eyes. She summoned every ounce of calmness she could muster. "Hello, Daryl." *There.* She even sounded cool, but her heart was racing with remembered hurt and anger.

Daryl glanced at her hands and the gorgeous engagement ring on her finger. "Can we talk?" he asked her in a strained voice. And to Christian, "Will you excuse her?"

Dosha shook her head vehemently. "We've nothing to say to each other, Daryl. We were finished long ago."

She made a step forward, but Daryl threw up his hand. "No, please, I've got to tell you how sorry I am. God, I was such a fool. I had to be crazy." There were tears in his eyes as he told her, "I'll always love you. I had time to realize that in prison. I haven't tried to contact you because I didn't know what to say. I felt I couldn't stand it if you slammed the door in my face. But I was always coming back to you. I'm down on my knees. Baby, I'm so sorry for what I did to you."

Her voice still cool, she told him, "I'm sorry, too, but as you can see I've moved on and this is my fiancé, Christian Montero. Chris, Daryl Stoner. I think we have to be going now."

But Daryl hung on doggedly. "I saw your picture in the wedding column in the *Post.* Lord, you're still so beautiful." He licked dry lips. "I came today to pick up my nephew. You remember Alan."

She nodded.

"I was going to call and apologize, ask if we could be together again. We *belong* together, babe."

Ah, yes, she thought, that was Daryl, throwing away what he had with little thought and clinging to what he had lost. Christian glanced from one to the other and wondered if she wasn't at least still a little in love with this man. He knew her well enough to know that her cool exterior masked deeper feelings. He took her hand, squeezed it and she relaxed. "Goodbye, Daryl."

Hot tears sprang to Daryl Stoner's eyes.

"If you ever need me, or need anything from me, you've got it. I'll always love you," he whined.

It was a jilted lover's plea and she was horrified. He was acting as if Christian didn't exist and she turned to her fiancé. "Let's go, love. We're going to be late."

Her words seemed to bring Daryl back to his senses and he placed a hand on Christian's arm. "Man, I want you to know that you've got the world's best in a woman when you got Dosha. Treat her right or you'll hear from me."

Dosha felt the edge of hysterical laughter. What in hell did Daryl know about treating any woman right? He had written the book on "playing" women. Her eyes pleaded with Christian to take her away from this place and this man. Christian's fingers gripped her arm and he led her away, leaving Daryl standing there, looking after them with haunted eyes.

In the car Christian got a couple of tissues from the dashboard pocket and handed it to her. "Thanks, but I'm not going to cry," she said. He leaned over and kissed her face, caught her hand and held it.

"That was quite a surprise," he said mildly. Might as well ask it now, he thought, and yes, he was more than a little jealous. Stoner was a handsome man. Christian wondered if he was a good lover. "Are you still in love with him?"

She didn't hesitate. "You ask me that knowing how I feel about you? No, my darling, I'm *not* still in love with Daryl. I thought I was, a little, even after falling in love with you. Now I know the Daryl I thought I loved was always a dream, a mirage. He has no integrity and no honor and I don't think he ever will have what you have to spare. If you'll kiss me, I think I can show you who I love."

His mouth on hers was savage then, claiming her and Dosha felt waves of love and lust sweep her tender body. She wished they were somewhere else instead of in a public parking lot.

They tore apart after a few minutes. "We had better go,"

he said huskily, "before I lose my head, kidnap you and race with you to the nearest motel."

She laughed delightedly. "That's what I love about you. You're a wicked man."

"You think making love is wicked?"

"You know I don't, but losing our heads in public is a tad racy."

"Ah, turns you on, does it?"

Her face grew earnest then as she touched his face. "Everything about you turns me on, in every way. In the meantime, if we don't get on to Roland's and my fitting, we're going to have a wedding with the bride in an old, bedraggled gown."

"Why not naked?" he teased her. "That would give the guests a show. But then I could not take all those eyes seeing the nakedness that belongs to me. Dosha, how long will it take to show you how much I love you?"

"About as long as it takes me to show you the same."

He patted her knee. "Let us go, love. One more step on the road to being together forever."

But a slight chill struck him then. Why had he repeated almost the same words Isabel had told him just before their wedding? Damn the stifling guilt that took over his mind from time to time. But he was guilty and he knew it. He had offered heartfelt prayers to God to forgive him his sin against Isabel, no matter that she had betrayed him. She *had* left him alive. *And he had killed her.*

He started the car then and eased out of the parking lot. Dosha looked at his profile with a slight frown on her face. He had gone into his other world again.

The man sat behind the driver's wheel of his rented Mercedes Benz. A sly smile played across his face as he picked up the cell phone beside him. He was parked in a two-hour space and he hated having to pay for more time than he needed. He dialed and the phone rang several times before a woman's musical voice picked up.

"I'm not here. Please leave a message. And, Damien, if this is you, Chris and I are going to Roland's Bridal Salon for a fitting after his presentation. It's three blocks above the tunnel on Connecticut Avenue. Bye."

A native of Spain's Canary Islands, the man had visited D.C. several times and liked it. He knew Dosha was a teacher and he'd been able to get her telephone number from the phone book.

Smiling, the man cut off the phone. He consulted the map spread out on the seat beside him. The bridal salon should be just a few blocks over. He would park nearby and walk around until he saw them walk into Roland's. He would meet them as they came out of the dress shop.

He felt a little edgy. He needed to see Christian, but he wanted the meeting to seem coincidental. He picked up a dark straw slouch hat and pulled it over his ears. It would not do to have Christian recognize him, he thought.

He crossed his fingers because he was a superstitious man. He had learned from Christian's grandmother, Socorro, to trust his gut feelings. And his gut told him that the promotion he desperately wanted might be given to Christian. Hadn't Ramon Muñoz, the Banc International director, indicated he favored Christian for the job?

The man wanted this job more than he had ever wanted anything in his life, even Isabel, and he intended to have it. Muñoz had been impressed with both men, until Christian became engaged. Munõz liked stable family men.

All his life he had competed with Christian. He was pure Castilian Spanish and that ought to mean something. Christian was a damned half-breed, a *mestizo*. He laughed narrowly. A mongrel.

But Christian's new fiancée was lovely. She had class and she was gifted and the fact that she belonged to Christian whetted his appetite for her.

Lucky him, there was a park across from Roland's. The sun was surely hot and he saw that the little park held few people. He didn't relish the thought of sitting in that heat, but there was one medium-sized tree and his wide-brimmed hat would shade him.

It seemed to take a long time, but finally he saw Dosha and Christian come down the avenue and he tensed. They and Roland's salon were opposite him. How long would they stay inside? He hoped not too long, but he was prepared to wait. It would be worth it to see the look on Christian's face.

Chapter 3

"Ah, Dosha, and you, Señor, it's such a pleasure to see you both. Please come this way."

The dress designer who specialized in ball and wedding gowns and called himself simply Roland greeted them at his door. As they walked through the vestibule of the salon that was done in varying shades of cream and aquamarine, they were watched by a big, white angora cat who finally came and sniffed them both.

"She likes you," Roland told them, "and she is as finicky about her people as she is about her food. It's not for nothing that I call her Fancy." He bent and stroked the cat for a brief moment.

"She's an exquisite animal." Dosha made a mental note to talk with Christian about getting a cat when they settled.

"One of the best." Roland stood with one finger poised on his cheek as they entered the spacious room with two fitting rooms to the side. Small-boned, ebony-hued man with elegant features, he took clients by appointment only. A small woman came into the suite and Roland introduced her to his clients. "This is Helena and she will help me with your gown," he said.

"It will be a pleasure," the woman told them.

Roland stood with his chin in one hand. "I asked that you bring an object dear to you. Show it to me, let me study it for further inspiration and tell me a bit about it. Already seeing your beautiful engagement ring has brought me visions."

"I didn't forget," Dosha told him. "I've so many objects I've come to treasure in my life, but this is something newly given me by Christian's grandmother." Reaching into her handbag, she found the leather case, took it out and opened it.

She handed the pendant to Roland, who held it gingerly. "Oh, my dear, this *is* a treasure. It's priceless and I don't need much time to gauge its spirit. This pendant is romance personified, the very essence of it." He shook his head. "You are so fortunate to be close to someone who would give you such a gift."

Dosha told him then about Socorro and the brief history she knew of the pearl pendant and Roland closed his eyes. "It comes in to me now. Lines and angles I had not thought to put into the finishing touches of this gown. The basic design and sewing is done, of course, and it still works very well in my mind, but there are changes, small additions and deletions. You'll see how it all comes together and you'll be pleased, I promise you."

He seated them on a deep, curved dark aquamarine sofa with a carved rosewood coffee table in front of it. The fragrance of fresh cut flowers filled the room and symphony music played softly in the background. Roland brought out sketches, notepads, sewing odds and ends and placed them on the coffee table.

Dosha felt a surge of excitement run through her and she pressed Christian's hand. He winked at her slowly and she caught her breath. She always called it his *turn-on* wink and he teased her with it when she least expected it.

She touched his face. "You're a rascal and a roué," she told him, "and I love every ounce of you."

"I am going to remember that and give you much more of the same," he promised.

Roland clapped a hand to his head as he handed her back the pearl and watched as she returned it to the case and placed it inside her purse. "I'm remiss. I was so caught up in seeing your precious object that I forgot to mention that Jimmy is looking forward to seeing you. You're one of his favorite customers, Dosha, and he told me to be sure to tell you that he has the special seafood salad and cherry pie you like so much."

Dosha's stomach rumbled a bit. She had only sampled the food at the presentation and she was hungry again. She pressed Christian's knee. "Remember, love, when we went by last time you were here? *Jimmy's Corner?*"

Christian grinned. "How could I forget? He took the trouble to make paella in my honor, and it was delicious."

"You will want to see the gorgeous fabrics your fiancée has chosen, Señor," Roland said.

"Please call me Christian."

"Thank you, and I, of course, am simply Roland, always. It seems to fit me."

Dosha felt relaxed now, looking forward to a good lunch and being with Christian. Roland left to get the fabrics and Christian kissed her with his eyes. Half closing them, he let his gaze rove her body, knowing how much it turned her on. Christian delighted in knowing that she was his, all over, completely his. He felt a surge of virility so strong it startled him.

Roland came back with the silk satin and lace wedding gown. Christian blinked again at the beauty of the fabrics and the fine workmanship. He shook his head. "You really are fantastic. I know little about design or materials, but I know expertise when I see it. You do my fiancée full justice and I thank you."

Roland looked up abruptly. He loved love and lovers and the very essence of romance was in this room. And Dosha was a favorite client. He had made her wonderful gowns for her to wear at concerts since she was very young. She passed up designers in New York where she attended Juilliard and always came home to him for her formal wear.

The assistant came to escort Dosha to the changing area for her final fitting. As she slipped off her garments and the assistant unzipped the wedding gown down the back and Dosha stepped into it, she felt her world begin to change. In a few days she would be Mrs. Dosha Montero. *Señora Montero.* She got the pendant from her purse and the assistant helped her fasten it. And looked at herself in the triple full length mirrors.

"Such lovely jewelry," the assistant murmured and Dosha thanked her.

This gown was magic, she thought. Not quite finished, it bespoke its promise. Off the shoulder with wide straps over her shoulders, the exquisite ivory silk flattered her skin the way nothing else but silk ever did. She wanted Christian to see her, but he must not. A bridegroom never saw his bride in her wedding finery until they stood together to say their vows.

Dosha ran her tongue into the corners of her mouth. "You're as lovely as the jewel, Miss," the assistant said as Roland entered and leaned against the wall.

"Only you do me and my designs justice," Roland told her. "If you are ever rich, I'll sew only for you."

Dosha laughed then. He was such a treasure. "You have your wedding invitation," she told him, "and invitations for whoever you wish to bring."

"I have them in a safe place and I'll bring just one guest. And I thank you."

"And my two sisters-in-law? Are their dresses finished?"

"Of course, and they're pleased. Yours will be a wedding fashioned in heaven. I can't tell you how good it is to see a couple so full of love the way you two are. I'm afraid ours has become a world where love is expendable. There's time only for computers and making money and more money..." His voice trailed off and for a moment he looked sad.

She asked him then about taking pictures for Socorro and said she had brought her camera. He shook his head.

"I have a new, state-of-the-art digital camera. It'll be just the thing."

He posed her to his satisfaction, fretting over every detail. "If I were not a designer I would be a photographer."

In a very short while he had emailed the pictures to Dosha's web address.

She thanked him and kissed his cheek. His face flushed hot and he smiled widely.

Back with Christian, Dosha kept feeling the excitement that had begun when she entered this salon. She hardly thought of Daryl at all. Or did she?

When she sat down, Christian took her hand. "You're not still upset?"

"About Daryl? A little, but believe me, Chris, you take all the bad feelings away. You look at me and I feel blessed. I'm full of wonder that you love me and I love you," she said.

"That goes double for me," he said quietly and at that moment he was with her all the way. There seemed no part of him living in the past in a black hole she could not reach.

They were interrupted by a very cheerful Roland. "I've

got something I think you'll like," he told them. "At your wedding I'll have my own photographer take pictures of you. Let me show you the alcove where I hang full length photos of my wedding gowns. Come with me."

He led them to a large alcove and they saw ten full length photographs of women in all their wedding glory. There was already a space reserved for Dosha with her name in gold lettering above the space.

"Oh, these are wonderful!" Dosha breathed.

"Fascinating." Christian felt joy at the thought of claiming this woman for his own and this was merely one of the steps. His loins expanded at the thought of what they had and what was to come.

Roland thrummed with excitement. "I may be moving to a larger place next spring. I'll expand on this gallery and this fall the fashion editor for the Post has asked to do a feature article on me. I guess you could say I've arrived."

Dosha raised her eyebrows. "I would say you arrived a long time ago."

"Thank you. I wanted you to have these." He went out and came back with a bouquet of multicolored roses in a crystal vase. "I've filled it with only a little water. Roses for a rose. And I hope, Señor, you don't mind."

Christian just smiled.

In the parking lot, the man watched as Dosha and Christian left Roland's salon. He would not trail and confront them now. He would follow them to their car. He crossed the street and set out, keeping a few yards behind them. He had expected them to go to their car, but they paused in front of a restaurant on the corner—at a place called Jimmy's Corner, then went in. The man took off the wide-brimmed hat and mopped his brow with his handkerchief. It was still so hot and he could use a long, cool drink.

As Dosha and Christian entered, Jimmy, the owner, a portly man with a beaming face, came forward. "Oh, my goodness, you're here. Roland called and said you were there for a fitting and I told him to make sure you knew about the cherry pies. You've got to taste some and I'm sending one home with you to your mother.

"You look lovely, my dear, and, sir, you look happy to be with such a beauty. I met you when you were here a couple of times before. Welcome back."

The men shook hands. "You always prefer the table by the window. As you can see, it's free and if it were not, I would see that it soon was," Jimmy chortled with delight. "Those roses are beautiful."

Dosha thanked him and set the roses on the table. Seated, Christian brushed a leg against Dosha's and grinned. "Claiming you, like the jealous man I am."

Dosha shook her head. "You aren't jealous, not really. I like the way you handle yourself around other men. You're attentive and just competitive enough." She broke off and looked at him from under long eyelashes. "But then I'm prejudiced. I think you're perfect."

"And I return that compliment."

Jimmy brought the salad himself. Christian swore he still couldn't eat much more and he only wanted a piece of pie. They both glanced at the man standing near the door with his back to them and Christian frowned. Was that not...?

The man turned and started toward them. "Francisco!" they both said at once as he reached their table.

He bowed. "I would kiss your hand, señorita," he said gravely, "but then I would interfere with your meal and it looks so delicious. The señorita is beautiful today, like the roses."

Christian felt a slow burn begin in his abdomen as Francisco smiled narrowly. Christian assessed Francisco's pale, smooth skin, dark brown hair and blue eyes. As usual, Francisco was immaculately dressed. The man was vain about his Castilian blood and never so much so as around his mestizo cousin.

"Well, cousin," Francisco said. "Will you invite me to sit down? I've come a long way and I'm a bit tired."

Dosha looked from one man to the other. She had talked with Francisco only a few times and Christian always seemed a bit angry around him, but he was more so today.

"Sit, man," Christian ordered and Francisco pulled out and slid into a chair. *More like slithered,* Christian thought.

Jimmy came over. "Welcome, sir. Will you be ordering?"

Francisco looked at the salad Dosha was eating. "*Sí.* I would very much like a salad like the señorita is eating. It looks delicious."

"Ah, the seafood salad is especially good today. Maryland blue crabs and the jumbo shrimp. It's the best I've made in a month of Sundays. I'll get it for you immediately." He turned to Christian. "And you, sir, will you take your pie now or wait for the lady?"

Christian chose to wait. When Jimmy left, Dosha turned to Francisco. "How on earth do you happen to be at this particular spot?"

Francisco spread his hands. "Coincidence. You know I visit Washington often. A friend introduced me to Dupont Circle and we—as he put it—*roamed* the area endlessly. The proprietor doesn't remember me, but I've been in this very restaurant." He paused, smiling. He was lying. He had never been here before, although he had been in Dupont Circle, but they didn't have to know that.

"I was walking behind you because I was sitting in the park, resting, when I saw you come out of a shop. I hurried over. I knew that my cousin was in Washington with you, señorita. Yes, well, coincidences are—well, coincidences."

It sounded suspicious to Christian. Since they were boys his first cousin had proven himself to be the slimiest of creatures, notwithstanding his vaunted and bragged-about Castilian blood. His mother had been Christian's father's sister.

"And *why* are you here?" Christian asked bluntly.

Francisco mused on that question. "For so many reasons. If I'm lucky and I get the job, then I'll need to be familiar with this area, as you know. Ah, cousin, this new job would be a plum, would it not?"

Dosha perked up. The word *plum* used this way was American in its usage. Had Francisco been studying to become more Americanized?

Christian felt a slight pain in his belly. This man had slyly tormented him all his life. Now Ramon Muñoz, Vice President for Human Affairs of Banc International, was in the process of deciding between him and Francisco for the post of Cultural Affairs Director. Grimly, Christian thought that his cousin was totally unqualified for the post. Surely Ramon would see Francisco for what he was, slick, unctuous and underhanded.

Francisco turned to Dosha. "You're quiet, Dosha. And you look as beautiful as you always do when I have the good fortune to be in your company. Cousin, does she not remind you of my aunt and your mother, Magdalena?"

"You *know* she does." Christian took Dosha's hand. "That's one of many reasons I love her so."

He wished Francisco wouldn't call him cousin; his name was sufficient. He hated being reminded of their kinship.

Dosha smiled deeply. "And I can never tell just why I love you so, honey. I only know that I do, and completely." She squeezed Christian's hand and he squeezed back.

"She also reminds me a bit of Isabel."

Christian blanched, but he said nothing.

"How is that?" Dosha asked. She had seen the pictures of the incomparable Isabel and she wasn't anything like her.

Francisco shrugged. "I'm not sure just what I mean, but like her, you are entrancing, elegant and unforgettable. It's the greatest compliment I can pay you and I pay it gladly. I hope to get to know you better."

Somehow Dosha felt a bit uncomfortable at Francisco's flattery.

"Not too much better, I hope. You and I have never been the best of friends and I don't foresee that changing. I think it would be far better if we continue to go our separate ways."

Francisco shrugged again. "Unfortunately, that may not always be possible, cousin. Ramon has plans for us both at the bank and no matter which one of us gets the promotion, we both will be working there. It's a situation I look forward to, but then I've always been fonder of you than you are of me."

The lying rascal, Christian thought. And Isabel's face rose before him, telling him her secret, breaking his heart. For one brief moment it hurt the way it had hurt then, but under the table Dosha's leg pressed his and he looked into her eyes. He knew then that he could always turn to her for solace and perhaps one day his wounds would heal.

Jimmy watched them with fond eyes. The piped music played pop tunes and a few of the milder rhythm and blues. Dosha finished her salad and patted her mouth with her napkin.

"And the salad was...?" Jimmy asked.

"Incomparable, but that's as usual."

"Would you like to rest and talk a while before I bring the pie? And you, sir, how did you find my salad?"

Francisco leaned back. "It's as the señorita says, incomparable. I've been here before. Do you remember me?"

Jimmy thought a moment, then shook his head. "No, I don't and I mostly remember faces, but then I slip sometimes."

"But you will remember me and I'll come again."

"I will and please do come again. Now, may I bring you my also incomparable cherry pie?" He looked at Dosha. "Now I made your portion with the skimmed milk whip. I add a little cream and voilà, no one can tell the difference between it and whipped cream."

"Ah, you're a magician for sure. Should I ever get rich, you're my chef." Dosha's face crinkled with laughter.

Francisco wanted cherry pie, too, and Jimmy left to get the order. They were so engrossed in their conversation that the three at the table were not aware of Damien Steele's presence until he cleared his throat. The six foot, three-inch Damien usually bore a rakish, amused air and he took the world on his terms.

Dosha got up with a glad cry and went into her twin's arms for his bear hug and quick, warm kiss. He held her a moment before he let her go and went to Christian.

"Brother-in-law, how're you holding up? You can always back out, you know," he told Christian, grinning.

Dosha laughed. "It took me long enough to find a man like Christian, and I *won't* let him back out."

Damien chuckled. "You're forgetting your manners and, yes, I'll have a seat. I've eaten so I don't need to order, but..." He looked up to see Jimmy coming up with three pieces of pie on a tray. "Ah, I never met a piece of Jimmy's cherry pie I didn't like. Now, my good man, you're not going to shut me out?"

"Damien!" Jimmy's face was wreathed in smiles. "What has Nashville got that keeps you so tied up down there? We need to see you more. Married yet?"

Damien groaned. "Not you, too. The world needs single men and the more the merrier. Who's gonna take up the slack, make the unhappy women happy? Man, when I get married, it'll be on billboards from coast to coast. And how's Millie and how are your five crumbcrushers?"

Jimmy shook his head, smiling. "My Millie's fine and the five boys are raising hell as usual. One day they'll grow up and their Ma and I will have some peace."

He left to get Damien's pie and the others waited until he brought it back. Then they all dug in as Jimmy stood by, "Just waiting for the compliments."

And the compliments came unreservedly. The four people ate slowly, savoring the cherries with the vanilla bean flavor and creamy filling and the flaky, melt-in-your-mouth crust.

They made the dessert last a long time, then offered endless kudos.

Damien leaned back. "Hail to the king!" he said happily.

Jimmy left to wait on another table, calling back over his shoulder. "Now don't forget Rispa's pie."

"Got a surprise for you," Damien told his sister.

"I'm almost afraid to ask what it is."

Damien reached inside his summer jacket pocket and took out two sheets of folded paper. He spread the paper open and studied them. "I can't let you see it yet, but it's a wedding song that I'm working on. The music's really good and the words ain't bad. I call it 'If Love Is Good to Me.'"

Dosha looked at him with love spreading through her. "Oh, that's beautiful. Thank you. When can I hear it?"

"I'm going to play it for you tonight. What do you think, Chris?"

"Like Dosha, I think it's a wonderful thing to do."

Francisco spoke up. "Then you, too, are a musician, like the talented Dosha."

Damien nodded, wondering why he didn't like this man he had just met. Too oily. Eyes a bit too shifty.

Francisco realized he was being studied and it irked him. Putting on the charm, Francisco told Damien, "Christian didn't say it, but he and I are first cousins."

Damien noted that Christian didn't respond except to nod. There seemed to be at least some bad blood here.

"You're here for the wedding?" Damien asked.

Francisco cleared his throat, looked woebegone. "Actually, I don't have an invitation, but I'm full of hope."

Damien looked from his sister to Christian. What the hell was going on here?

"Are you inviting the man?" Damien asked bluntly, feeling like a bull in the proverbial china shop.

And Dosha looked at Christian, put her hand over his. "Honey, we have a few invitations left. He is your family."

But Christian would be damned if he would be more than civil; he wasn't about to be gracious. "Invite him if you wish," he said shortly.

Dosha reached down into her tote. "I brought a few invites with me in case I ran into people I had forgotten," she said. She scrawled Francisco's name on the envelope and on the invitation and handed it to him. "I'm assuming you are alone."

"Yes, I'm alone," Francisco said gravely, "and I thank you more than I can say. You *are* too kind." He looked at Christian. "I thank you both."

Dosha smiled, but Christian's look was grave. And Damien continued to study all three people and with his artist's imagination, conjuring up possibilities as to what the strains were that seemed to exist between the two cousins.

Chapter 4

"Damn, but my luck is holding these days," Francisco chortled as he sat in his car on a quiet, dark street in Dupont Circle with Juan, the nephew of Christian's house caretakers.

"God is with us this time," Juan agreed. "Is there anything more I can do to help?"

"You may be sure there will be more. And to think that Christian invited you to come with him as his valet, as if he were a gentleman."

"You really hate him," Juan mused.

Francisco grimaced. "I certainly do not *like* my cousin. It's just that I believe in the order of things. Some are born on a higher order and it should remain that way. Did you mail the package?"

"*Sí.* The first day I came."

"Very good. If all goes as I planned, my cousin will have a wedding-day surprise. And you, Juan, are lucky that you are earning such a tidy sum from me. Continue to do your work well, and if I get the promotion at the bank, there will be even more in it for you."

Francisco coughed a moment thinking he really ought to stop smoking because he planned to live a very long time. "Make sure no one sees us together. And remember, you are to watch carefully for anything that might interest me. You are to call me at the first signs of turmoil in that house."

Chapter 5

It was late afternoon at Rispa and Mel Steele's. The sun was sinking a bit and it was still hot, but a mild breeze had sprung up. Two giant oaks provided shade in the backyard that had been under preparation all year for the wedding. Massive flower beds had been planted with impatiens. Black dahlias, peonies and gladioli lined the edges of the yard and big stone pots of fern sat near the place where Dosha and Christian would take their vows.

As Dosha and Christian strolled through the garden, he put an arm around her shoulders, squeezing her gently.

"Getting cold feet?" he teased.

She grinned. "Nope, but I'm hoping that you won't change your mind and run away."

"*Querida,* that will never happen."

Dosha closed her eyes then and saw her siblings and herself as children playing in this backyard in summers when the house had not been as large. Her father was a master carpenter and a singer. He never tired of adding on to the big stone house they loved. And today they were all there, with spouses, children and the house was filled with the same happiness that had existed since her childhood.

Her brother Damien walked over to Dosha and Christian. "Bro," he said to Christian, "could I please borrow my twin for a few minutes? I want to instruct her on how to be a good wife to you."

Christian laughed delightedly. "I think she already knows, but of course you may. Please don't keep her too long."

Damien took his twin's arm and they walked a fair distance over to a grove of sycamores. A manmade lake lay just beyond the trees. He took out a handkerchief and spread it on a little hillock for her to sit on and he squatted. "You really love him, don't you?"

"I love him more than I thought I would ever love anyone again," she said.

"And I'm glad, really glad for you two. Chris is a great guy and you'll be good for one another. Daryl hurt you so. The lowlife bastard. I could've killed him."

Damien's voice was tight with memory of when he had been afraid for his sister and what she was suffering. "But life has a way of righting itself if we let it," he said now. "Let yourself go with Chris. Love him with all your heart because he's worth it."

"Damien, I always had doubts about Daryl, doubts I couldn't put my finger on and I ignored. I wanted to be married. There were warning dreams where he walked away from me and I cried. I told him about those dreams and he just laughed at me, but he never tried to reassure me. I told myself what I wanted to hear and I was in love. How could I not know he would betray me the way he did?"

Damien took her hand. "Look, babe, you're looking at a man who never married and probably never will. The woman

I loved wrote the book on betrayal. It happens, but it won't happen to me again."

She pressed his hand. "You can't let yourself still be so bitter, Damien. There are other women out there waiting for you, crying in their loneliness for you. Find one, or let one find *you.* Oh Damien, I want the best for you. I want love for you the way Chris and I have it now."

Damien laughed. She was getting to him and he didn't want to talk about it. He had loved and lost and it had hurt too much to try again. He told himself vehemently he wasn't going that route again anytime soon. He had pushed himself to become a player's player, not really by choice, but to survive his heartache.

They talked a little more about love and marriage and she listened quietly, wondering if he knew how bereft he sounded. Then they both got up and she kissed his cheek. They walked back to where Christian stood holding her brother Marty and Caitlin's twins, Malinda and Caleb Myles, one in each arm. They stroked his face and hugged his neck and called him "Uncle Chris."

Chris grinned at Dosha. "They set me dreaming," he told Dosha. He turned to Damien. "You've instructed her on how to keep me happy?"

"I gave her my best advice on the care and feeding of a husband."

Christian smiled. "I have *her.* That is all I need."

Marty's baritone voice came from behind Chris as he faced his brother. "And how in hell would *you* know? You're a man who runs from commitment like a thief in the night. You say you like fine women and we've introduced you to some great ones, but you always run like the coward you are."

Dosha saw the pain on Damien's face and her heart went out to him. She reached out and patted his shoulder. "All in good time," she said softly.

Caitlin frowned as her twins waved at her. "Sweetheart, please," she said to Marty. "Don't tease him. We all do the things we will at the time we will. *We* were lucky. Remember that."

Adam Steele came up then to join his siblings and sister-in-law. He had lingered on the edges of the conversation, listening with his detective's ear. "And, yeah, we have to remember that sometimes we make our own luck. We've all been hurt, man, but we move on...."

And as his voice drifted off, Caitlin remembered her love for her late husband Sylvan and how she had fought loving Marty. Now she was happy with him and her twins. Before Marty she would never have imagined the joyful depth of the life she now knew. And Marty had brought it all about. She felt her heart expand with love and wished they could help Damien find someone.

Mel and Rispa and Adam's wife, Raven, joined them. Damien always flirted with Raven and she took it good-naturedly.

Now Damien bent and took Raven's hand, kissed it. "Now grow me a woman like Raven and I'll bite," he said.

And Adam growled, "Yeah, Bro, you may be a player, but you've played your last hand if you ever try to mess with *my* wife. I'll put a hurting on you that will make you wish you *could* die in prison."

Damien grinned and raised his eyebrows. "Some women are worth dying for."

Adam shook his head. He wasn't altogether comfortable with Damien when he got in this mood. Now he took Raven's hand, kissed it. "Where's the baby?" Adam asked his wife.

She smiled softly at him. "Dead asleep, I'm afraid. She had worn herself out."

Rispa went close to her husband. She and Mel had matching bright silver hair and slim bodies. Even though they had been together for years, anyone could tell that he still made her heart race when he gave her that special look. They still loved each other.

Chris looked around him. His father would arrive in the States that night and the wedding would take place the next day. Excitement climbed in his loins. One more day and Dosha would be his forever.

"I'm really looking forward to meeting your dad," Adam said to Chris. "It will be nice to have another policeman in the family. How long will he be here?"

"Just three days," Christian said. "We'll be back in Puerto before he gets back."

Damien grinned. "On your *hon-ey-moon.* Hm-m-m."

"You'll never grow up." Dosha shook a finger at him, but she felt a hard thrill go through her.

"It was good enough for Peter Pan. And, oh, yes, Sis and Chris, you know that song I promised you and had to keep working on it? Well, I've got it ready and when we go in, after dinner, I'll sing it to you. I've got a new Zemaitis guitar and the sound of it's going to fill your very soul."

"The guy from London who made the fabulous guitars?" Dosha asked.

"You've heard of him?"

"Yes. When I was in Puerto, a guitarist played in Charcot del Plaza and he told us about the wonderful instrument he played, and the man who made them by hand, Tony Zemaitis."

"I wish I could have heard him play." Damien looked wistful.

Then he turned to his niece and nephew who were standing on either side of Chris, playing peekaboo.

"Last year you guys were in the middle of your terrible two's," Damien told the children. "You wore out the word 'No.' What are you saying these days?"

The twins stopped stock still and stared at him. Malinda turned and buried her face in Chris's pants leg, but Caleb Myles shouted at him, "Yes!"

The little boy thrummed with nearly violent energy and Damien shook his head as he told his brother Marty, "Lord, give you strength, because with this hombre, you're gonna need it."

Later, the family gathered at the pool to relax. Rispa and Caitlin decided not to go in, but the men, Dosha and Raven were all eager for a cooling dip. And the twins were nearly hysterical with joy. They both loved the pool and they looked darling—Malinda in a little white ruffle-skirted suit and Caleb Myles in red trunks. Rispa opened the gate to the pool that had been kept locked once the twins became old enough to get around.

Caitlin lined her brothers-in-law, Dosha and Chris and the kids up for a quick photo. "My, my. I haven't seen so much beefcake since I was in charge of buying the meat for the church picnic last month. We really ought to start selling beefcake calendars. The church could use the money," Rispa said, eyeing the group with her hands on her hips.

She gave a special glance to Mel who was still in good shape as a result of regular exercise, healthy food and Rispa's ardent love.

Mel looked at his family and blushed to think that in this time and in this place and with these people he had it all.

Christian and Dosha had eyes only for each other. In her black two-piece she looked fabulous to him. His eyes went to her hips and he half closed them thinking of the child those hips would bear from his seed and to the tender, full breasts that would nourish that child. For a moment wildfire raced along his veins and he could barely get his breath.

Christian wore black trunks and Dosha felt her libido

surge just looking at him. She smiled as if she knew exactly what he was thinking. Her honeymoon couldn't come soon enough for her. His body thrilled her the way it always did, but the love with which his glance swept over her thrilled her even more. He was so dear and as they sat on the edge of the pool, a bit away from the others, their feet dangling in the water, she turned and smiled at him. He caught her hand, squeezed it and they were silent and happy.

Marty helped Malinda who was becoming fairly adept at treading water and Adam helped Caleb Myles. After a few minutes, he called to the boy's father, "Hey, this kid will soon be better than I am. Talk about a natural. But then, Marty, you were always the best swimmer in the family."

The pool and the atmosphere rang with merry voices when Adam's tall, thin teenage son, Ricky, and Merla, Raven's nine-year-old daughter, came out in their swimming gear and slipped into the pool.

"Glad you got here. What took you so long?" Adam asked Ricky.

"Mrs. Reuben couldn't give us a lift right away." Mrs. Reuben was their housekeeper. "Hey, Dad, race me."

"Okay, but I hate to see a young boy cry."

The others moved to the side as the boy and his father began at one end of the large pool. They were both expert swimmers and they plowed through the water effortlessly. By the end of the first lap, Adam was ahead. "Well, Turk," he teased his son. "I thought you said you had been practicing at school."

Ricky ducked and came up with water streaming down his face. "It ain't over 'til it's over," he teased back, shaking some of the water off.

The agreement was that they would do four laps and by the end of the third lap, Ricky was pulling harder and felt more certain of himself. Adam could have burst with pride at the prowess of his gangling son. His lessons had borne fruit, and the boy was in fine shape. In the fourth lap it happened. Ricky soon pulled ahead and stayed ahead until the end of the race. As his father finished, Ricky let out a victorious warrior's yell.

Rispa and Raven cheered from the sidelines and the bathers laughed and slapped Ricky on the back. "You really aced that one, kid," Marty complimented his nephew. "Your old man will never be the same."

Ricky looked sideways as he stood near his father at the shallow end of the pool. "Dad, I dunno," he said sadly. "I dunno if I *want* to beat you—at anything."

Adam took his son in his arms. "It's the way of nature," he told him. "Out with the old, in with the new. You were born to beat me one day. When that day comes, you'll leave my house and be your own man." And Adam felt his heart grow just a bit sad because his little boy was fast growing up and sooner than he had expected. Was any father ever ready when it happened? he wondered.

Merla swam to her brother and hugged him fiercely. "You were so good," she told him. "Congratulations." Then ever the diplomat, she turned to Adam. "You were very good, too, Dad. You'll probably beat him next time."

Adam hugged his daughter, smoothed her hair. "It's all right, love," he assured her. "Your old man doesn't mind losing to someone he loves."

Raven swam alongside Christian and Dosha. "The pond is beautiful today," she told them. "You should walk Christian down to the pond. It's gorgeous by moonlight. Last week Adam and I walked down there and it seemed like Eden," she said to Dosha.

Christian laughed. "If we go down there, we may not come back. This whole place is so beautiful. You all have a standing invitation to visit us in Puerto."

"And I for one intend to honor that. As for coming back..."

They went inside and changed, but the merry mood did not. The sun had set and it was cooler. Rain had been forecast but it had not come. The family sprawled over the living room and the parlor, both rooms done in dark and light plum with white woodwork. Big, deep sofas sat in both rooms and the carpeting was plush dark plum. It was a place to dream in, Christian thought.

Dinner was simple. Crisp fried catfish, potato salad, green beans with slivered almonds, Mel's beloved baked beans, zucchini squash and a big crystal bowl filled with lush varieties of crisp lettuce, tomatoes, cucumbers and other fruits of the garden. Black and pimento-filled olives. Christian thought food had never tasted so good and he smiled with pleasure at the thought that Dosha's mother had cared enough to serve his country's dishes.

Roy stood about and waited for Sarah, his wife, to come in. "My little honey of a wife is lost."

Sarah came in as he spoke. "Now nobody is going to mistake me for little."

The family smiled as Roy looked at his wife's ample form fondly. "Lord, how I love your big body. Don't lose a pound."

"Sit down, you two, and join us," Mel ordered. "Take a load off your feet and enjoy this delicious meal you've prepared. Roy, we outdid ourselves this season with the tomatoes. And every restaurant owner in D.C. would kill for lettuce like this."

"Not to mention the cucumbers and the squash," Marty added.

The couple sat down and Sarah told them, "You're really going to brag when you taste the strawberry ice cream Roy made. And I did the lemon pound cake. You said you like that kind of cake, Christian."

"Thank you," Christian said, giving her his best smile. "I've enjoyed every mouthful I've eaten tonight."

"Gramps," Ricky said, "your baked beans taste better every time I eat them, but I've got a complaint."

"What is that?" Mel fixed a loving glance on his grandson.

"You don't do them often enough."

Mel smiled. "Thank you."

"You promised to teach me to bake beans when I'm eighteen," Ricky reminded his grandfather.

Mel nodded, smiling. "Oh, I'll be certain to do that."

Adam's eyes met Ricky's and he laughed. "No chance of you letting him forget."

Christian thought of the twins sleeping in their cribs in one of the bedrooms and he dreamed again of the children he and Dosha would have. And the look that passed between them was lost on no one.

After dinner everyone sat around the dinner table listening to crickets and other night sounds. The two old hound dogs, Red and Blue, had been hunting with a neighbor all day. Now, fed and happy, they lay near the back door waiting for Mel to tell them good-night. Finally, Damien announced that he was ready to entertain them.

"Oh, lovely," Rispa said. "I'll help Minnie load the dishwasher and we'll all be in."

Damien and the others trooped into the living room and Damien got his guitar out of the hall closet, brought it back with a flourish. "I won't open this baby until Mom and Sarah get here," he declared.

They all took seats and waited with eager anticipation until the two women came in and sat down. Dosha sat on a loveseat in the curve of Christian's arm and wondered at the happiness that filled her.

Damien took the guitar out of its black leather sack with

autographs of famous guitarists and they all gasped at the beauty of the instrument. "It's a 'pearly,'" he explained. "That's in-the-know jargon for pearl-front. The poor guy couldn't keep up with the demand. Everybody wanted a Zemaitis, and not everybody got one. I was lucky. I got mine from a friend of his and even so, I paid plenty, but it's worth it." He struck a few chords and Dosha was electrified by the purity and the depth of sound from the guitar. She had seldom heard anything like it and she glanced at Christian who had tensed with pleasure and squeezed her shoulder.

Damien got a high stool from the wet bar, sat and played his new tune through for them, delighting in the look of rapture on their faces. Mel was a consummate musician and he thought he had never heard such music. Whatever Damien had paid—mild chills raced along his spine and the sound of the splendid guitar brought back his youth when he and his children had traveled America and Europe as The Singing Steeles.

At the end of the song, Damien stopped playing and announced. "To my beloved twin sister, Dosha, and her—well, it's so close I can just say her husband, Christian. This is my musical toast to their love. No two people deserve happiness more. 'If Love Is Good to Me.' And I predict that love *will* be good to them."

In a very good baritone he began.

Stars flung across a midnight sky
You in my arms, full moon on high.
You by my side our whole life through;
Each day as old dreams become the new.

All this and ecstasy,
IF LOVE IS GOOD TO ME!

Come, let us walk along the shore,
Like the sea, we'll last forevermore.
Each tender look becomes a thrill.
I need you now; I always will.

All this and ecstasy,
IF LOVE IS GOOD TO ME!

I know all life's a mystery,
I know how dear you are to me.
I offer you a heart that's true.
In all this world, my best to you.

All this and ecstasy,
IF LOVE IS GOOD TO ME!

Christian thought the music was like the best champagne. When Damien had finished, the room was still, then Marty sang out, "Encore, Bro. Encore!" And the others took up the cry.

Smiling broadly, pleased at the response, Damien looked at the engaged couple and his heart warmed at the pleasure mirrored on their faces. Being single had been great as long as his twin was single, too. Now he, alone of the Steele children, was unmarried. He shrugged. Thank God, it was now a world where many didn't marry. Ruthlessly he crushed the desire to meld with someone else; it simply wasn't for him.

This time Damien played the song in a slower tempo, letting the richness of the melody wash over him and the group. Damn, he thought, he had really done himself proud. And it came not of his own volition, seeping into his brain and clinging there—"All this and ecstasy, If love is good to me."

Damien bowed his head when he finished. At first they were all silent, then Ricky broke the ice. "Unk, that's one of your great ones."

"Bee-yoo-ti-ful!" Merla enthused. "Thank you, Uncle Damien." She went to her uncle, hugged and kissed him, touched his guitar.

"That guitar is so fine it talks to me," Ricky told him.

The family clustered around him with congratulations. Dosha pulled him to his feet and gave him a fervent hug. "You're the world's best twin," she told him and there were tears in her eyes.

"You ain't seen nothing yet. I've made you a CD with only me singing as I play this beauty. And there's another recording with full orchestra—violins, the works," he said.

"Oh, Damien," Dosha breathed. "How can we thank you?"

Damien turned to Christian. "You had better make her happy, Chris. I won't stand for anything less. You hurt her and you're dead meat." He grinned. "But then, Sis, you had better be good to him, too. Chris is the best."

They were seated again and Damien was going to play as they sang the Golden Oldies. Dosha looked at her watch. "We're going to walk down to the pond and hope the rain doesn't catch us."

Sarah raised her eyebrows. "Oh, I sneaked a peek outside before we came in here and it's clearing a bit, but it still smells damp. Ought to be a great night for a walk. That's one big, fat moon favoring us tonight."

Christian and Dosha went out the back door and walked slowly down the wide wagon path to the pond. It did smell damp, Dosha thought, fresh, inviting. There were not enough numbers in the world to count the stars that blanketed the heavens, Dosha thought. *And, oh, that moon!* She turned to

Christian. "Ever wish you could live in the sky for a while and enjoy all that glory closeup?"

"If I could take you to live with me." They walked on.

The three-and-a-half acre catfish pond glittered in the moonlight. Even at night catfish leapt. And the full moon reflected the beauty of the multicolored water lilies that grew on the edges. There were hyacinths on one small section just outside the pond and a quartet of swans, three white and one black, nestled in a corner near the stately flowers.

Two canoes sat just at the edge of the pond with the grove of sycamores several yards away to the left of them. As they stood there, she asked him, "Would you like to take a canoe out?"

"Maybe a bit later. In a minute, I want to indulge myself with something I've been aching to do all day."

She came close to him. "And that would be?"

"As if you didn't know." He pulled her to him and his mouth went to the hollows of her throat, nuzzling. He licked her lightly and she shivered. With a slightly hoarse voice, she told him, "I've been thinking. Let's deprive ourselves of lovemaking until the honeymoon. That way we'll be *starving* for each other."

"Anything you want, love. I can wait until our honeymoon. But, *querida,* once we are married I will never be able to get enough of you. Perhaps after we have a few babies and we are both tired, but even then..." Dosha felt a thrill go through her as she listened to him.

"Let's walk to the sycamores," he told her. "We can watch the pond from there."

And at the nearest pale-barked sycamore tree he smiled and took her in his arms. "I do not want bugs to bite you."

She shook her head. "Dad sprays the trees so there aren't many. No bugs. What do you want to do?"

"Just this." He pressed her against the tree, his arms encircling her so that she felt imprisoned in his embrace and her knees went weak. The taste of the strawberry ice cream was still in their mouths as he kissed her so deeply she nearly fainted with excitement. They were never going to be able to wait for him to be inside her, she thought.

His big hands roamed her body, eliciting moans of desire from her. This wasn't the right time to make love, Dosha thought.

But Christian held her close and pressed his shaft swelling against her softer body. His back was to the moon, but he didn't need it. She was his moon and his stars and his mouth on hers was merciless with desire. Their tongues slowly and feverishly tangled and teased. He wanted to reach beneath her clothes and put his hand on her secret place, feel the intense heat of her wanting him, but there wasn't time for what would surely follow and he wasn't a man who liked to hurry.

He stroked her sides and put his face in her soft, sweet-smelling hair. And her light jasmine perfume blended with the night smells of flowers, summer trees and coming rain. Her face in the moonlight was entrancing. She was his dream as he was hers.

She let her fingers slide over the rippling muscles of his arms and across his back as an owl hooted in the next tree. One lonely night bird sang a mournful song and she felt herself drowning in the glory of his passion and his love.

"You are so beautiful," he told her.

"No. It's just that you love me." She placed her index finger beside his mouth and he turned and took the finger into his mouth, sucked on it. "Go ahead," she murmured. "Burn me up. Then you'll have ashes for a wife."

He shook his head. "In you I have a flame. I love you, *querida.* I will always love you. I know now I have waited all my life for you."

She wondered about Isabel then the way that Christian had felt for his first wife. She wanted to ask Christian about Isabel, but couldn't. Instead, she lost herself in the kisses that he rained onto her face and in the fierceness of his tongue as it seemed to devour her.

"Honey," she finally managed to break free and tell him. "We're going to have to go back before I can't walk back."

"I'll carry you."

"You may have to."

Reluctantly they turned and walked slowly back to the house. Then he pressed her against the stone exterior of the house and kissed her again, imagining the syrupy wetness of her and he knew he would need lots of coffee to last the rest of the evening. But even more, he needed her.

Chapter 6

On the way to Dosha's apartment, Marty, Dosha and Christian were merry, full of the camaraderie they had just shared with the Steele family. "I want you to get to the airport in plenty of time to meet Captain Montero," Dosha said to Christian, "so don't see me in. I'll be fine."

She sat between the two men and Christian took her hand. "No, *querida.* We will get there in plenty of time. I will see you to your door." And he grinned at her, thinking he needed another kiss. The last one had left him in a bad way and he groaned inwardly. He could never quite believe the passion he had for this woman.

They pulled up at Dosha's apartment building and Marty waited as the two went in. Going through the lobby, the desk clerk stopped them.

"Ms. Steele, you have a special delivery package." The older woman smiled at the couple. She often talked with

Dosha about the families of both and was delighted at the coming marriage.

The woman reached under the counter and got a large, flat package. It was the size a painting would be and Dosha wondered if it was a wedding gift. They examined the package and it seemed safe enough to open. Letter bomb packages were a fact of life nowadays, but this one was neatly wrapped in heavy white paper, had a proper return address with all lettering done in bold, clear type.

Christian took the package and they went to Dosha's apartment. He insisted on going inside where he put the package on a living room table and took her in his arms.

She laughed a bit, but she clung to him. "I knew there was a method to your madness in bringing me in. You get one kiss and no more, señor."

"*Two* short ones?"

"With you, there is no such thing as a short kiss. One." He held her hard against him and his mouth ravaged her. "Honey, you're going to leave me steaming. Be kind," she begged.

"Why? You were not kind to me by the pond. Woman, do you know what you do to me?"

Dosha took her mouth from his and took his face in her hands. "I can't really know, but I have an idea, and I surely know what you do to *me*. Day after tomorrow we'll be man and wife and the next day we'll be in Puerto and on our honeymoon. Look forward to that and it will cool you."

He shook his head. "By then I'll be a cinder." He nuzzled her neck, feeling glued to her body.

"Go!" she commanded. "You've got a father to meet and you don't want to be late."

"I've a sweetheart to kiss once more."

Dosha laughed. "Oh, you're an insatiable lover and I wouldn't have you any other way." She hugged him fiercely, gave him one wild, quick kiss and pulled away.

He looked at her. "You are going to pay for that last quick kiss," he told her.

"Your emotional currency is good in my bank any time."

He left then and she sat a moment on the sofa with her eyes closed, letting the spell of his kisses wash over her. He was so precious. Then opening her eyes, she glanced at the package. Getting a sharp knife, she undid the wrapping. Was Marty surprising her with a painting? It would be just like him. It had been so much fun getting her splendid presents. Friends and acquaintances had been more than kind. And generous.

Holding the painting up, she blinked for a moment and her blood ran ice cold. Goose pimples peppered her arms. What on earth? Maybe she was too close to it to see it clearly, but no—she blinked fast again. *Was this a dream?* She had bad dreams sometime. Not looking at the photo, she carried it over to the sideboard and set it down, stood back and forced herself to really look at it.

There was no mistake! This was the photograph of Dosha dressed in a beautiful white wedding gown with a veil atop her hair, but it wasn't the gown Roland had made. Then a thought hit her. The woman in the picture was her, but more beautiful than she had ever been. Evidently a photo had been retouched and it was a masterpiece. The woman in the photo lay on a chaise lounge and her lifeless hand and arm dangled. Oh, yes, this woman was very beautiful. *And very dead.*

Dosha felt her knees begin to shake so badly she had to sit down. Who? And why? A whimper began in her throat, though her eyes were dry and aching. She wanted Christian, but her mind cleared somewhat then and she realized that Adam would still be at their parents' house. With shaking hands she called him, told him what had happened. And she waited, willing herself to be calm.

He was at her apartment in a few minutes. Looking at

the photograph, rage filled him. What lowlife would do a thing like this? he wondered. But Adam was a detective and he knew very well that the world was full of sick people who would do this, and worse. He examined the wrappings carefully.

"There's a return address, but it might not be real." He sat on the sofa beside Dosha who felt numb and unbelieving. "Think, Sis. Who do you know who could possibly do something like this? Take your time."

Her mind worked swiftly then and she could think of no one. She didn't make enemies. She was a levelheaded, no-nonsense woman who didn't play games, but did play fair and square. Most people liked her and those that didn't knew she wasn't to be trifled with.

"You can be sure I'll check out the address and do everything I can to get to the bottom of this." Adam reached over and pulled his sister to him, hugged her and stroked her back. "You're going to be all right, honey. We'll get on this right away."

But Adam's breath was shallow. *How* would they get to the bottom of it? He prayed that somehow the address was a right one, that an unthinking nut had put his own address on the package, but he was doubtful. Holding Dosha, he studied the photo from across the room. Great camerawork. Dosha's photo had been in the Post from an article done on the college where she taught. Retouching was easy. For a moment he clenched his teeth. He dealt with crime every day, but not since his wife Raven's stalking had it hit so close to home.

Adam told his parents and siblings about the troubling photo that night. He also told Marty and Christian. He prepared to call on Marty's cell phone when a call came from Christian that they were on their way. Adam told Christian what had happened, but just that it was an unsettling photo.

"Unsettling *how,* Adam?" Christian demanded. "Is Dosha all right? How is she taking this?"

"Simmer down, Chris," Adam told him. "It's a photo. My wife is at my parents' house. Take your father there, then you and Marty come here. Dosha needs you."

"No," Christian said. "Do not forget Dad is Puerto's chief of homicide. He will insist on giving you what help he can."

"Okay, do it that way then."

By then everyone in the family knew of the "photo" and there were expressions of shock all around. Mel cursed under his breath. He didn't understand the way the world moved these days. His daughter's marriage was only one day away and he wanted things *right* for her. He could have crushed the skull of whoever was doing this to her.

But it was only when Christian arrived and with his father studied the photo that Christian saw depths that the others had not seen. Those dead, therefore unseeing eyes haunted him. Those lifeless hands. And it came to him with a shock. *His late wife Isabel had looked just like that.*

The telephone rang. Rispa picked it up and told Christian it was for him. To his surprise, it was Socorro.

"My darling," she said slowly. "I called the number you gave me and they transferred me to this number." She hesitated for a moment. "Christian, I had trouble deciding whether or not to call, but something is pushing me. You know my spirits guide me and they crowd me now. Again, I do not get a clear vision, but there is trouble or there will be shortly. It is not too bad and you can handle it, but I want you and Dosha to be very, very careful.

"I feel it all the way through me, lies and deceit and betrayal. You *will* be careful? Did your father arrive safely?"

"He has arrived. We're all at Dosha's. *Abuela,* I love you, and yes, we will both be careful."

"Has anything happened?"

He thought for a moment and decided not to tell her. She would worry too much. "Everything is fine."

"You know you have my blessings for your wedding day, and Christian, I sent a ring to Dosha a couple of days ago. Have you gotten it? I marked it special attention and sent it by courier mail."

Christian turned and asked Dosha if she had gotten a package from Socorro and she said no, but Rispa slapped her hand to her head. "Yes, you did. In the rush this afternoon I forgot to tell you and to give it to you."

"Grandmother," Christian told her, "your gift has arrived."

"Good, because it's the jade ring your grandfather gave me. I have two rings so I'm not without. Please let me talk with Dosha."

Listening to Dosha's voice, Socorro went into her special place. "You sound a bit disturbed," she said immediately. "Is something wrong?" Because the spirits were pressing in on her and the voices of others always told her so much.

Dosha steadied herself and turned her back to the photograph. "I'm jittery the way all brides-to-be get, I think."

But no, Socorro thought, there was something beyond that. Were they being truthful with her? She didn't doubt her spirits and her visions. They were off sometimes, but never completely wrong.

The call came to Francisco as he lay in his hotel room and Juan's voice was full of laughter. "Señor, I watch the house of the señorita. The package was delivered this afternoon. Christian and one of the brothers brought her home, then left, I suppose to meet Captain Montero. I wasn't there this afternoon at the Steeles, but as you know, I've been there and offered what help I could and they spoke of the Captain's coming..."

"Your words wander," Francisco said abruptly. "Have you special news to tell me?"

"Oh yes, forgive me. The Steeles all came to this building where the señorita lives and they seemed very anxious. So our play is beginning." He waited for Francisco to dismiss him, to show appreciation, but no appreciation was forthcoming.

Instead, Francisco commanded, "Watch carefully and keep me informed. It'll be well worth your time."

Francisco hung up and Juan sat in his car, smiling. Francisco was a cold man, but he paid well and Juan would need that money to leave Puerto and settle in a new place where he could live the way he had always dreamed of living.

After the others left, Christian spent the night with Dosha, holding her, seeing that she slept some. He prepared a light meal for her late the next morning and was pleased to see that she no longer seemed so haunted. It had sunk in then that this was someone's idea of a joke, a very sick joke.

He helped her to pull herself together. Adam had taken the photo and the wrappings with him, but in her mind's eye she could still see it. Rispa sent the package with the jade ring over by Juan who had come by, offering to help. Ah, he thought, he was in luck. The señorita answered the door and she had looked worried. There would be more news for Francisco who would be pleased.

Slipping the beautiful, large jade stone with its gleaming gold setting on her right hand as Socorro had instructed, Dosha felt a measure of peace. Christian kissed her hand and held it to his heart. "Like the pearl pendant," he said, "it's one of her dearest possessions. She loves you as I love you."

But Dosha thought sadly that someone did *not* love her. Someone hated her and wanted her dead.

In his office Adam pondered Dosha's package. The return address on the wrapping of the package was for a seedy part of town. It turned out that the address was a deserted building. The building was abandoned, slated to be torn down, boarded up and filled with squatters—crack junkies and prostitutes. He would have someone check the post offices to see if anyone remembered processing the package. It was a long shot and budget restraints didn't really permit much investigation, but dammit, this was his sister and he didn't intend to let anyone hurt her.

Dosha came awake the next morning with Christian lying beside her propped on his elbow peering down at her. Deep concern was mirrored on his face.

"Good morning, love," he said. "How do you feel?"

For a brief moment she was only aware of his beloved presence in his white tee shirt and blue boxer shorts and her body began to warm at his presence. Then she remembered the photograph and stiffened. No one had spoken of Daryl, her ex-fiancé.

Now she said, "Christian, what about Daryl as a suspect? It's the kind of thing he would do."

He looked surprised. "But he seemed so cordial, so contrite."

Anger rose in her breast. "Daryl is like Dr. Jekyll and Mr. Hyde. He has a split personality and his right hand seldom knows what his left hand is doing. Oh, Lord, why didn't I think of him last night?"

"You were still in a state of shock, love." He leaned over further and kissed the corner of her mouth, nuzzled her face and began to kiss her. She shook her head.

"Give me a minute," she told him. "I need to at least rinse my mouth."

He got up and got a package of mints from his shirt pocket, came back to the bed and held the package out to her. She took one and put it in her mouth, instantly feeling refreshed.

"One quick kiss," he said, "then you do your toilette because I want more. Meanwhile I'll hold you for a minute, then fix you some breakfast. What do you want to eat?"

She didn't want anything to eat. What she wanted was to be away from all memory of the hideous photograph. But she saw he wanted to do something for her, so as he held her she told him she wanted only orange juice, a raisin bagel with cream cheese. He kissed her lightly then. "Maybe you're right and it *is* Daryl. If it is, Adam will put a stop to his nonsense," Christian said.

"Daryl used to drink heavily," she said slowly, "and I'm told he sometimes did cocaine. I hardly believe prison changed him. At least if it is him, we know where it's coming from. What if it's not?"

"I do not know, love, but I'm prepared to move heaven and earth to help your brother find out who sent that package." But holding her, Christian thought he had seldom felt so helpless.

In the bathroom, Dosha looked at herself in the mirror. She seemed a little drained and her eyes were frightened. She did her ablutions quickly, hating to be alone and, slipping into the rose summer dressing gown she had brought in with her, went back to her bedroom. She had begun to pace a bit alongside the bed when the phone rang. It was Caitlin.

"Hello, lovey." Caitlin's voice was tender, concerned. "How do you feel this morning?"

"I'm holding up, holding on. How're *you?*"

"I'm fine. Listen, I know Christian spent the night with you, but would you like for me to come over? It's a hell of a thing that happened last night. Marty and I are still upset."

"I know you are," Dosha said slowly. "I'm thinking now it could be Daryl. And somehow that helps."

"Yes," Caitlin said. "Daryl Stoner. You said you saw him out at the college. How did he act?"

"Like the king he has always imagined himself to be. But Daryl is crazy, Cait. Now I can understand why we broke up several times."

"Lovey, the twins are up and no man rests when that happens. Marty wants to speak with you."

Marty's deep, rich voice came over. "Sweetheart, how're you feeling this morning?"

She told him what she had told Caitlin and he expelled a harsh sigh. "Stoner can be a real bastard all right. We've all had good evidence of that. And you're right, it might be a good thing if he *is* the culprit. Adam will clip his wings in short shrift. Try to relax, Sis, and that's saying a helluva lot because I don't imagine you can. Know that you have a solid family behind you, an adoring brother who will get to Stoner and a father and two other brothers who will beat him up if necessary."

Dosha's voice caught with laughter that made her feel better.

"Eat something now," Marty said. "You always used to stop eating when you were even a little upset. Promise me you'll eat something?"

"Chris is fixing my breakfast now. He and all of you are so wonderful and I think you know how much I appreciate it. I love you all so much and you make me feel so much better."

"And we love you. You've got a great guy in Chris, Sis. He's as solid as a rock. I was in emotional tatters when you were tied up with Stoner. I never understood what you saw in him and I was *glad* when he went to prison. I'm not going to lie about that."

"Daryl was the mistake of my life," she said sadly. "I haven't made too many."

"You bet you haven't. You're a smart woman. Chris proves that." Marty made a kissing sound then and signed off as Christian came into the room with a crystal tray set with dishes holding her breakfast. He had clipped a yellow rose from the bouquet Roland had given her and put it in a bud vase. She smiled at him, blew him a kiss. "You are talented," she told him. "That's a mighty pretty tray."

"For a pretty lady." He put the tray on the night table and sat beside her. "No more excuses. I'm taking a kiss from those luscious lips." He held her warm body close to him and she responded, but couldn't suppress last night's memory. Lord, let there be some break on who was doing this and why.

He stroked her back and felt her tremble. "*Querida,*" he said softly. "If you can't kiss me, I certainly understand how upset you are."

She took his hand then and looked deep into his eyes. "My darling," she said softly. "The devil himself couldn't stop me from wanting to kiss you. Yes, I'm upset, bothered, more than afraid, though. I guess I remember Socorro's warning and her urgent voice last night. But I'll kiss you and you tell me whether I want to kiss you."

She poured her heart and soul into that kiss and they both caught fire. But the passion in their bodies was nothing compared to the passion in their hearts. They were holding back, saving themselves for their honeymoon. But for a moment she wavered. She needed him so. What happened last night had really shaken her. She began to moan softly and stroke his back. He held her tightly.

The phone rang and for a moment neither quite heard it. Then groggily she leaned forward and picked it up. It was Adam.

"I waited a bit," he said "to give you time to sleep longer. I won't even ask how you feel, Sis. How *can* you feel other than bothered and angry?"

"Adam, right now I feel better than I ever could have

expcctcd. I've been thinking that Daryl could be behind this. Last night he didn't cross my mind."

"He damned sure crossed mine. I stopped by Stoner's house this morning and questioned him. I don't know how much was him and how much was liquor and cocaine talking. He'd been drinking and it showed. Guilty conscience? You tell me."

"Oh, Adam, did he say anything incriminating?"

"Plenty. That he loved you too much to do a thing like that. Of course, he seemed shocked. That he wished you well and hoped you would be happy. That he liked on sight the man you were going to marry. That he knew he had never been good enough for you. I remembered everything you'd ever told me about him and it helped some, but he is something else. He's a consummate liar and I couldn't tell if he was telling the truth or not.

"Sis, I'm putting a tail on him. That should stop him from trying anything else. And I'm having your building watched. If another package comes in, we'll know who brought it. I've already talked to your building manager and the morning desk clerk. The wedding's tomorrow and that will be watched too. By the next day you'll be in Puerto de la Cruz on your honeymoon and hopefully safe.

"We're checking the post offices to see if anyone remembers a package like this being mailed since it was sent special delivery and was fairly large. But this is going to be a task because we don't have the manpower or the budget to do it. A couple of my retired policeman friends are on it and will report back to me. I'm working, baby, and when I work, I usually get results."

Adam stopped and cleared his throat. "Sis, let me speak with Christian, please."

Dosha handed the phone to Christian and got up feeling much better. Adam had always made her feel so protected;

all three of her brothers and her father had. And her twin, Damien? What to say about Damien? He had always been a wild man in his defense of her. When Daryl had been indicted, Damien had wanted to tear him limb from limb. It had taken their father and his two brothers to dissuade him. She hated having Damien know that they suspected Daryl of this. There was no telling what Damien would do to Daryl.

"How's it going, Adam?" Christian asked.

"Well enough. My investigation is underway. My sister says she's doing okay, but I want to hear it from you. *Is* she doing okay?"

Christian glanced at Dosha who half lay on a chaise lounge across the room, her shapely legs inviting him. "I'd say she's doing better. Dosha's a strong woman and she's resilient. It'll take more than this to send her down."

Adam repeated the information he had given Dosha and Christian listened carefully and found himself relaxing. Marty was his best friend, but he felt close to all her family and Adam always reminded him of his own father, Puerto's chief of homicide, Captain Montero.

Now Adam said, "You met Daryl Stoner. What did you think of him?"

Christian thought a moment. "He seemed a decent enough man. Dosha tells me that he's also a deceptive man."

"You had better believe it. He managed to hornswoggle the judge into giving him just five years in prison when he should've gotten twenty. Stoner comes from a wealthy family and there's no excuse for what he did. Some of the people he worked the Ponzi scheme on could take the loss and they were just greedy. But many people were poor to begin with, desperate for a change in their fortunes. They lost their homes and in one case a man committed suicide.

"I don't mind telling you I despise Stoner. I have from the beginning, even when I thought I had no reason to." He paused a long while. "Chris, I'm picking up your father this morning and he's visiting with me today. I'm going to be busy on this Stoner thing, but my assistant will show him around. He'll also spend the day with me the day after the wedding. You've got a great father; we clicked on sight." He paused a moment, chuckling. "And for the record, tell my sister she's made the catch of her life in you."

Christian blushed. "It's I who have made the catch of my life. I love your sister the way I thought I would never love again. Thank you all for being the people you are, so that she is the person she is."

And Dosha sat on the chaise lounge studying her beloved. Already the hated photograph had begun to recede from her mind. With men around her like the men she knew, who could hurt her? But, she thought now, she would be a fool not to heed Soccoro's warnings.

Sitting there, she wondered about the love that ran so deep it went to the marrow of her bones and at last she had a man worthy of her love. Chris smiled at her, blew her a kiss and she shuddered with delicious delight.

Francisco sat up in bed holding the phone.

"The house was in an uproar," Juan said. "You would've been pleased."

Francisco's face was wreathed in smiles. "I've seen fit to take you into my confidence, so you know the story. You'll keep Christian unsettled and upset as we bedevil his wife with threats and more threats. He can't do his best work, can't comport himself with the necessary aplomb when his wife is suffering. He's that kind of tender, weak man. So it was with Isabel." He paused. "I can only hope it won't become necessary to hurt her. Or worse."

Juan shivered with the mention of Isabel Montero's name. She had flirted outrageously with him and he had always wondered if she would have become his lover if he had been fool enough to risk it. He was an attractive, compelling, virile man. She had been a beautiful woman who lived life and cared nothing about what others thought. He knew that Francisco had been her lover, and it was rumored there had been others. She had been careful with Francisco and it had not become gossip. Juan wondered if Christian had known.

Now Francisco said. "Tomorrow you'll mingle with the other servants and guests and make good use of your time. Prove to me that you're loyal. Watch carefully and bring me information that will be useful to me. You'll never be sorry that you did."

Chapter 7

The day of the wedding dawned and held fair and clear as Dosha had prayed it would. The horizon was blush pink and beautiful beyond description. Now it was six o'clock in the morning and the guests were gathered in the huge back and side yards of the elder Steeles' home. It was an elegant setting for a sunrise wedding and the family had spent the entire year planning and preparing for the event. The yard was like something out of "House and Gardens" magazine and even the old, stately oaks seemed to know that they were part of a special occasion.

The hound dogs, Red and Blue, had been taken to the neighbors for the day. "Otherwise, they'd make themselves sick as *dogs* begging and eating leftovers," Mel had joked.

And Jimmy's best catering employees were busy in the Steeles' big kitchen preparing food for the reception which would also be held on the grounds. With his hands behind his back, Mel surveyed the scene and thought that by the end of the day he would only have one unmarried child left, Damien. Damien, he thought, was unlikely ever to wed. That fact made his father sad.

Beige canopies stretched across the yard to protect the guests from the July heat, that could be intense even in the early morning, and rain. Rented blue plush chairs were lined across the yard and in front of the podium that was banked with white cattleya orchids, roses and maidenhair fern. It was a large wedding and guests had begun to arrive as early as five o'clock. Now everyone was seated and their anticipation was palpable.

Rispa couldn't stop bustling about, checking on last minute details. Mel went to her. "Baby, if you don't slow down you're going to collapse. You've been up since four."

Rispa touched his hand. "I could've stayed up all night."

She was ecstatic. "Just look at that sky, honey. Isn't it the most beautiful thing you've ever seen?"

Mel smiled. "Nope. This morning our daughter is the most beautiful thing I've ever seen, besides you."

She flashed him a quick smile. The sun had begun to rise on their only daughter's wedding and they were enthralled.

In her old bedroom, Dosha could hardly contain her excitement. A sunrise wedding to the man she adored. Rispa came in. "Checking. Just checking, honey. Are you all right?"

Dosha nodded. Like her mother, the photograph of the dead woman was in the back of her mind. She firmly pushed the image away. Someone had meant to spoil her happiness at her wedding, and maybe it was a warning of truly bad things to come, but this day was hers and she intended to enjoy it. Still, the feeling lingered.

So far, a check of the post offices had turned up nothing and no further incidents had marred her life. She kissed her mother's cheek and her two bridesmaids hovered around her. Her sister-in-law Raven, and Viveca, Raven's and Dosha's friend, were beautifully gowned in pastel pink silk crepe. Her matron of honor, Caitlin, wore aquamarine silk. Caitlin looked at her best friend and sister-in-law. Dosha's wedding gown was the stuff of dreams, she thought.

Caitlin kissed Dosha's cheek. "You're so beautiful. This marriage thing is everything it's cracked up to be—and more," she murmured.

Dosha laughed. "You don't have to convince me. I'm totally converted already."

Viveca stood back a bit. "I'm looking at that pearl pendant you have on, girl, and I need a new word to describe it."

Dosha smiled. "You don't need a new word. *Treasure* is just fine."

"I'll say," Raven amended.

"Let's see now," Caitlin continued, checking off items on her fingers. "You've got my blue ruffled garter for something blue, your mom's old white lace handkerchief. You've got a new gold vanity case from me and you borrowed Raven's white Bible And, Lord, you've got a hunk of a man for a groom in Christian. Girlfriend, you're all set."

And a happy Raven commented, "You have the world to gain, love. Your vows are all written, so you can't forget them. And my hat is off to you and Christian for writing those vows. When Merla gets married, I'll remember them. I've never seen you look better, Dosha, or happier." But she thought she saw a shadow cross Raven's face and she thought it had to do with the hated photograph.

"Ladies," Rispa announced, straightening Dosha's veil a bit, "Let's get the show on the road. The sun's rising fast."

Taking a deep breath, Dosha closed her eyes and smiled as the group started out onto the beige carpet that led to her groom and her future. With her on his arm, Mel was ten feet tall.

· And by the podium that was banked with orchids, fern, and roses, their minister presided, his round, dark brown face wreathed with smiles. He couldn't remember in fifty years marrying a better suited and happier couple.

In front of him, awaiting the bride, Christian stood, nervous and highly excited at once. Was it really happening? Was this vision really going to belong to him?

Because Dosha was coming up the aisle on Mel's arm and she was resplendent in her wedding gown. It displayed her silken nutmeg skin to perfection. A short veil of ivory tulle lifted off her brow and she carried a bouquet of white orchids.

Christian thought she had never looked so beautiful and he felt his whole being flame with love and desire, together with a passion to protect her with everything that was in him. Her eyes met his and a murmur rose from the crowd. They caught the wonder and the deep love that flourished between the couple and it thrilled them.

Christian and his best man, Marty, had decided on unadorned black tuxedos. The two men were handsome and full of their mission. Marty looked at his sister and found it hard to believe that she had once been a tomboy. Now she couldn't have been more demure and feminine.

Mel's firstborn son, Frank, of the famous Singing Steeles, was there with his wife, Caroline, and their three grown and very prosperous children—Ashley, Whit and Annice. The families were so close that it was as if the four siblings were whole. But Mel had had one son with his first wife who had left him, and four with Rispa. Today Mel felt like the luckiest man in the world. A man loved his sons, but a daughter was special. You worried more about her in a world like this, he now thought. And there had been the debacle with that scoundrel, Daryl Stoner. He had thought she would go under, but she had not. Her family and her own strength had pulled her through. Now she was at a splendid stage in her life with a man he had begun to love like a son.

The flower girl and the ringbearer were children of Raven's cousin and they were precious. The little girl carried a basket of white orchids and ferns and the little boy carried the beautiful platinum band of diamonds on a white satin pillow.

Dosha felt as if she moved in a dream. She and Christian were linking for all time and she felt butterflies take off in her stomach as Ashley, her half sister, the world famous gospel diva, took the microphone and began to sing the ever beautiful "O, Promise Me." Her gorgeous contralto drew every bit of magic from the music and she held the crowd in the palm of her hands.

At the end of the song, Nick Redmond, onstage, handsome in his tuxedo, played his piano softly and was accompanied by his combo. He loved weddings and this one was special. The Steeles were old friends of his and his wife, Janet, and today his music carried a special significance.

There was a rustle of paper in the audience as people looked at their programs that outlined the wedding service. The second and third pages held a copy of the vows the couple had written themselves and they listened raptly.

"Dearly beloved, we're gathered here today." Time honored and time tested, the minister's voice and his presence belonged to this time and this place and these people.

In a minute the vows began as Dosha and Christian held hands that trembled with hope and passion.

"I, Dosha Marletta Steele," she began, looking at Christian with moist, loving eyes.

"I, Christian Paulo Montero." His voice caught as he looked at her and his breath was shallowed with wanting her.

They began to recite together:

"In our love we have decided to marry, to join together as man and wife, as one, to love, respect, honor, treasure and protect each other with all our strength and all our power.

"For love and respect are the hope of the world and our love and respect are boundless. Love like ours is our hope and our world. If we would but love and value to the utmost what we love, what wonders could be achieved. We would live close to Paradise and God then.

"If we would but value highly our dreams of begetting, bearing and raising our children, love them, respect them, sustain them and bring them into a society we helped to foster, with integrity, we would know joy unending.

"If we would but live sublimely in a world of our peers and others, giving and being given to, helping and accepting help, praying to the God we serve and believe in, ever rich in belief in that God and his Heavens and the world He has made."

Dosha felt lightheaded with happiness. "If we would do these things then the world we hold dear will be ours and our love will be whole and safe from harm. Dearly beloved, let us do these things and be such people and hold these things dear.

"We'll be joined, oh, Lord, we'll be joined together in love and passion and tender desire without end forever. Amen."

Mel felt warm with happiness as he gave his girl away thinking it was a far cry from the way it would have been with Stoner.

The minister pronounced them man and wife and the ringbearer handed the ring to Christian who slipped the band on Dosha's finger. He smiled at her with promises of joy almost without end once they were at last alone.

To Christian it seemed to take forever before the minister said, "I now pronounce you man and wife. You may kiss the bride."

And kissing her Christian whispered, "I promise you all of me forever."

"And I promise you the same," she whispered back.

The sun spread its soft, yet brilliant colors across the sky and a robin began a merry trill to comment on the festivities. This was his yard and these were his people. Predators had spared him to enjoy the birdhouse and the birdbath here. And there were always crumbs aplenty on the kitchen windowsill.

Nick's group began the recessional, from Mendelsohn's *A Midsummer Night's Dream.* And Christian offered Dosha his arm. They moved slowly past the myriad faces that were turned toward their happiness and their own faces sparkled with intense joy. As they moved along, Rispa looked up at them and her smile was wide, beatific. As if of one mind, Marty and Adam blew them kisses and Damien rose and bowed low as they came to his end seat.

Dosha and Christian smiled at Damien and his heart lifted. Christian had come to be like one of his brothers and he knew he held his twin's love forever. Yes, a part of him felt deserted and alone and he felt he was never going to know this kind of joy. Another part of him groused, because he was never again going to go through the risk of the kind of pain it could take to get there.

The seven-tiered wedding cake was Jimmy's crowning glory—and that was saying something because he was renowned for his pies and cakes. This one was chock full of sweetmeats and nuts and covered in a whipped cream cheese icing made from Jimmy's secret and much coveted recipe. A smiling plastic bride and groom topped the cake.

Dosha looked at Christian as his hand met hers to cut the cake and a familiar electricity jolted them both. She fed him the first bite of cake from her fingers as was the tradition in the Steele family; both felt lightheaded with happiness.

At the side door with wedding guests now beginning to congratulate them, Christian took Dosha's hand. "Your bridesmaids and your matron of honor will soon be with you. Do not get tied up in the girl talk. Hurry back, because I need you for support."

In Dosha's bedroom, Dosha, Caitlin, Raven and Viveca giggled like high school girls as the latter three helped Dosha take off her wedding finery.

Viveca whistled a wolf whistle. "Wow! That lingerie is sexy plus. It's wasted on anything but a honeymoon first night." The others agreed that the sheer cream lace panties and bra was something else. Viveca looked at Dosha and said drolly. "Honey, I hope you've got plenty of thongs. They really drive men crazy."

Caitlin laughed. "I have them, but it doesn't take them to turn my sweetie on."

Raven cleared her throat. "Dosha, love, we three had a special honeymoon package for you. Unfortunately, it was so popular it was on back order. The company says it will take anywhere from six weeks to three months to get it back in stock. It's got to come from Paris. You know Sileia and Mick?"

Dosha thought a moment. "I sure do. Mick's that great sound engineer. Damien comes all the way from Nashville to have Mick record his soundtracks and he sends all his artists to Mick. He met Sileia in Tahiti. They are quite a couple."

"Well," Raven said, "Sileia swears this setup will put you in passion's heaven and she's usually right about things."

Dosha perked up further. "Give me a hint," she begged.

"You've heard of monoi oil?" Viveca looked merrily sly now.

"I can't say I have." Dosha wondered what they were up to.

Viveca closed her eyes. "Oh, it's great. All of us have tried it. We wanted to wait until now to tell you about it and to give you the package. Well, it's a special massage oil Tahitians use. You can get the new version that smells and tastes like peppermint and it can be—" Here she raised her eyebrows and giggled. "*Ingested.* So kiss away, lick away and be carried to heaven. Oh, there's more. A special rose-colored very soft plastic sheet so you can go wild without dreading the cleanup. Just throw the sheet in the washing machine. Sound good to you?"

Dosha smiled. "Uh-hum-m-m. It also sounds very expensive."

"What are friends for?" Caitlin demanded. "Well, enough of this. I'm sure you and Christian are fully capable of taking care of the romance department. But we'll send the monoi oil package along by courier mail the second we get it. Are you all packed?"

"I am."

At a knock on the door, Rispa came in, surveyed the group and smiled. "You ladies look like you're up to no good," she said. "I wish you could see the cat and canary look on your faces, but I'm not asking any questions."

Raven threw back her head, laughing. "Mom, you probably could guess in a heartbeat." Both daughters-in-law called Rispa mom.

Rispa went to the bed and held up the wedding gown. "You were so beautiful, love. Now do hurry and get downstairs, the lot of you. The food is scrumptious. You know Jimmy outdid himself. Nick is playing his heart out, and the sound system is working perfectly. People are dancing on the ceiling. Lord, we have a crowd. That lingerie you're wearing reminds me of my wedding day, sweetie. Come on now, let's move it."

Juan had insisted on helping the caterers with their serving and they let him. Francisco found him near a rose-draped fence and smiled at him with hooded eyes.

"It's quite a gathering," Francisco commented. "The caper we pulled does not seem to have done much damage, but I think it did no good. From time to time I've watched and Dosha has seemed haunted. Then she recovers. She is a tough lady."

Juan nodded. "They speak of someone called Daryl Stoner, I think he is her ex-fiancé. They suspect *him* of sending the photograph."

"Wonderful!" Francisco chortled. "I couldn't have planned it better. Now in Puerto I have other happenings coming up and I'll need your help... If things go my way, I may not need to hurt my cousin further. If not..."

"Always you have me."

"And what an advantage you will have, Juan, living in the house near them, a completely trusted nephew of Christian's caretakers. God himself couldn't have favored us more. I'm coming to know the new Mrs. Montero and I'm impressed. It's too bad that it may be necessary to hurt her."

Juan raised his eyebrows. "You have superb connections, señor. Perhaps this job you want will be yours without too much further effort."

Francisco clasped his hands behind his back. "Pray that you are right. Intrigue is the stuff of my life. Violence is not something I'm too fond of, but I'll do whatever is necessary. Come, man, and let's sample the food. The guests are saying that the paella is wonderful."

Rispa came to them and Francisco bowed low, lifted and kissed her hand. "How gallant you are," she told him. "Are you enjoying yourselves?" They both paid her high compliments and she said to Juan, "We're grateful for your help. It was so kind of you."

Juan smiled with all the charm he could muster. "Señor Montero thought I would be willing to help and I will, of course, save you the trouble of packing up things that will be shipped back to Puerto. It's been a pleasure."

Dosha met Christian at the bottom of the stairs. He stood for a moment looking up at her before she reached his level. "*Querida,* you are a vision in that dress, as you were in your wedding gown." And Dosha *felt* lovely in her low cut clinging silk jersey that was intricately draped. Periwinkle blue was one of her best colors and she wore sparkling gold jewelry. Mel came to her, held out his hand.

She smiled at Christian and waltzed away with her father. "I'm having trouble keeping myself from bursting with pride," he told her. "We're going to miss having you around, baby."

"We'll be back at the beginning of next year and you're coming to Puerto, I'm sure."

"Can't wait."

The music was soft and dreamy, then lively by turns. Today Nick Redmond really strutted his stuff. Listening to his combo play, you knew why they were on the top of the crossover charts.

Roland found Dosha as Christian came to her again. "Mr. and Mrs. Montero," Roland said now. "I've never created a greater masterpiece and, my dear, you are divine. If every bride I created for wore my gowns with the grace you have, my fortune would be made, and will you save a dance for me?"

Dosha smiled. "You are very kind, and, yes, you know I will."

Damien came to them as Marty came up, too. "Lord, I miss the little twins," Damien said. "I'm going to have Caleb Myles for my ringbearer."

"By then," Marty growled, "he'll be married and have his own kids."

Dosha saw the hurt look cross Damien's face and she scolded Marty, "Don't tease him so, love. It's not like marriage is something he doesn't want."

Damien flashed her a grateful smile but said nothing and Marty desisted. Christian looked from one twin to the other. He found the Steele family fascinating and was glad he fit in like a glove, as Dosha fit into his family.

Mel came back with his firstborn son, Frank, and his wife Caroline. They reached the couple, beaming. "My three kids have long ago tied the knot," Frank said. "Now you have only one left." He turned to Damien. "Bro, you've done well for yourself. Pay no mind to folks who push you to get married. It can be heaven or it can be hell. So make your own choice in your own time."

Damien threw back his head, laughing at his older half brother. "Now I know why I love you, Bro."

And Frank's three children and their mates were all there: Ashley and her husband, Derrick, Whit and his wife, Dani, Annice and her husband, Luke. All were in happy marriages.

Jimmy came up, wiping his face with a white handkerchief. He took Dosha's hand. "My dear, the gods are looking after you two. I oversaw the preparation of your food with all my love." A small, dark brown woman moved to stand at his side and Dosha greeted her. "Reese." The two women hugged and Dosha told her, "You lucked out when you got Jimmy, and I'm sure he did with you."

Reese thanked her and Jimmy mopped his brow again. He looked at Christian. "The paella is fabulous, I promise you. Four kinds. It's catching on in D.C."

Christian thanked him. "This is like going home again before I get there."

Dosha and Christian danced then, a slow dance, and he held her tightly, kissed her earlobe, getting a whiff of her perfume. "I'll let others dance with you," he murmured, "because I can't stand to have your body pressed so close to mine. I keep wondering how I'm going to last until we get to Puerto."

"We'll be so tired when we get there, we'll probably sleep for a day or a full night."

He pulled her closer. "No, we won't. By the time we get in our cottage, I'll be crazy for you. I'll lock us into our little love nest, and…I can't stop dreaming. It's madness to torment myself like this."

Dosha's half sister Ashley's husband, Derrick, cut in then and swept her away. Derrick and Ashley owned a large and thriving farm in the Tidewater Area of Virginia. Dosha and Christian had been down there once or twice, but Dosha had visited them often.

"Beautiful wedding," Derrick told her. "You and Christian seem so happy. You know Ashley and I wish you all the best. You all are like my family now."

"Yes," Dosha told him. She was dancing with him, but her body was still with Christian. Derrick was an expert dancer and he guided her through a long waltz.

Nick Redmond sang Damien's song for the couple, "If Love Is Good to Me," pouring his heart into it and a few people stopped and went to the bandstand to listen more closely. A brisk breeze had sprung up. Couples danced in the living room, the dining room, the parlor and the family room, as well as out in the yard. A sound system had been put in to carry the music throughout the downstairs area and outside.

Now Nick came off the stage and found Christian and Dosha. He shook his head. "Well, it looks like you two have it all," he said, "and it couldn't happen to better people." He held out his hand to Dosha, "May I have this dance, if the groom can spare you for a few minutes?"

Christian liked the musician very much and he grinned. "Reluctantly. Please bring her back soon."

In Nick's arms, Dosha radiated happiness. "You and your group are fabulous today," she told him. "I've never heard you play so well."

"Thank you. It's all for you. They say all brides are beautiful and I know mine was, but you are outstanding. Dosha, I'm glad you found someone worthy of you, and I hope you'll always be happy." He remembered well the torment she had gone through with Daryl Stoner and he felt a bit angry thinking of that bad time now.

He had been a good friend during that time. Now Dosha told him, "You and Janet and your kid have a standing invitation to visit us in Puerto. You've never visited there?"

"No, but I hear it's beautiful. One of Europe's playgrounds."

"Yes, and not enough Americans visit. They don't advertise because they don't need to."

"We *will* come. I promise."

Christian stood alone for a few minutes, just long enough for an unwanted vision of his marriage to Isabel to invade his mind. That had been a splendid wedding of pomp and circumstance. Isabel was one of two spoiled and headstrong daughters of Raoul Martinez, a wealthy builder.

Raoul had not thought Christian good enough for Isabel at first, although he respected the family and swore by Socorro. But Isabel had put her foot down. She found Christian exotic because he was a Brown Baby. He was handsome and he had narrowly missed being a toreador. Later, Raoul had grown fond of Christian.

At first Christian had been happy and he was never certain when that happiness began to fade. He only knew that bitterness had corroded him until he had killed her.

Christian jumped as Rispa spoke at his elbow. "My dear, you were lost in fantasyland. Come back to us."

He breathed a sigh of relief and held out his hand. Rispa was still a good-looking woman, her skin still smooth and lovely. "May I have this dance?" he asked her.

Dosha's next dance was with Carey Sloan, Viveca's husband. With his curly brown hair, fair skin and sky blue eyes, Carey was an engaging man and an excellent dancer. He was only a little taller than Dosha and he led her easily and expertly.

Carey was very much at ease in a multicultural setting. His father trained master printers at Hampton University in Virginia and his mother had taught physical education there. He and Viveca had married while both were college students.

"You and Christian have got my wife demanding we go to Puerto de la Cruz for the carnival season." He laughed. "I guess I'd love that, too."

"Come," she urged. "We have a big house and Christian's father has a big house. Say you'll come."

"Prepare for guests."

Dosha's next dance was with Captain Montero who found himself enjoying his stay and this wedding more than he had enjoyed himself since his beloved Magdalena had died.

"You're a very good dancer," she told him.

"And you're wonderful to lead. Dosha, how can I tell you how glad I am you are marrying my son. He has talked with you about his mother, the love of my life as you are of his."

Francisco came to them, tapped Captain Montero on the shoulder. "El Capitano, Americans have a custom called 'cutting in' and here it's permitted. Please relinquish this beautiful lady to my care."

With raised eyebrows, Captain Montero moved away cautioning in only half-jest that Francisco was a rogue and she should be careful with him.

Dosha was glad it wasn't a slow dance because she didn't want to be too close to Christian's enemy.

"You look ravishing," he told her. "If this were a samba, I could watch your lovely body sway and be even more entranced."

She refused him the entry he sought, asking vaguely, "Are you enjoying yourself?"

He saw that she half rebuffed him, but took it in stride. *Sí,* she was a cool woman, but he was a man who liked challenges. If he had to hurt her, perhaps even destroy her, he needed to know much more about her.

Dosha found Christian and together they went to the white damask-covered banquet tables that were set up in the house and on the huge, screened in back porch.

Jimmy was right; he had outdone himself. Baked hams and chicken, cornish hens, fried chicken and roast beef. A whole baked pig, Jimmy was also famous for his macaroni and cheese and his collard greens. There were huge crystal bowls of vegetable salads and platters of carved vegetables.

The scrumptious cakes and pies were fast disappearing.

Christian and Dosha ate slowly, savoring each morsel. She took small samples of the food and stopped before the plates were too loaded.

After they finished eating, he took flutes of champagne from a passing waiter and toasted her. "To us and the children we'll raise. May our love last forever."

Two hours later, Dosha was dressed and ready to go to the airport with Christian. Marty would drive them. In her bedroom, Rispa and Caitlin helped her dress as Rispa cried and held her. "My baby," Rispa said forlornly before smiles broke through. "But you are happy and with Christian you're going to *stay* happy. Make us a granddaughter or a grandson in a hurry and write and send pictures, you hear."

Dosha laughed and hugged her mother, then Caitlin who told her, "I don't know what I'm going to do without you. Who will I tell all my hot secrets to?"

"There's such a thing as a telephone, you know," Dosha said.

"And my bill is going to go through the ceiling. We'll all probably be over to Puerto before your honeymoon is over. We're clinging to you. It's the price you pay for being so lovable."

Dosha hugged them both again as they surveyed her, finally dressed in her dark navy silk faille suit with a sheer white, embroidered chiffon blouse. Her accessories were dark red and blended perfectly.

"Hey, you three, hurry and come out," Mel called from the hallway. "You've got a lot of goodbyes to say."

Christian and Dosha took their leave and there were hugs and kisses and tears all around. Finally suitcases were put in the back and the three were seated in the front seat of Marty's black Porsche on their way to Dulles Airport.

"Maybe I'll just keep driving in circles and we'll find ourselves back home. I hate like hell to see you both go. Sis, the only time you ever spent away from home was your four years at Juilliard. Even then, you were back as often as you could swing it." He paused a long moment. "But I know you'll be happy together and that's what matters. You're going to find that marriage is all it's cracked up to be, and more."

Dosha nodded. "I get after you, I know, about ragging Damien, but keep it up. Just be more encouraging rather than teasing him. You and Adam have great marriages. Frank and his children all have great marriages. You'd think Damien would take a clue from that."

Marty grew thoughtful. "Damien has always been different. He's just more sensitive. He's always seemed to hurt more when things happen. We all had pets. They died and we were sad, but only Damien cried, gave them funerals. And this woman he was so in love with for so long, I could've strangled her for the way she savaged him. And he still sees her. He says they're friends, but he no longer really cares about her. Who knows? Well, I keep praying…"

"And *I* keep praying," Dosha said softly.

They stopped at a red light about ten blocks from the house on the only route they could take to the airport. Dosha felt compelled to look at a man dressed in old, worn clothes who stood on the street between cars. He wore a battered, old hat and she thought she recognized him. Then he pulled off his hat and she looked straight into Daryl Stoner's eyes. His look was fierce and relentless and she couldn't tell what message those strange eyes held. It seemed the light held for so long and for a minute she had trouble getting her breath.

Then Marty and Christian both looked and Marty swore. Christian grabbed her hand and held it tightly. "Are you all right, *querida?*" he asked.

"I'm okay, love," she said quickly and she patted his hand with her other hand. "I really *am* okay."

Driving again, Marty's forehead creased in a deep frown. "I'll say this for the bastard," he told them. "He has a world of nerve. I'll bet he parked there because he knew we'd have to pass that spot. Well, he had his chance and he blew it. The luckiest thing you ever did, Sis, was dumping him."

Chapter 8

"Señor, Señora Montero, welcome to our honeymoon cottage in the hills. Your place is ready for you, my wife and I personally saw to that. There is champagne and many delicacies for you to savor."

Cedric, the manager for the Cielito Linda Cottages, bowed and kissed Dosha's hand. "I'm charmed. You are tired from your long journey?"

"Surprisingly, no," Christian told him. "We slept a lot on the plane. Were you able to prepare the waterfall site?"

The manager's smile was wide. "*Sí.* It's all prepared. Your luggage will be in shortly. There is an incredible moon tonight and we have no rain forecast for days. The weather is perfect."

He handed them the keys and they thanked him and walked the distance from the office to their spacious rose stucco cottage, with a tan tiled roof.

Inside, Dosha found it lovely, furnished with wood furniture from Tahiti and romantic colors with hemp-covered floors and big, deep area rugs. But she only saw this at a glance before Christian locked the door and they were in each other's arms. They walked through the living and dining rooms and into the bedroom with its kingsize bed and its white eyelet cover.

"My love," he whispered softly. "Feel what you do to me. I would swear it has been months since I've been inside your body."

He placed her slender hand on his shaft and she held her mouth to his and kissed him first. Then they were drowning in each other and she stripped his clothes from him quickly, flinging the garments onto a chair. Breathing hard, he tried to be slow in removing her clothes and found himself frantically unfastening the hooks and eyes of her bra. In a haze he saw her low-cut navy satin bra and thong as she deftly unfastened the bra and released her satiny brown breasts. He looked down at the navy thong, caught her buttocks in his hands, pulled her to him and began to feast on her gorgeous breasts. His shaft pressed her center as he suckled and she moaned aloud. Dizzy, he regained a bit of composure, drew away a bit and bending, stripped the thong from her body and flung it onto the chair.

Her body smelled of the earth and flowers and he had to taste her—right then. He couldn't think what he wanted to do first. He had to have it all and quickly, so he would sample each act and move on to fulfillment. She was completely and fully compliant as he stroked her with long, slow, voluptuous strokes and she knew what it cost him to hold back.

He lifted her and carried her to the bed. She leaned forward to pull the coverlet back, but he whispered, "There is no time… We've waited so long."

And even in the heat of passion, Dosha chuckled. It had

been three days and yes, he was right, it *seemed* like months. But he was here now and she lay across the firm king-sized bed and he was on his knees kissing her inner thighs, his lips slowly moving up to her belly. His tongue flicked lightly into her navel indention, then moved down again with tantalizing precision to her belly, then her physical center. He was expert and he was intent on bringing her to her fullest pleasure. She cried his name and threading her fingers in his hair, held his head in closer to her aching body.

Lightly licking and sucking, he tenderly tormented her swollen sensitive bud and the surrounding flesh until she was sick with wanting. "Honey," she told him, her voice a bit hoarse with passion, "go slow. I'm on the edge and I don't want to finish yet."

He wanted to satisfy her this way first, but he had other plans he knew she would love. This was a first step only and he had to make her come quickly to get to the deeper part of what he had in mind. So his tongue flicked wildly, savoring the fruity, sweet juices of her body, thrilling at the way she always totally surrendered to him. His shaft seemed to him about to burst and he knew he would be gone once he entered her. It would be a long, heavenly night and he dreamed, even while he was living in the dream.

His tongue in her center darted and thrust hard and he felt her go far over the edge as her first orgasm began and knew there would soon be others. This time she screamed his name in the soundproofed room and her voice was music to his ears, the music of love and communion. They were blessed. They both often had multiple orgasms during their lovemaking.

He continued stroking her. She was so silken. He stood up and she smiled at him, sat up and took his love-swollen shaft in her hands, but he stayed her. "No, *querida,* I couldn't stand it. Please."

He opened her legs and entered her willing body and thrilled again at the knowledge that he always came home when he entered her. Her inner walls clutched him greedily, fed on him. "You are so big," she whispered, "and I love you so much." But she thought then that he could have been much smaller and the passion would be the same because she loved him with everything within her. He tried to hold back at least a little, but his need was too great and the raging fire in them both was out of control.

The blood erupted in his loins and he exploded with the pent-up fury of dynamite, unleashing the hot fluid to flood her womb with his seed. And she was only a little behind him as she felt her body begin to quake with wave after wave of ecstatic wonder. Then there was the rhythmic, even gripping and release again and again that continued a long while as they lay still, thankful to each other. His shaft throbbed slowly inside her and her inner walls grew quiescent.

"Maybe we made a baby, *querida,*" he whispered. "Do you think so?"

She smiled. "The doctors say you can't tell by how much you enjoyed it. But if you could, we'll make a lot of babies tonight. I can never quite believe our lovemaking. How can it be so good?"

He nuzzled her throat. "Because we love each other and we're so deeply in love with each other. We don't hold back anything. And we trust each other. God, how we *trust* each other."

And as he spoke, he thought about Daryl on the street the day before as they left Minden. But mostly he thought briefly about Isabel and her betrayal and how much he had loved her. How had he come to trust *this* woman so completely? He only knew he did and he thanked heaven for that trust.

He was fully prepared to go deeper into their lovemaking, but they fell into a fast sleep and didn't awaken for a couple of hours. And they both came fully awake at about the same time, laughing and rubbing their eyes.

"I guess we were tireder than we thought," he said. "Are you hungry? We ate little on the plane."

"I am and I'm willing to bet that all that food waiting under covered dishes is good."

"This place is famous. I have part interest in it. It has been in operation a very long time. The night's just beginning. Do you have the stamina to last it through?"

"You know I do."

He kissed her slowly, then got up and started away from her as she saw him glance down at his body. Tonight she had not been aware of the deep scars that went across his upper belly and halfway across his back. Those were grievous scars left by El Diablo. He turned and saw her looking at those scars and he wondered.

"Come here," she told him. He came to her and she sat up, stroked his scars and kissed them, running her tongue lightly over them.

"My scars have never seemed to turn you off," he said in wonder. "The first night we made love, you said the same thing to me: 'Come here,' and you kissed my scars and they have never bothered me since."

And it came to his mind without his wanting it to that Isabel had hated those same scars, but said they fascinated her because the world of danger and men who lived dangerous lives fascinated her. But he would be damned if he was going to think about Isabel tonight.

He drew on his boxers and got the suitcases from outside their front door.

The food was superb and Dosha made up the silver trays. Roast beef, ham, roast chicken, already sliced and made into delicious sandwiches on wheat and black bread. There was the ever present paella, this time with pimentos, pickles, black and green olives, big crisp potato chips and huge strawberries and cherries half-dipped in chocolate. All the food was covered and set on warming or cooling trays.

"I'm pretty sure we'll find ice cream in the refrigerator," Christian said. They looked and sure enough there was even the Neapolitan ice cream he had told the manager he wanted stocked.

Dosha kissed the tip of his nose. "No wonder I respond to you the way I do. My center just runs and grabs you when I'm anywhere near you and I dream of you when you're not."

"Don't remind me," he growled, "or you will find yourself carried back to bed."

They ate in companionable silence, stealing lover's glances at each other.

Finally he said, "That was a great beginning. Sleepy?"

"Not at all. And, yes, that *was* great. I wish I could give every hungry-for-love woman a man like you."

"I wish a woman like you for every man."

The food tasted really good to Dosha who enjoyed the spiciness of Spanish dishes. Christian thought she glowed from his lovemaking and his mind was on his next move, but Dosha had her own ideas. They both sampled the chocolate-dipped cherries and strawberries, decided they would save the ice cream for another time. The sangria wine was delicious and they savored the taste and the warmth as it went down.

"We could use some music," she told him.

"You *are* music, *querida.*"

"And you have a honey tongue. Flattery will get you anywhere you care to go."

"It's not flattery to tell a rose that it's beautiful, completely beautiful."

"Thank you. I'm glad you think so. There must be a sound system around somewhere."

"You're right. I'll turn it on. What would you like to hear?"

She laughed aloud. "I packed several of Barry White's best. A couple of Luther Vandross's extra specials. I know where I put everything. I'll just open the suitcases and get those articles."

"You'll need more."

At her raised eyebrows he smiled. "Later we'll walk a mile to the waterfall and spend the rest of the night there with the heavens, then watch a spectacular sunrise."

She got up, went and unpacked the articles they would need and came back with one Barry White CD and one Luther Vandross. Both had quickly become favorites of Christian. He went into the living room and set up the music which was piped all over the cottage. Sitting down, he felt her pedicured foot caress his calf, then his thigh and his crotch. "You're being provocative, my wife. Don't complain if it leads to things you're not quite ready for."

On impulse she got up, walked around the table and stood by his side. "Please, *querido,*" she said, "move your chair back from the table."

His look questioned her, but he did as she asked. She straddled him, put her arms around his neck and held him in a searching kiss. Her naked buttocks were very warm on his lap and she pressed down, loving the enraptured expression on his face. Her heat radiated across his body and for a moment he shuddered, his shaft growing and hardening to steel.

"Like this?" she murmured.

"*Love* this."

She kissed his face lightly, letting her tongue go over the smooth, leathery flesh, then she cupped his face in her hands and kissed him, her tongue exploring the warm, slightly salty hollows of his mouth. "You're so precious to me," she whispered.

He let her play him and he was silent, unmoving until an inherent masculinity asserted itself and he took off his boxers and unloosed his powerful instrument, letting it slide into her waiting body slowly as she moaned softly in the back of her throat.

And he teased her. "Like this?"

"You know damned well I love it."

"Then prove it. Work your hips against me the way only you can do."

And she did as he wanted, moving slowly, her full breasts begging for his mouth on them, her belly burning up with lust and passion. She felt his muscular arms and placed her hand flat against his wide, hard chest. His strength came to her and she was thrilling beyond belief.

He placed the flat of his hands against the back of her buttocks and pressed hard, rubbed the melting soft flesh and squeezed it with his big hands. He thought then that if he died this minute, the world owed him nothing. In her, he had everything he wanted, had ever wanted.

He throbbed mightily inside her as he began to suckle her breasts at last, groaning, half panting with lust and wonder. Her tough-tender inner walls held him in a loving powerful grip and he passed her womb and went into a deeper place. Later, by the waterfall, when he had her legs over his shoulder, he would enter her completely with deeper thrusts and higher heaven. Lord, she was good as she leaned in on him, kissing his scalp, his face, lightly biting his ear in a way that enthralled him. Then he thought that he wouldn't wait for the waterfall. He had another idea.

His mouth waxed and waned on her breasts as he suckled tenderly, then greedily. If a baby came from all this passion, he thought, then what a child that would be. He ran his free hand slowly up and down her back, caressing, pressing. With an index finger, he traced her spine. "There is something else I want to try."

She breathed harder, not wanting to move from this position. "It's so good this way."

"I promise you even more passion my way."

And his way was to place her on the polished wood of the table and enter her again, drive into her with tender fury, slowly and expertly, until she cried out. His shaft was completely swollen now, rock hard, and he pulled her legs around his shoulders and pressed his face into the hollows of her throat.

Barry White lured them on with his tender words and groans of passion. As his haunting, mesmerizing voice massaged their ears, fed their hearts with a love as great as their own, they felt awe at the love and desire and passion shimmering in waves around them.

"I love you now," he whispered. "I'll always love you. Please do not ever leave me. Do not ever stop loving me."

She pressed more kisses onto his face. "You know I never will and I'll love you forever."

They were still in heat of passion and the fury with which they met couldn't last very long.

With him throbbing inside her, she laughed a bit. "We're not teenagers, nor even in our twenties. But I think you and I behave like teenagers sometimes."

"For us, the thirties is a hungry age, too. We've both been without for so long. We've so much time to make up."

A storm of passion hit her then and she begged him with a few tears in her eyes. "Don't talk. Just love me, love me..."

Chapter 9

It was two in the morning when they set out for the waterfall. He wore shorts and a tee shirt and she was naked under a blue shift. They held hands as they traversed a long, sandy road. After only a few minutes, she stopped and he stopped with her. She put her arms around his neck and drew his head to her, with her mouth close to his ear. In a low, sultry voice she dared him, "Lover, catch me if you can."

"I'll do better than that," he told her. "I'll even give you a head start. You won't be able to get far before I take you down."

Laughing, she was off and running while he held back. Cool air filled her lungs and almost from the beginning she felt a runner's high. She didn't look back, but kept running, the flat ballerina shoes comfortable and helpful in her flight. She had closed her eyes and swept on when he caught her from behind and slowly bore himself and her half onto the soft, black sand and half onto the crisp, green grass. They were cushioned by the blanket and the pillows.

With his face in her hair, he held her close and murmured, "Run away from me, will you? You little devil. In a minute, I'll make you pay for running. I'll pin you to me with my love shaft and I won't let you get away."

"I won't even try," she whispered.

They lay still together, resting for a moment before they sat up and both looked up at the dark blue sky and the countless spangled silver stars and full moon. "Are we under the full moon's spell?" he asked.

"I expect we are. But when did we ever need a full moon?" Her face was serious in the bright moonlight. "We're passionate people, love. We're blessed that way."

Very quietly he said, "Passion so deeply felt can also be a curse."

She thought of Daryl then and of Isabel and nodded. "But we're grown up enough to handle our passion. The hurt we've known has taught us valuable lessons. I don't think we'll ever really hurt each other, but if I ever hurt you, tell me and I'll move heaven and earth to make it up to you."

He laughed softly. "I feel the same way about you. Come here."

"I'm already here. How close can I get to you?"

"You're closer than you dream. Love, you're so much a part of me it frightens me, but I wouldn't have it any other way. If you ever hurt me, I'll take it and remember what we know now. I could sit here all night, but I've dreamed of making love to you by the waterfall on our honeymoon, so let's go. I've got a surprise for you."

And when they reached it she was surprised because she had seen the waterfall on a couple of her visits to Puerto de la Cruz and he had had multicolored orchids planted to the area. A wide patch of black sand sparkled like diamonds in the moonlight.

"Oh, Lord, it's beautiful," she told him. "You did this for me. Thank you." She kissed his neck and he held her to him.

"For us. I want us to remember this night always. When I do things you may not like, when I get too involved with work or when we have babies that keep us both up all night, remember these perfect nights together."

"Just having you in my life is all I need to make it perfect," she murmured.

"You're kind. That's the way I feel about you."

The wide waterfall spilling over a slope that was half quartz rock and half grass was gorgeous in the moonlight. It sparkled even more than the glittering black sand. A few night birds sang, and suddenly there was a wondrous trill of music from a joyous bird. She listened and after a moment queried, "A nightingale?"

"Yes. They come around sometimes. I had hoped he would come tonight and here he is. *Querida,* even nature knows how much I love you."

They stood, silent, letting the nightingale's song caress their ears and feeling the gentle breezes caress their bodies. "You are even more beautiful in the moonlight," he told her and drew her closer. His big hand began to pull up her shift. "Is it safe here?" she asked, "and will some other ardent lovers come here looking for what we've found?"

He laughed. "It is safe. This whole area is patrolled by well-trained men. They know how close by to stay to ensure safety and how far to stay away. We have that trellis of roses to shield us and I gave orders that we're to be left alone. Don't worry about anything but me. You might be in danger of my gobbling you up. Then I would have you forever."

She stroked his face and he turned and walked a short distance to the rose trellis. She watched as he stripped a red rose from the trellis and brought it back to her. The heavenly odor filled their nostrils as he stripped the leaves from the stalk, checked for thorns and put the flower behind her ear. Putting his arms around her, he searched her face in the moonlight, then his lips barely grazed hers. She pressed closer, hungry for him now, her belly flashing fire.

"How could I want you again so much so soon?" she whispered as molten honey filled her veins.

"We want each other, *querida.* Deep loving makes us this way." He stroked her back in long, tender movements and pressed her buttocks in to him. She ran her hands over his rippling biceps and muscular back. Drawing her down onto the very warm sand, they were on their knees facing each other as his lips darted hot kisses all over her face and throat. She moaned low and trembled in his arms as he pulled off her shift and his clothing.

He spread the blanket and threw the pillows onto it. Then he took her down and lay poised over her as she touched his shaft, stroked it tenderly, then bent and kissed it a lingering kiss.

"He's even crazier about you than I am," he told her, "if that is possible. You kiss me there and I'm yours for all time. You do know that?"

She smiled. "I only know I'm yours."

Parting her legs, he entered her with easy, deft strokes as she crossed her ankles over his back and held him prisoner. He worked her then expertly with loving pressure and his tongue roved her face and throat as she breathed raggedly. This was the essence of romantic love, of love itself, she thought, as he throbbed inside her. Then she cried his name because he had slid past her womb into a deeper place and waves of pure pleasure filled her veins with liquid fire.

Christian was nearly blind with rapture as thrill after thrill flashed through them both. Inside her body, he was a god, but he worshipped the beloved woman beneath him. They were slow, with him thrusting gently now, filling her with his love as well as his shaft.

"Honey," she murmured, her voice slightly hoarse with wanting.

"Yes, love." His own voice was hoarser.

"Make it last a long time. You feel so good inside me."

"That's the very reason it's so hard to make it last, but I'll try. Calm your walls inside and make them stop grabbing me, drawing all my seed. Make them behave."

"They love you too much." She stopped moving her hips in the slow, concentric circles and settled down.

"Okay. That is better. You were bringing me on in a hurry. Now we can both be still."

They lay there with the smell of roses surrounding them, the warm, warm sand under their bodies and the singing of other birds they couldn't identify. After a little while he hugged her lightly and quickly, kissed her fingers and her arms. His mouth fastened gently on her breasts and he suckled with alternating teasing passion and tender hunger. His mouth on her breasts brought desire to the surface again and she locked her ankles around his.

Withdrawing, he began kissing her, beginning with her scalp with the fruity smell of her shampoo. She shuddered with wonderment and ravening desire as his mouth traversed her body. His tongue was wild in her navel indention, hot on her belly and down into her center. She bucked under him and cried his name, increasing his ardor before he moved on to her thighs, calves and her silken feet.

Turning her over, he tongue-kissed her back and her buttocks, stroked and kissed her thighs and calves. And he finally sat up grinning. "Like that, do you?"

She didn't answer, just laughed lightly in her throat, pushed him flat on his back and began the same movements on his body. "You're a good teacher," she murmured. "Now I'm going to drive you right out of your mind."

She licked his flat nipples and he shuddered, loving the

circular movements she made with her tongue. His shaft was swollen with raging need and he stopped her, turned her onto her back and entered her again with more haste now. He pulled her legs over his shoulders and his tongue in her mouth was ravaging and sugar sweet. He stopped for a moment and pulled a pillow under her hips, then entered her again. This time they were both panting with wave after wave of desire filling them to bursting as they came to climax in a special world made for lovers like them.

He felt like a god bestriding a mountaintop with her by his side and his loins felt a glory he couldn't remember ever feeling before as his seed poured into her. She was a creature of the sea with waves crashing through her tender body until some force of nature caught and held her, shaking her with loving hands until she took in his precious seed deep in her body and, seeking, held it. And both lay drunk with what they had just known and the child they both hoped would come from it.

Chapter 10

"Oh, my dears, you both look so happy, and I'm happy for you."

In her apartment, Socorro hugged the two newlyweds, noting that this was their first day down from the hills and their week-long honeymoon.

It was early morning and she asked, "Shall I get coffee for you, or tea?"

They both shook their heads, having already had coffee downstairs. Socorro couldn't stop smiling at them. She thought Christian had never looked this happy and Dosha was glowing. They all sat on the plush chairs Socorro favored.

"I was going to offer to read the Tarot for you as a beginning," Socorro said, "but the spirits are not with me just now. I'm getting lovely vibrations from the universe, but I sense a little disturbance. Ah, as I get older, I get more wisdom, but things are sometimes not as clear."

She broke off for a moment. "Oh, yes, I asked Estela to bring Marta to meet you. I do not know why, but I wanted to be with you when you were introduced. The girl is seventeen, a distant cousin of Estela and was with us when Isabel was here. In fact, it was Isabel who brought her here. She took ill and had to go home shortly after Isabel died. She wanted to come back after all this time and I let her, on condition that you like her. My dear, it's entirely in your hands."

Dosha sat reflecting that Christian had told her that Estela and her husband, Pablo, had been caretakers of this estate for many years. In their early fifties, they were superb servants who loved and were loved by the whole family. Juan, who had gone to D.C. with Christian for the latter's wedding, helped them when something needed fixing. Juan was very adept and even knew something about electronics.

Dosha nodded as a knock sounded. At Socorro's answer, Estela and a young woman who might have been pretty had she not seemed so sullen came in. Estela introduced her as Marta and to Dosha's surprise, she curtsied.

"Thank you for letting me live here again," Marta said drily.

Socorro raised her eyebrows. "Do your job well and we'll all be content. Señora Montero will talk with you about what she wants your duties to be."

Estela smiled broadly, "Oh, señora, I'll see that she talks with Señora Montero as soon as the señora wishes her to."

Estela and Marta didn't tarry and closed the door softly behind them. Dosha thought a strange expression crossed Christian's face, but it was quickly gone. They settled down to a leisurely conversation about the wedding and the honeymoon.

"Such a short honeymoon," Socorro said, shrugging. "New couples need much more time to get closer."

"My boss has promised us three weeks in Tahiti if we can

hold out for five months. There's so much work to be done in setting up this new territory for the bank." He grinned at Dosha. "We may go on a second honeymoon with her pregnant." Half closing his eyes, he focused on Dosha and their glances held. Socorro watched the interplay and delight filled her. Christian was her heart, so much like her late and precious Magdalena, his mother.

"I'm going to leave you two ladies to chat," he told them. And to Dosha, "Do not let my abuela charm you so that you forget to come to me." He stood up, bent and kissed Dosha's cheek.

Socorro smiled. "She is completely taken with you as you are with her. She will listen to me with half an ear, I assure you."

Christian chuckled. "I'm going to walk about a bit checking downstairs and deciding on a few things about the house I wish to talk with you about. When you come down, we'll have breakfast and walk around the grounds. Have you had breakfast, Abuela?"

Socorro shook her head. "I wanted a late breakfast this morning. Pablo is fixing me waffles..."

"That's what he's making for us," Dosha exclaimed. "Why don't you eat downstairs with us?"

Socorro smiled. "Thank you for the kind invitation, but I remember the early days of my marriage and my parents left us alone as much as possible when we lived with them. It's so wonderful that you both wanted me to remain here. I'm more grateful than I could ever tell you. Know that my spirit's with you constantly. Much later, perhaps, I'll take a few meals with you."

Christian went to Socorro's chair, bent and kissed her brow, ruffled her silken white curls. She caught his hand and pressed it.

Once he had gone, Socorro was silent a long while.

Finally she said, "There's so much I want to tell you about my late husband, Isaac, and me. I think my story aches to be told because our happiness was like Christian's and yours."

"I'll love hearing this story and thank you for telling me."

Socorro looked at the lovely jade ring on Dosha's finger. "Wear it always," she said softly. "Jade is said to give power and strength and to protect you."

"I *will* wear it always. You're so kind."

Socorro smiled. "Life's been kind to me. I simply pass it on."

Socorro digressed a moment, said abruptly, "You'll see a haunted look cross your husband's face from time to time and it may bother you. It has always been my feeling that he is remembering the incredible torment he finally knew with Isabel. She hurt him so badly for so long. His father and I were afraid for his sanity, for his very life. We're people who love with all our hearts and such people can be grievously wounded. We'll talk more about this later."

Socorro smiled then and closed her eyes for only a moment. Then she began after drawing a deep breath. "Let's talk about my husband. Isaac's car went off a road when the brakes of the Army jeep he was riding in failed. We lived in the wooded section of the hills and I found him unconscious as I rode my bicycle. I knew a bit about first aid and I got my father who got others and we took him home. Medical men and supplies were hard to come by during the war, but we were fortunate. One of the neighbors had been medically trained in the Spanish Army and he examined Isaac, said there were no life-threatening signs.

"Isaac got in touch with his company and they came out with better medical supplies and treated him further. He asked and to our surprise his commanding officer permitted him to stay with us until he was well enough to travel."

Her eyes misted then. "We fell in love from the beginning.

I with my Spanish-Gypsy-African bloodlines and he with African, white and Indian blood running in his veins. Yes, he was handsome, and I saw him as a godsend. Puerto is not a place for hatred. God has been too good to us, but my *madre*—mother—who was a mestizo worried that I wouldn't find a husband who was good enough. My father, a Spaniard, always said he would be happy to have me on their hands for the rest of their lives and mine."

Socorro's eyes crinkled with smiles and she was beautiful remembering. "Both my parents loved Isaac from the beginning. He showed us all photographs of his family, his mother and father and his one brother. They lived in a place called Yazoo City in Mississippi and were very prosperous farmers." Socorro chuckled. "People teased us, said he probably had a wife and children waiting for him back home, but I knew better. The spirits told me that this was my intended mate and not to let him go."

She was thoughtful for a very long time before she sighed. "There were letters from his parents and his brother. We exchanged photographs. We weren't wealthy, but we wanted for little, except that there was rationing with a war going on. His family invited me to visit them when the war was over and I accepted. I invited them here. Oh, their material life was much grander than mine. They lived in a big, white country house with acres of yard, pecan, peach, apple orchards. They farmed beautiful fields of cotton, corn and soybeans. His brother was what your country's people call 4-F, unfit for military service, left that way by rheumatic fever."

Socorro grew warm with memories. "Isaac didn't formally propose to me. As we sat on the porch when he could first get around, he simply said he would ask his brother to be his best man. And he looked at me shyly and I cried. 'You are asking me to marry you,' I could only whisper.

"'Yes,' he said. 'Why are you crying?'

"'Because I love you and I'm so happy.'

"In a week or so he went back to his company and he was shipped to Hawaii for recreation and rest. Within a couple of weeks I received a beautiful diamond engagement ring." She held up her hand and touched the two rings on her finger. The large diamond and the heavy, plain gold band sparkled and gleamed in the sunlight. Then she kissed the rings and her lips lingered on them.

"The war ended and Isaac came back for me and we were married. We talked of my going back with him to the States, but he liked it here. He said he liked the peace and quiet. His father and his brother told him they could manage well without him. There was turmoil in the south and he hated that turmoil. So we settled here and he worked with my father in his blacksmith shop and we prospered."

Socorro paused for long moments, then continued. "We visited Mississippi and his family was wonderful to me. Theirs was one of the largest and loveliest farms I've ever seen. His mother told me she had always wanted a daughter. Now she had me. I loved both his parents and his brother on sight." Then she said almost as an afterthought, "His brother never married.

"Then something else wondrous happened. They struck oil on Isaac's family's property and they were suddenly rich. He never really cared about money and neither did I, but his father shared equally with him and his brother. With money, we visited back and forth often, and when Magdalena was born, she could have been a princess with all the attention and gifts she got."

Socorro's face was alight with memory. "Rafael Montero fell in love with my beautiful Magdalena and begged—not asked—for her hand. They were married, Christian was born and my world has long been complete. And so it went until later when Isaac's parents died within months of each other, and his brother and Isaac inherited the farm. They were fortunate to find a competent manager. Then the brother and Isaac died many years later and I was left with the farm. I sold it for an astonishing price, keeping large shares of the mineral rights. So I'm a rich old woman..."

"What a beautiful story," Dosha murmured.

"Yes. My life was a beautiful story until Magdalena died at thirty-five of scarlet fever. We were all inconsolable, but Christian was shattered. He had been so close to his mother. At sixteen he began to be interested in bullfighting and to go to Pamplona in the spring to run with the bulls.

"His goring by El Diablo a year or so later was both fortune and misfortune. I had many intimations of his death by violence. There were too many women pursuing him, some far too old for him. And he drank too much. But he will tell you this if he has not already."

"He's told me a little. He told me he was brutally hurt by his mother's death."

"Yes, but he's also very close to his father, so Rafael persuaded him to take the necessary exams and enter the university at nearly eighteen. He graduated with highest honors and chose to go into banking, about as far away as you can get from bullfighting."

Socorro shook her head. "Scars left by that goring were horrendous and I wet them all with my tears." She paused a long moment, then looked at Dosha. "Do you find his scars unsightly, my dear?"

Dosha smiled softly. "I find the scars and Christian beautiful beyond words. I love him so much."

"I know you do and I pray you both will have that love always." She moved easily to the next topic. "You may find Marta a bit difficult. She was so heartbroken after Isabel died, I'm shocked to find she wanted to come back. Estela tells me she is a devoted worker and very useful. She is a sullen creature, though, and if she gives you any trouble, let her go. You are far too happy to have it spoiled in any way. Now, I'm sure you are famished for the sight of your beloved. I can't tell you how happy I am that you came to see me."

"Oh, we would have come last night, but it was late."

"I'm happy in your happiness and my only prayer is that it will continue. Get pregnant soon. You both deserve that pleasure. Desire is never so strong as when a baby is demanding to be conceived. I know it was so with me before I conceived Magdalena."

Downstairs the big house hummed with early-morning activity. The smell of grilled bacon and other breakfast foods filled the air, making Dosha hungry. She turned on music from an entertainment center and the soft sounds of Debussy's *Afternoon of a Faun* swelled forth. For just a moment she closed her eyes and, smiling, went to look for Christian.

She found him in the large alcove at the end of the living room where Marty's magnificent portrait of a radiantly beautiful Isabel in a one-of-a-kind red silk satin ball gown held sway. His tall body seemed very tense to her, even from behind and he didn't hear her come up.

After a moment she spoke. "Chris?"

When he turned, his face bore the familiar haunted expression before he relaxed and smiled, took several steps to where she stood and hugged her, asking, "Did you and Abuela have a good visit?'

"Um-m. Your grandmother has to be one of the most interesting people on earth."

"But not more than you are, my love."

"Or you." She bit her bottom lip. Should she ask him?

"You seem so bothered, honey. Marty really showed his genius when he painted that portrait."

Christian nodded. "It was the talk of Puerto. Every woman who could afford it wanted him to paint her. He could be doing a rushing business today if he chose." They looked at the other walls that were lined with portraits and photographs. "Socorro, Isaac, her beloved, her passion for all time." Christian's mother and Socorro's daughter—Magdalena. His grandparents. His father, Captain Montero. Some of the photographs were very old, some more recent.

The soft ecru of the room and the soft lighting enhanced the paintings and the photographs. It was a mini-museum, she thought.

He cleared his throat. "I've decided to send Isabel's portrait to Puerto's museum." She saw that his face was set in suddenly hard lines.

"But why? It's such a glorious painting."

He placed a hand on the side of each shoulder and drew her to him. "Dosha, this is *your* house now. My grandmother has decreed that it be. If the house weren't so precious to her, I would build you a new one—just for you. You deserve that much and I intend to give you everything you deserve, everything you want."

"I love this house," she told him, "love having Socorro live with us. The painting is one of Marty's finest and I enjoy looking at it. But if it hurts you too badly…"

He didn't comment on her last sentence. "You can enjoy looking at a woman I once loved unwisely?" He shook his head. "But not the way I've come to love you."

"Yes, I can enjoy it because I feel in the marrow of my bones that you love me as I love you. *Does* the painting hurt you so much?"

He held her away from him and his eyes lovingly roved her body. "Not if it doesn't bother you. I'll let it stay for the time being. Marty told me when we go back to D.C., he will paint you in your wedding finery. That will go in the alcove around the corner all by itself, or wherever you choose."

"I'll look forward to that."

"And so will I."

But the lighthearted conversation they were having didn't erase the pained expression on his face when he had turned as she saw him looking again at Isabel's portrait. Isabel had hurt him deeply, he had said that much, but she longed to know the particulars of that hurt.

Marta came to them, her face somber, "Excuse me, señor, señora, your breakfast is served. I set places on the patio as you instructed."

As the girl left, Dosha said, "Doesn't she ever smile?"

"In all the time she has worked here, I don't believe I've ever seen her smile. Estela says she's led a hard life as one of ten children on a farm that barely provides a living."

"That probably explains a lot. Socorro says she was close to Isabel."

"Yes. Isabel said she once told her that she wanted to be her personal maid. She worshipped Isabel. She was quite young when she was last here and Isabel tutored her. They were very close."

Breakfast on the patio was pleasant, beginning with melon wedges and orange juice, then waffles with fruit syrup, bacon strips and eggs scrambled with scallions and sharp cheese. A robin watched and sang to them from the branch of a nearby tree and farther away a Drago tree stood in all its ancient majesty.

They ate slowly as a soft breeze caressed their faces and were finished when Marta brought Dosha the telephone. "Señora, the señor says he is your brother."

Dosha took the phone to hear Adam's lively voice. "Adam!" She felt her spirits lift even more.

"I hate interrupting a honeymoon, but you need to hear this."

"We came off honeymoon last night. Work made us cut it short and for this, we'll be given a three-week stay in Tahiti later on."

"Lord, the life of some people. I've got to take Ricky to a school meeting, so I'm going to be brief. I've talked with Stoner since you left. Grilled him. Raked him over the coals. He apologized for waiting for you to pass on the way to the airport. Swore he wouldn't bother you again. He offered to take any kind of test I wanted him to take to prove he didn't send the photograph of the dead woman who looked like you. And I took him at his word. He passed a lie detector test. He's either one of the best liars I've ever seen, or he's telling the truth.

"But there's one other thing. He's nothing if not psychotic and those birds can often pass any test because they *believe* their lies." He sighed. "Be careful, Sis, and keep your eyes and ears at the ready. Stoner's got money to go anywhere he wants to go and Puerto's not difficult to get to. I'd say he's got the kind of crazy love for you that you neither need nor want. He said he's in love with you and always will be, that you'll come back to him, that the two of you can only love each other."

"Oh, really." Her voice was sharp, sarcastic. A small shudder ran the length of her body as she thought about Daryl's wild eyes when they passed him on the way to the airport. Would he come to Puerto? She prayed he wouldn't.

She envisioned Adam's big, athletic frame as he said, "I love you, kid."

"You nut. You're the youngest."

"Only chronologically. I'm an old man in wisdom. Raven and the kids send their love and we'll all be talking en masse soon. Is Chris around?"

She sent her love to Adam's family and handed Christian the phone. The two men chatted for a short while with Christian's face wreathed in smiles. Finally he hung up. "That's quite a family you've got. They feel like my own."

"They *are* yours—your family is mine."

Dosha and Christian spent the rest of the morning walking the grounds and talking with Estela and Pablo. "Oh, señora, we're delighted to have you here," Estela said. "Along with Señora Johnson, I can see you'll be a dream to work for."

"And, of course, I feel the same about you and Pablo," Dosha replied graciously.

They retired to their suite after an early dinner and began listening to Verdi's *La Traviata*.

Before the popular opera began, Dosha said thoughtfully. "Some of the composers have stranger lives than their opera schemes. And I'm reminded of a country singer who says he's sorry for anyone who's not him tonight."

Christian laughed. "That's the way I feel. And you're the sole reason for it. I love you, *novia*. Do not let me forget to tell you all the time."

Dosha sat on the sofa as Christian lay with his head in her lap. He picked up the jacket of the opera album and studied it for long moments. Finally he said grimly, "A beautiful woman pursued by many men. It's an old story." His voice sounded suddenly bitter.

She was silent for a few moments, but she wanted to help ease his pain.

"You're thinking about Isabel."

"Yes. When the stories about her and lovers—not just one—began to filter back to me, I laughed it off. Jealousy, I thought. She's so beautiful and she's mine. And she assured me that she was. I wanted many children. She wanted no more than one, if that. 'God,' she would say, 'I don't want to see my body ruined with childbearing the way I've seen it happen to my friends.' I pointed out to her that marriages are based on love and children born to those in love. I could never reach her."

"But you were happy at first?" She ran her fingers over his leathery cheeks.

"I was. Isabel got along with everybody. She was an excellent hostess. Oh, she flirted, but I dismissed that as a beautiful woman demanding her due. She was spoiled, her father's favorite, and I knew it. I did well at the bank. She and her sister were heiresses. So there was plenty of money to indulge ourselves.

"I sensed that Socorro didn't altogether like Isabel and that bothered me because Socorro and I have always been so close. Then after about the third year, I thought I saw that Isabel wasn't going to get pregnant anytime soon and I demanded that we talk. I was right. She wasn't sure she wanted a mestizo child, but she said she was thinking about it. I was stunned and I pointed out that she knew my bloodlines when she married me.

"She said my bloodlines excited her more than anything she had ever known. She knew her father liked and approved of me and our marriage and thought that having a mestizo grandchild was fine. He was an unusual man, Puerto to the bone."

Christian was silent for a very long time as she stroked his body and the opera played on, largely unheard. "Then I began to hear stories about her and Francisco, my cousin, Francisco. This time the pain was intense. She swore it was all a lie and I watched, but found nothing. My father thought I should get a divorce, but I was still in love. He suggested I get a mistress to heal some of the hurt, but I'm a faithful man.

"So in less than three years my happy marriage was beginning to unravel. When I pressed her one night to tell me when she would bear me a child, she told me that she was in love with someone..." His voice had become labored and harsh with memory. Suddenly he burst out, "Dear God, I can't talk about this right now."

"Then don't," she murmured as he sat up and drew her to him.

"You need to know and I need to talk about it, but right now I just cannot," he said.

Her voice was calm, soothing with love. "Then *don't,* my darling. Just wait until you can."

She turned off the opera and they undressed and went to bed, lay in each other's arms for a long while before he turned to her and took her with breathtaking fury that was sweeter and more poignant than at any other time.

They both fell asleep immediately and it was after two by the luminous dial of the bedside clock. Dosha awakened, thirsty. She wanted a drink of water. She got up and slipped into a robe, stepped out into the hall. At the end of the corridor she saw a small female figure turn the corner and she walked on to find the figure halfway down that corridor. "Marta," she called softly.

At first the girl hurried on until Dosha called a second time more sharply and her own footsteps hurried until she caught up with her.

"You were coming from our corridor. Why at this time of the morning?" she demanded.

The girl's face was frightened and sullen at once. "Oh, señora," she said breathlessly. "I don't sleep well and I walk along *all* the corridors. Please forgive me. I meant no harm."

But when Dosha put out her hand to reassure her, the girl drew away, saying, "Forgive me."

Dosha nodded. "It's all right. I've herbs that can make you sleep better. I'll give them to you later today."

"*Gracias*. You are kind. May I go now?"

"Yes, of course."

Dosha stared at the girl until she turned another corridor corner and went down the stairs.

She followed her down and went to the kitchen, got her water and drank it slowly. Why had the girl been near their bedroom, and was she lying? She had adored Isabel. Was she envious of Dosha? Some disturbing sixth sense filled her. She didn't like Marta, didn't trust her for a minute. For some reason she thought more sharply then of Adam's call and she had not for most of the day.

She shook her head. "Welcome to Puerto," she murmured to herself, "and I thought the intrigue ended when I left Daryl and the United States."

Chapter 11

"You're early and that's always good. I'm so glad to see you both again."

An effusive Ramon Muñoz, Christian's boss, greeted them in Ramon's lavishly appointed office just off the Charcot del Plaza. The building was new black granite and designed by one of Europe's foremost architects. A small, dapper man of enormous charm and energy, Ramon shook hands with Christian and kissed Dosha's cheek. Dosha had met him only once while visiting Puerto and they had liked each other on sight.

"My wife is about somewhere," Ramon said, "and will join us shortly." He pointed to the heavy silver coffee set. "This morning the brew is superb, but my wife will kill me if I pour before she gets back."

Dosha laughed merrily. She had found Ramon's use of American terminology one of the most attractive things about him. A very attractive woman exquisitely dressed in shades of blue who was a little taller in heels than her husband came in and walked over to them. "You're here. Oh, Christian, your wife is lovely."

As she had liked the husband, so Dosha was immediately attracted to Pia, the wife. It was going to be easy to work with these two, Dosha thought. She was glad she had worn one of her most attractive outfits, a soft yellow silk slub jacket over a matching sheath. Tan strap shoes and a tan Coach bag completed her outfit.

The coffee *was* superb, served in Limoges cups and saucers and the hot, buttered scones served with delicious strawberry jam brought their taste buds alive. For a few moments, they ate in silence before Ramon began. "I wanted to see you both because I have wonderful news. You'll be working together for at least a while, and, if I can get this through, for the duration."

"That's wonderful news," Christian said.

Ramon looked thoughtful. "As you are aware, you've been one of our most useful and valued employees. It's past time that you are rewarded for your truly excellent work."

"Thank you," Christian said gravely.

Ramon smiled. "You'll thank me more, I think. As you know, if Señor Jaime Garcia, our CEO, selects you, you'll head the administrative segment of the Arts Section of Banc International. This is completely new and it will be up to you to develop the nuts and bolts of it. Finances. How much money is to be allocated. You're magnificent when it comes to working with others and I'm sure you'll do your best as always.

"Now this is where Dosha comes in. She's a gifted musician, a teacher, and she'll oversee the awarding of scholarships to the most gifted young musicians. She will, of course, have a committee to help her, but the main thrust will be hers..."

Dosha looked up, startled. She hadn't expected anything so encompassing. This was a real plum, as interesting as Christian's position.

"Thank you," Dosha said softly. "I hardly know what to say. This is something I'll love and it's kind of you to think of me."

Ramon leaned back. "Not kind, my dear. We pride ourselves on picking the best people for our jobs. You're spoken of as a genius with all the best credentials, and Christian's gifts have long enhanced Banc International. You would be monitored by a couple of the best musical names in the business who are far older than you, thus far more experienced, but you will hold your own. Of that, I'm certain. It's a trial run, subject to your approval and ours. Lean heavily on me and I'll guide you to those who can best direct you."

Ramon stopped for a moment then, smiling widely. "Of course, I'll keep in mind that you're newlyweds. The job begins in October and you'll be inundated with meetings. The CEO of Banc International himself, Jaime Garcia, is very interested in this project and is very anxious that it succeed."

Christian nodded. "I don't have to tell you how much we would appreciate this opportunity to work together."

"Yes. You'll live here in Puerto for six months of the year and six months in Washington, D.C. Here and in the U.S. you will make contacts for Europe and for America. We'll begin small, with these countries, but later Señor Garcia wishes to branch out to Africa and South and Central America. We've often talked and he has long felt that the arts can bring the world together in a way that nothing else can. This can be your crowning achievement."

Dosha and Christian both nodded, thrumming with excitement. Then Ramon's eyes narrowed. "Of course there's Francisco..."

"What about my cousin?" Christian demanded.

Ramon's voice went dry. "What indeed? Francisco has ties to two of the top people in the bank and they want *him* for this job. But I happen to have Señor Garcia's ear and he holds you in very high esteem, as I hold you." He smiled, then looked somber. "He was a friend of Francisco's late father and he is fond of Francisco."

Christian sat with excitement flooding him. The job wasn't his yet, but should it become his, this could be the culmination of a dream. To be part of making his world a better place had been his wish since he had been grown up. Now he smiled at Dosha, reached over and pressed her hand.

Ramon leaned forward. "You're not a man given to hatred, but I think you need to be careful about Francisco. He's a man given to deep hatred, grudges and angers. Should you be chosen, he'll be angry that you were chosen over him and he'll do what he can to undermine and hurt you. You *will* be careful and keep me apprised of any untoward move he makes?"

Christian nodded. "You may be sure I will."

"Good. There will be several meetings for you both at first. And day after tomorrow there is a meeting set up for you and Señor Garcia." Here he looked at Dosha, smiling charmingly. "I'll need to take him away from you for afternoon and evening meetings, and it's best that he plan to spend the night. Bear with us and think of the glorious prolonged honeymoon you'll later have in Tahiti."

Dosha smiled, as did Pia, and Ramon continued. "We'll take this slowly at first and you'll both be superbly trained. We'll meet often, talk much, but right now, I must meet with Christian for an hour or so. Pia, I leave Dosha in your hands to entertain as only you can do."

"Of course." Pia got up and Dosha rose with her, but Dosha stopped to press Christian's hand and smile at him.

He returned the smile with narrowed eyes that signaled her a message of love and sensuality and brief fire raced along her veins. They had known each other for over a year, she thought now, and they were more deeply drawn all the time. How blessed they were.

Pia took Dosha to a breathtakingly beautiful small room in the same building; they were alone. Green, growing plants were everywhere and there were gorgeous orchid plants that reminded Dosha of the orchids at the waterfall the night of their honeymoon. She and Pia sat in a nest of deep sofas near floor-to-ceiling windows that threw bright sunlight. A fountain in the middle of the room splashed into a black marble basin below. Like the orchids, the fountain brought recent memories of the waterfall on their honeymoon.

"I'm so sorry business has come up so soon," Pia said. "You needed more time alone together. But after the first few times, you'll be left alone for a time. My husband is a kind man who sincerely believes in fostering love where he can."

"You're both kind," Dosha murmured. Pia was such a lovely, forthcoming woman, she thought, with her thin, shapely body and medium brown curly hair.

Now she looked at Dosha. "I hope we'll become very good friends. I love Socorro and it seems I've always known Christian. Unfortunately, I was away the times you visited while you two were engaged. I travel for my husband. But now that I know you..."

"I think we'll be friends," Dosha assured her. "Christian is so fond of you and Ramon."

Pia raised her eyebrows. "Christian and I are both descendants of Spanish Brown Babies. My mother and Christian's mother were friends." She looked mournful then. "Now both are gone." Her eyes were bright with tears.

Dosha leaned over and put her hand over Pia's. "I've

talked with Socorro about the Brown Baby phenomenon," Dosha told her. "I'd also love to talk with you about your mother."

"I'll be happy to and we will. But just now there's something I want to mention to you." Pia paused and drew a deep breath. Her expression said she was marshaling her thoughts. "In October there'll be a grand ball, the *Baile de Isabel.* It's one of the social highlights of the season in Puerto and I don't have to tell you why. Isabel sought to make herself a goddess and in many ways I suppose she succeeded. When she died, her sister, Antonia, set this ball in motion in honor of the good deeds Isabel had done...."

Here she paused and her eyes narrowed. "I suppose this was also an attempt to balance the hell she strewed about in her wake." Pia leaned forward. "I want you to have the most beautiful gown imaginable made for yourself." She looked Dosha over, head to one side, eyes half closed. "Perhaps something in ivory, which would be wonderful for your magnificent brown skin and hair."

Pia chuckled softly. "Ah, yes, I can see it now. You come in on Christian's arm and for the first time the *Baile de Isabel* is *yours*, not hers. I'm glad you are beautiful. It will do so much to erase the stain of her evil. And, oh, I'm glad that Christian has found someone to love the way he loves you."

"I'll do my best," Dosha said, already caught up in the intrigue. From the beginning she had hated this Isabel who had caused her beloved such pain.

"And there's one other thing. You have Antonia Hidalgo's invitation to dinner next week?"

"Yes."

"Be very careful of two people in Puerto. One is Francisco and the other is Antonia. Now, there was no love between Antonia and her sister, Isabel. Antonia is a plain woman and a bloodless woman. Her husband, Huarto, makes up in heat for what she lacks, but he's a man of no morals whatsoever. He takes his pleasure where he finds it and dares her to do anything about it.

"To live the social life she worships, Antonia needs to be the wife of somebody rich and she is and has stayed his wife. The Hidalgos were once a rich, old family. But Antonia is an unhappy woman and she creates and spreads mistrust and intrigue. She has the tongue of an adder, is a vicious gossip and possesses a foul temperament. Even her daughter, Carmela, long ago emotionally fled her. She forced the girl into a loveless marriage and has always dominated her ruthlessly. Fortunately for Carmela, her husband who was like her father died of a heart attack not too long after their marriage."

Pia spread her hands. "Here I accuse Antonia of gossiping and I'm doing the same thing, but you need to know about her. You *will* be careful of her and of Francisco?"

"Yes, I'll be careful, and thank you for telling me."

"It's nothing. Now let me take you around this beautiful building. You'll be coming here often later. It'll be your second home. My husband is very much taken with you and I'm certain that the CEO of the bank will be, too. He's greatly taken by women with charm and you have it, as you Americans say, in spades."

Chapter 12

Antonia Hidalgo's house was one of the most lavish in Puerto. The furnishings were mostly the Italian provincial she favored, with huge, ornate gold leaf-trimmed mirrors and Persian rugs worthy of a sultan's castle. She maintained a small staff of superbly trained servants, and her small dinner parties were the envy of other Puerto hostesses.

Antonia's husband, Huarto, needed her to entertain the customers he had as a highly successful, well-known jeweler and she always came through admirably. Dosha felt comfortable in a pale peach linen sheath and creamy cultured pearls. Antonia looked at her and purred, "What a nice little outfit, my dear, but I must introduce you to my dressmaker." Antonia felt no one could hold a candle to her when it came to clothes. She mostly favored Parisian designers, but she didn't think this American woman would go that route.

Dosha saw the patronizing look in Antonia's eyes and coolly answered, "I appreciate your concern, but I already have a wonderful dressmaker back in Washington that I'll continue to patronize. You look lovely."

The warm smell of expensive perfume permeated the air and Beethoven's Sixth Symphony played softly. It was one of Dosha's favorites.

Now dressed in Armani's black that would have defeated a lesser woman, Antonia's dazzling white skin was perfection itself. But Christian looked around him at the women and smiled to himself. Hands down, Dosha would be the most beautiful woman here. Not that she needed that accolade; he loved his wife and that was enough for him. It was just that Antonia had always been a thorn in his side from the time he had been married to her late sister, Isabel.

Huarto, Antonia's husband, narrowed his eyes as he looked at Dosha. He was a connoisseur of the finer things of this world, and women were his favorites. From a youth, he had made no secret of his penchant for womanizing. He had sought and found a wife who didn't care what he did as long as he provided her with the money she craved to live her life. Antonia and her younger sister, Isabel, came from a once-wealthy family that had fallen on hard times. Her indifference left him free to pursue his passion—beautiful women. And Dosha was such a women.

Now Huarto turned to Christian. "I offer you services of my humble shop to provide this treasure who is your wife gems that will do her full justice. I must congratulate you on your choice of women."

Christian smiled and thanked him. Huarto drank as much as he roved and at parties people often took bets on what the hour would be when he passed out and Antonia had to take or send him home. Antonia came to them, took her husband's arm, "Darling, could you check on Francisco? He was supposed to be here quite a while ago."

Huarto drew a deep breath. "Francisco is a grown man,

with a grown man's business to attend to. If he's late, what does it matter?"

Antonia bit her lip. So Huarto was going to be difficult tonight. This meant he was interested in this particular woman, she thought. People often commented on the fact that Antonia seemed to appear out of nowhere just when her husband got most interested in another woman and this time his attention had begun early.

Francisco came through the archway and Antonia suddenly turned, saying "Ah, there you are, you bad boy. I asked that you be early."

"Por qué?" But why? Francisco was suave in his expensively tailored, elegant black suit and snow white linen. He intended to have fun tonight, at Christian's expense if at all possible. He had had just enough to drink to make him lively. He quickly assessed the situation and saw that Huarto was busy charming Christian's wife. Well, he thought, he was going to rival Huarto's legendary charms tonight.

Antonia frowned. So both her husband and her friend, Francisco, were going to be difficult tonight and all over Christian's wife. She decided to take Christian's side and be blunt about it. As Francisco's eyes went over Dosha, Antonia smiled at Christian. "I see that two men are taken with your new wife, Christian." Then to Dosha, "Please pay them no mind. They are *infamous* womanizers, both of them. Were you to choose either, you'd have to share them with more women than you would care to."

Her remark left her husband irritable; he didn't like being reduced to his juvenile emotional skeleton. But Francisco laughed uproariously and said to Huarto, "I'm afraid she has our number, my friend. Ah well, there are three of us men here so far and Christian is a safe enough man. Right, amigo?"

Dosha sweetly took Christian's arm. "He is not safe. He's

the most dangerous, the most magnetic man on earth. But it's a danger that's not destructive; it just draws you closer for more and more." Her voice had gone dulcet and Christian grinned as Francisco smiled. "Touché."

Antonia and Huarto's daughter, Carmela, came into the room then. A young woman in her twenties, she was a study in dark blonde hair and creamy porcelain skin. At a first glance, she looked far plainer than she actually was. She was somber as she met and acknowledged an introduction to Dosha, and greeted Christian and Francisco.

"You're a lovely woman," she said to Dosha. "I can easily see why Christian chose you. You'll be an asset to him in every way."

Francisco's eyes narrowed here. He really needed a wife, he thought now. Carmela was right, Dosha was an asset to Christian. Well, that was easily arranged. Women could be handily found. He knew several right then who would jump at the chance to marry him.

Now Carmela said to Dosha. "If I weren't so busy, we'd have a lot to talk about. As Christian has probably told you, I work with orphans at a place called Children of the Hill. It's located in the hills. I lost my husband a short while after we were married several years back when I was very young. I grieved hard, but the children have helped fill my life. I'm thinking of adopting one of them."

Antonia looked startled, "But you never told me this, my dear."

Carmela looked at her mother levelly. "Mother, remember, we're not really close the way many mothers and daughters are. You've always been busy with your social life with time for little else." She shrugged and smiled a bit. "At any rate, you know it now."

"We'll discuss this further." Antonia's voice was tight as Carmela turned back to Dosha. "I understand you're a marvelous pianist and a teacher. I dabble in music. Francisco and I sometimes get together for a duet; I on the piano, he on the violin. Perhaps you'll play something for us tonight?"

Francisco's eyes caressed Dosha's face. "Ah, I would like you to accompany me on some lovely piece of your choice."

He was not jealous, but Christian's eyes claimed his wife. Since childhood there had been this rivalry between Francisco and him. "Only if she really wants to play. People can be thoughtless in asking an artist to perform." He hugged her to him. "I need her to keep me company. Were it not for a glitch at the bank, we would still be on our honeymoon."

At the word *honeymoon,* Christian's eyes locked with Dosha's and there may as well not have been anyone else in the room. She felt shivers of pure delight race up and down her spine and her blood ran hot. He knew he could do this to her, she thought, and she was going to get him once they got home. But she grinned a little inside; he was going to get her, too.

The Muñozes came then, Pia in aquamarine with gold jewelry and Ramon in an earthbrown suit from London's Savile Row. They greeted Dosha and Christian effusively and Francisco couldn't court Pia enough, but he was discreet. In no way did he intend to offend a man he needed to assure his place at Banc International.

"You always look like an angel," Francisco told Pia. Then to Ramon, "Like Christian, you're fortunate to have such a wife. I'm rethinking my priorities."

Christian couldn't resist the barb. "I would think a wife would have a hard time keeping up with you."

Francisco's face was grave. "I can and perhaps soon will settle down. You'll see." And he wondered if he didn't see a glimmer of interest on Ramon's face that had not been there.

Pia drew Dosha aside, laughing. "Christian is stuck to you like your glue tonight. Oh, he loves you so. And you love him so. I'm happy for the both of you." She lowered her voice to a near whisper. "I'm praying that Christian is the final choice for the Cultural Affairs Director at the bank. I don't mind telling you I don't like Francisco Salazar all that much." She shuddered a bit. "He and Huarto and all those women they string along. It offends me to see women used like that."

A beaming Captain Montero was announced and came to the two women. "I get to you two first, so my first greetings will be for you. Ladies, you are both beautiful."

Antonia bore down on them, gushing. "*El Capitano,* my favorite policeman. How many murderers and thieves did you lock up today?"

Captain Montero smiled. "Today, none I'm afraid, but please don't ask about yesterday."

Antonia laughed and patted him on the arm. "I feel safe in Puerto as long as you're head of the homicide division."

"Dad, you're here." Christian came to them. "I was afraid something had happened."

"No. For once I get a chance to enjoy a decent meal." He tapped lightly on a nearby table top. "Knock on wood."

Antonia looked at Dosha then. "I would like to show you my newly redone kitchen. Perhaps it will give you ideas about changing yours should you wish to."

Dosha didn't much feel like going with her, but she turned to the others and excused herself. Christian caught her hand. "Ten minutes is your limit away from me tonight or I shall come and get you. Is that understood?"

His eyes were merry as his glance tangled with hers and she murmured impishly, "Yes, master," to Captain Montero and Pia's laughter.

The smile had left Antonia's face when they reached a corner of the busy kitchen where a feast was being prepared. The kitchen was as large as the average living room and servants nodded and bowed as they passed. Shiny brown tiles covered the floor and the appliances were brown and beige, with much stainless steel. Dosha found it imposing, but like the owner, cold.

"Would you like a drink while we're here?" Antonia asked.

"No. I really do want to get back to my husband as soon as possible."

Antonia's glance was chilly. "I'm sure he'll survive." They stood by the patio doors when Antonia placed a hand on Dosha's arm. "I just want you to know early that my heart goes out to you. Yours won't be an easy life, for my late sister will be a terribly difficult woman for you to follow. Isabel and I got along poorly as all Puerto knows, but I admired her extravagantly. She was a formidable, ruthless woman, but incredibly beautiful and stunning in her power. Half the men in Puerto—indeed, in the Canaries—were in love with her." Here her mouth went down at the corners, "Including my husband, Huarto."

Dosha was silent. There was no comment she cared to make. Antonia continued. "I'm not sure Christian will ever really be in love again, but a man in his position must have someone to entertain his guests and business relations." She paused a long moment and her eyes glittered with malice. "And, of course, to warm his bed."

Dosha spoke from the heart then. "Christian and I love each other as much as either one of us could ever hope to love. We've both been hurt, but we're healing ourselves and each other. I'll be fine, thank you, because *I believe* in our love. I think not too many others can say the same."

She saw at a glance that she had drawn blood and possibly made an enemy, but she didn't care. She knew what she was talking about. Antonia bit her bottom lip. She hadn't loved Huarto even at the beginning, but it always scorched her to know that he preferred even the servant women to her.

"Forewarned is forearmed if we let it be so," Antonia said then. "In many ways I'm sorry for you. You'll learn when it's perhaps too late."

For the dinner, Antonia's table was set as elegantly as for a state dinner. Snowy white fine damask, Waterford crystal, Lenox china, specially fashioned sterling silverware all gleamed and sparkled in the light of the massive crystal chandeliers. Antonia had outdone herself and Christian felt it was for the Muñozes that she shone. Francisco was her friend and anything she could do to impress Ramon she would do.

"I can never give or attend a dinner like this and not think about the great dinners Isabel used to give. Oh, she was such a great hostess." She sighed again. "My sister was incomparable."

Dosha sought Christian's eyes, but he looked down with a distant expression on his face.

Captain Montero frowned and shot Antonia an angry look. The tense, faraway look on his son's face bothered him greatly. Damn Antonia, he thought heatedly.

Huarto sent his wife a scathing glance. "We wish to enjoy our dinner in the present, my good wife. Be kind and let us bury the dead."

Huarto's words cleared the air and lightened everyone's mood. Glancing at Christian again, Dosha found Christian gazing warmly at her. Her heart lifted, but she was troubled. More and more she felt his alienation. Isabel's name came up and he emotionally fled everyone. Did he still love Isabel so much?

With the first course of clear consommé with thin lemon slices, Antonia turned to Captain Montero and said brightly, "Ah, *el capitano,* you should have let me invite you a dinner companion, but no, you insisted that tonight you want no company. Are you perhaps hiding a secret love?"

Captain Montero smiled broadly. "No. It's simply that I work on a special case and when I do, I make poor company. My mind is completely taken with the case. Any woman would be bored."

It was Antonia's turn to smile now. "Next time perhaps you won't be working on a case. I've several women friends who admire you. You've been too long alone."

Captain Montero looked somber then. "Memories can sometimes be the best company of all."

Antonia's eyes on him were noncommittal, but Huarto said with surprising sympathy, "I remember Magdalena well. Beautiful woman. I can see why you're still taken with her."

Christian looked at his father sharply and his heart hurt a little for him because his father and his mother had known a great love like the one he and Dosha knew. Now in many ways his father had not moved on with his life, nor did he seem to want to.

A small dish of excellent mixed seafood in frosty bowls came next. Dosha found the blended flavors of shrimp, crabmeat and lobster excellent and the crisply curled lettuce surrounding it added its own fresh flavor. She sat between Christian and Francisco, across from Captain Montero. Now Christian's leg brushed hers in an intimate gesture and she smiled inwardly and looked down. He was building her up for the night after they left here and her flesh tingled at the thought. Lovemaking had been very good when they were courting, then engaged. Now it was beyond belief. It delighted her that he claimed her at every turn and she responded with deep desire.

Dosha came back to herself to find Carmela saying, "Well, Ramon, please tell us how things are going at the bank. Francisco mentioned that you're getting a Cultural Affairs Director. I always thought banks were stuffy old institutions. What is this all about?"

Ramon waggled his eyebrows at Carmela who was one of his favorite people. "Our CEO, Señor Garcia, is a cultured man and he feels as you express that banks are stuffy old institutions. He intends to change that image for Banc International. The new director who heads that division will work now in the United States and in Europe, a bit later in Africa. We want to engage the talents of youth here as well as older and aspiring artists, through scholarships, fellowships, grants. The greatest countries have been those that espouse and support their artists. There will be a man to head the division and a woman to work closely with him."

Carmela nodded. "A worthy undertaking."

Antonia's voice seemed to purr here. "You've someone in mind to head this division, Ramon?"

Ramon nodded. "We have two people in mind, but I'm not at liberty to say who."

Christian tensed a bit. He hadn't wanted for much in this world that he hadn't gotten, but he wanted this job for the good he could do. Yet, if the job didn't become his, he still had his beloved Dosha. Her body thrummed beside him now, sending him waves of love and support. For a moment he turned to her as she turned to him and both smiled. Looking at them, Captain Montero felt his breath catch in his throat. This was the way Magdalena and he had once looked at each other, and a wave of sadness washed over him.

The main course was lavish and consisted of several meat dishes: Tender chicken in a delicious garlic sauce, Salmorejo rabbit, a highly spiced dish, cooked long hours in a clay pot, which drew out incredible flavors, rack of lamb. There were potatoes done in butter and rock salt and garbanzo beans in a rich sauce. There was tender asparagus and zucchini squash, then a humongous salad of several kinds of lettuce, tomatoes, cucumbers, pimentos. The salad lent color and crispness and the vinaigrette dressing was delicious.

The wines were wonderful, with a different wine for each course and wines of choice for the main course. Both Christian and Dosha preferred warm red wine and pretty much stuck to that throughout the meal. The wine they favored had a delicate bouquet and slightly tingled the palate.

The food was so good they were silent often as they ate. The white-coated butler moved about, quietly serving, and Beethoven's Sixth Symphony played throughout the meal. It was all so pleasant, Christian thought. A miracle that a woman like Antonia could give a dinner like this with all the warmth and camaraderie when strife and turmoil were her stock in trade.

"Very well," Antonia said now. "You can't tell us who's likely to be your choice for a Cultural Affairs Director. How soon will you get started?"

Ramon shrugged. "That, as Americans say, is up for grabs. I know our CEO is anxious to get everything underway. My guess would be at any moment the selection will be made."

Francisco leaned back in his chair. He knew from talking with Ramon and other contacts at the bank that a married man would be preferable. But dammit, he, Francisco, had the edge of his late father's having been boyhood friends with the CEO. Still, the urbane Ramon was a man who wielded enormous influence and he favored Christian.

Francisco thought, too, of his unmarried state. But his mind was easier here. The CEO who favored him had assured him that a certain highly regarded woman employee could be chosen to work with him, so that wasn't really an issue. Now Francisco's face lit up as he looked across the table at Carmela. Why had he never realized how attractive she was with that mass of dark blonde hair, a lovely face and her deep reserve. She would make a *perfect* bank director's wife. With his reputation, wooing her might not be easy, but sometimes the shyer woman preferred a rakehell man.

"A penny for your thoughts, Francisco," Antonia said.

Huarto looked up quickly. "Francisco's thoughts would probably make you blush to the roots of your hair," he said drily.

Antonia glanced at her husband. His wit was keen and often risqué, but was he drinking too much again? And when did he not drink too much these days? She inadvertently sighed and smiled tightly. "We're all adults. There's nothing to blush about. He is a highly eligible bachelor."

And Francisco mused about what she would think if she knew he was considering her daughter as a wife. She had approved of Carmela's late husband, Arturo, but Carmela had married him anyway, for once not fighting with Antonia. Had they been happy? The husband had led a dissolute life, even as her father still led a dissolute life. Francisco knew himself to be a rake, but he was urbane, sophisticated and it was a smooth, accomplished way of life with him. He was brilliant where the other two were not. Ah well.

Captain Montero smiled as he said, "After all this splendor, I can only hope we have a dessert that does it justice."

Antonia raised her arched eyebrows. "In fact we have two. I asked Christian to tell me your favorite and it's Yam truchas which we're having, and Christian's favorite, Ice with Bienm."

Christian's mouth watered at the thought of the delicious almond flavored ice cream and the yam dessert so like the American sweet potato pie. This in spite of the full meal he had just eaten.

They lingered a long time over the dessert. Then, after small cups of Turkish coffee, the men retired to a room where they smoked Havana cigars and the women into the parlor where they sipped tiny glasses of liqueurs and paid Antonia lavish compliments on the dinner.

With the party gathered again in the living room, Antonia turned to Dosha.

"My dear, we would be so happy if you were to play something for us. Anything at all."

Dosha thought a moment. Yes, there was her unfinished concerto. Long worked on, but unfinished, this was a good place to try it out. She smiled at Christian. "You know the concerto I'm working on. Oh, if only you could accompany me on your violin."

"I'm sure your playing will be wonderful on its own," Christian replied gallantly. Francisco said nothing further about accompanying her.

"Very well," Dosha said, getting up and going to the grand piano. She sat down and ran her hands over the keys. The room was hushed then as she played the introduction of her concerto and segued into the melody. She hadn't realized how exquisite it was, flowing from her fingers like water from a crystal clear woodland brook. She quickly grew engrossed in the music and it filled her body and her spirit as she played. Crescendos and trills. Pianissimo. Fortissimo.

In the music the waters flowed gently, then they rushed as swollen streams will rush after a heavy rain. Was it as beautiful as she thought it was?

Looking at his wife and listening as she played, Christian sat with half closed eyes and felt his heart nearly burst with love and appreciation. She played for him and really no one else. He had heard her practice this music, had thrilled to it before when she didn't know he was in the room listening. And one night after hearing her play he had picked her up when she had finished, carried her to their bedroom, undressed her and made tender, passionate love. She did that to him, moved him so greatly he could hardly contain himself.

Christian's eyes on her were full of love and Captain Montero was happy for his son and his daughter-in-law. Ramon and Pia enjoyed themselves hugely as they listened to the beautiful music and thought how lucky they were to have friends like Christian and Dosha.

Carmela felt her heart fill. Dosha played so beautifully and she was so happy. She wondered if she would ever be that happy again. Then she chided herself. Of course, she had her work in the hills with the children, so she had a high degree of happiness. Francisco caught her eye and smiled. Her heart lifted. Did he look at her in a different way tonight? Or did she imagine it?

Antonia sat wishing she could play like this or do something as spectacular. Sometimes she grew weary of entertaining others.

And Huarto sat, too, full of the excellent food and liquor his wife had served, surrounded by elegant, beautiful women and one who played like an angel. What it must be like to have a woman like this, hold her, yes, make love to her again and again. He envied Christian sharply. He would have liked to stake his claim to Dosha, cuckold his former brother-in-law, but he knew that Christian would surely kill him and he had too much to live for.

That night in their bedroom, Christian turned to Dosha. "I'm sorry, *querida.* I should've defended you against Antonia's cruelty. *You* are the incomparable one, not Isabel."

He kissed her hands and his words warmed her. She wanted so badly to ask him what hurt him like this, but she sensed he was at his breaking point tonight.

They lay in each other's arms and didn't discuss the dinner party further. Unbidden it came to mind that he and Isabel had made passionate love and she was jealous for the first time.

It was several hours later that she came awake to find him thrashing in his sleep. She began to wake him and ask what he was dreaming about when she heard him call Isabel's name. Nothing could stop her from listening more intently then.

"Dear God, Isabel, *no!* You cannot *do* this thing to me. Please don't leave me. I love you…."

He jerked awake then and sat up, looking wildly around him. He was suddenly drenched with perspiration.

Dosha turned on the lamp and cradled his damp body. "It's all right," she soothed him.

"Please tell me what I said."

She told him and he groaned. "That love I spoke of was a long time ago. It's you I love now and will love forever."

His eyes pleaded with her to believe him and she did. But she also believed that he would also love Isabel forever.

He took her hand. "Dios mio, I'm a mess. I'll take a quick shower.

He got pajamas from the dresser drawer and went into the bathroom. He could have wept with frustration. He thought he didn't deserve Dosha's love. How ever to explain to her that he and he alone had killed Isabel?

Chapter 13

Three days later, in the late afternoon, Dosha and Christian were in their bedroom as she helped him pull together an overnight bag. Ramon had summoned him to a luxury hotel where Banc International officials were holding meetings and Christian would find out more about his possible promotion.

"Cross your fingers for me," he told her.

"Will you know if you get the job when this meeting is over?"

"Ramon says no, not quite yet. There're holdouts, but he thinks I'm the likely candidate. Francisco has a vice president firmly in his corner. I'll be talking with the CEO again. He has praised my father to me. An uncle dear to him was murdered and it was a difficult case that my father was instrumental in solving. The CEO has always been grateful. But he was Francisco's late father's friend, so it's a tossup."

Christian stood near the windows and Dosha came to

him. He pulled her close as she took the two sides of his collar and pulled his face to hers. "I hate it when you leave me even for a little while," she whispered.

"And I hate it more," he answered. "But we spent the morning making love, and I will return early tomorrow morning."

"Not soon enough. I'll dream of you, feel you beside me and inside me although you're not there."

"I will be here in raging spirit. And in the next meeting, Ramon tells me that you'll be included and your job will be finalized if I'm the choice."

"How could you *not* be the choice?"

"Others are not so prejudiced as you are."

Her body against his was limpid now as she stroked his back, felt the scars beneath his shirt and undershirt.

"It thrills me when you do that," he told her.

"Does it? You thrill me when you just look at me."

He kissed her throat. "When we're in Tahiti next spring, I'll never leave your side for the whole three weeks."

"I'll make you swear that in blood."

"Consider it done."

Christian left around five p.m. and Dosha wandered onto the patio to find Socorro seated on a padded rattan chair. The old woman's face lighted up. "Come here and give me a hug."

"I was going to do just that." She hugged Socorro tightly and held her for a few minutes before she sat beside her.

"Christian came by just before he left for his precious meeting. Oh, my dear, I'm praying that he gets this job. It means so much to him."

"Yes, it does."

"And if he gets it, you'll be working with him. What a joy that will be, to utilize your tremendous talents and be with the one you love. Isaac and I worked together in so many ways. He always took my advice."

"And you two were so happy."

"The way you and Christian are today."

Suddenly Socorro found herself looking keenly at Dosha and she frowned.

"What is it?" Dosha asked.

Socorro didn't answer for a moment. "I'm seeing a vision," she said, "of you and a man who is not Christian. Indeed, Christian is in the background and he's not pleased."

"Oh, my goodness. Who is this other man?"

"I don't know. Only that he definitely is interested in you and pays court. I can feel my grandson's anger. Oh, Christian is a calm one, but he has a fierce temper when it's aroused."

"I know."

Socorro closed her eyes again and this time she stiffened and seemed far away. Dosha was reminded of how Christian seemed far away at times, but he never spoke of visions. After a few minutes, Socorro came back to herself with a slight shudder. "In this small vision, you seemed to be in some kind of trouble. You were very, very tense and your eyes were wide, I think with fear. But I couldn't see what it was that you were so afraid of."

Socorro sighed then. "The way of a *cartamantica* is never easy. We pay in blood for what we do. The ones of us who simply read the cards travel an easier road, but I've an added gift, to sometimes know the future. I only wish it could be plainer."

Dosha cleared her throat. "This fear, Abuela, is this to come soon?"

Very slowly Socorro answered, "This I don't know. I only know that it *will* come. Just promise me you'll be very aware of where you are and who you are with."

"Oh, I will."

They talked about Banc International, Isaac and Puerto

An Important Message from the Publisher

Dear Reader,

Because you've chosen to read one of our fine novels, I'd like to say "thank you"! And, as a special way to say thank you, I'm offering to send you two more Kimani Romance novels and two surprise gifts – absolutely FREE! These books will keep it real with true-to-life African American characters that turn up the heat and sizzle with passion.

Please enjoy the free books and gifts with our compliments...

Linda Gill

Publisher, Kimani Press

...off Seal and Place Inside...

PUBLISHER'S FREE GIFT SEAL THANK YOU

We'd like to send you two free books to introduce you to our brand-new line – Kimani Romance™! These novels feature strong, sexy women, and African-American heroes that are charming, loving and true. Our authors fill each page with exceptional dialogue, exciting plot twists, and enough sizzling romance to keep you rivetec until the very end!

KIMANI ROMANCE ... LOVE'S ULTIMATE DESTINATION

KIMANI ROMANCE
DONNA HILL
Love Becomes Her

KIMANI ROMANCE
USA TODAY BESTSELLING AUTHOR
BRENDA JACKSON
solidSOUL

KIMANI ROMANCE
MARCIA KING-GAMBLE
FLAMINGO PLACE

KIMANI ROMANCE
her secret life
National bestselling author
GWYNNE FORSTER

KIMANI ROMANCE
KAREN WHITE-OWENS
Someone to LOVE

Your two books have a combined cover price o $11.98 in the U.S. and $13.98 in Canada, but are yours **FREE!** We' even send you two wonderful surprise gifts. You can't lose

2 Free Bonus Gifts!

We'll send you two wonderful surprise gifts, absolutely FREE, just for giving KIMANI ROMANCE books a try! Don't miss out — MAIL THE REPLY CARD TODAY!

www.KimaniPress.com

Two NEW Kimani Romance™ Novels

Two exciting surprise gifts

DETACH AND MAIL CARD TODAY!

168 XDL EF2G 368 XDL EF2S

FIRST NAME LAST NAME

ADDRESS

APT.# CITY

STATE/PROV. ZIP/POSTAL CODE

Thank You!

Please allow 4 to 6 weeks for delivery. Offer limited to one per household and not valid to current subscribers of Kimani Romance. All orders subject to approval. Credit or debit balances in a customer's account(s) may be offset by any other outstanding balance owed by or to the customer. ® and ™ are trademarks owned and used by the trademark owner and/or its licensee. © 2006 Kimani Press.

(K-ROM-10/06)

The Reader Service — Here's How It Works:

Accepting your 2 free books and gifts places you under no obligation to buy anything. You may keep the books and gifts and return the shipping statement marked "cancel." If you do not cancel, about a month later we'll send you 4 additional books and bill you just $4.69 each in the U.S., or $5.24 each in Canada, plus 25¢ shipping & handling per book and applicable taxes if any.* That's the complete price and — compared to cover prices of $5.99 each in the U.S. and $6.99 each in Canada — it's quite a bargain! You may cancel at any time, but if you choose to continue, every month we'll send you 4 more books, which you may either purchase at the discount price or return to us and cancel your subscription.

*Terms and prices subject to change without notice. Sales tax applicable in N.Y. Canadian residents will be charged applicable provincial taxes and GST.

If offer card is missing write to: The Reader Service, 3010 Walden Ave., P.O. Box 1867, Buffalo, NY 14240-1867

POSTAGE WILL BE PAID BY ADDRESSEE

THE READER SERVICE
3010 WALDEN AVE
PO BOX 1867
BUFFALO NY 14240-9952

and had milk shakes served by Pablo on the patio. Dosha kissed Socorro's cheek again and brushed her silken white curls. Socorro caught her hand, "I can see that you miss him even for this short time."

"I'm afraid I do, but I'm going to soak myself in a wonderful bath of soda and French lavender oil and dream of him."

Socorro laughed. "To watch you, to listen to you talk of your beloved is to watch and listen to myself so many years ago. Ah, I'm not going in just now. I'll watch the blazing stars and the pale moon."

Inside the house, Dosha wandered around a bit downstairs. She ran her fingers over the keyboard of the grand piano, but didn't feel like playing, so she climbed the stairs to prepare for her bath.

A little later, immersed in the soft water with the scent of French lavender surrounding her, she relaxed completely. The dinner party of a few nights before came to mind and she smiled to herself. She would make a better hostess than Antonia because she had heart and soul where Antonia had little. But her role would also be to work at Christian's side as they brought wondrous culture to the masses. Christian *would* get the job. He had to get it because it meant so much to him and he had so much to offer.

The bathroom door was closed. Dosha thought she heard a soft knock, but she came away from her thoughts and listened, heard nothing else. When she got out of the tub much later, the huge rose bath towel enveloped her as she blotted herself partially dry, then completely dried off under the jet dryer.

She slipped on a cream nylon tricot gown and began to listen to tapes by Luther Vandross, Teddy Pendergrass, Barry White and other lesser known artists. After making a choice of a few tapes to entice her husband when he returned, she finally got into bed and switched off the light on the night table. Glancing at the luminous dial, she saw that it was 11 p.m. and fell fast asleep.

Her dreams were benign and thrilling, filled, of course, with Christian. She put slender fingers over her abdomen now as in the dream she held a baby and Christian held them both. They sat in a meadow of red clover with brilliant sunlight warming them and they were deliriously happy. They would always be happy. But suddenly there were black clouds and an angry swarm of bees surrounded them as Socorro cried, "Run! You must get away from this danger! You will be hurt, perhaps killed!"

And as the dream interwove with reality, she thought that this evening when they had talked, Socorro had not known to warn her of being killed.

She came awake in a cold sweat and abruptly sat up, trembling. Reaching over, she snapped on the night table light and looked wildly around, breathing hard, her heart racing. Almost immediately she saw the big, hideous and hairy black spider and she knew enough to know that it was a tarantula advancing on her. She screamed then, involuntarily, but she moved, too, getting up and snatching a magazine blessedly there on the night table. She crushed the spider with all her might and got out of bed.

In a very short while, there were knocks on her door as Pablo and Estela, then Socorro came into the room.

"What happened, señora?" Pablo asked first.

And Socorro came to where Dosha stood and quickly demanded, "What *is* it, *querida?* What has happened here?"

Numbly Dosha stood beside the bed, her heart still racing, and before she could point they saw the crushed spider.

"My God!" Socorro breathed nearly as fast as Dosha. "A *tarantula.* How did it get here? They're not common to Puerto."

Marta came then, rubbing her eyes. "I heard you scream, señora? What is wrong?"

Socorro looked at the girl narrowly. "The señora was nearly bitten by a tarantula," Socorro said shortly and the girl said nothing more, but her mouth opened with surprise.

"This is terrible," Socorro and Pablo said in one voice as Estela wrung her hands.

"And Christian is away," Socorro said then. "I'll call Rafael."

"No, please," Dosha said. "It's over now. There's no need."

"Nonsense. We'll stay here while you get a few things and come with me. *Tonight* Rafael can have the rooms searched for more of these monsters and we can be sure that you're safe."

Socorro made the call from downstairs and took Dosha in her arms, hugged her, soothed her, rocked her as if she were a baby. "I'm sorry to be so frightened," Dosha said. "I was fortunate enough not to have been bitten, but I can't seem to stop shaking. You gave a warning of trouble, but I didn't dream it would come so soon."

Grimly Socorro said, "And neither did I, or that it was possibly deadly."

It was only when she was in Socorro's apartment that Dosha began to breathe a little more regularly again, but her blood was still chilled when Captain Montero came a short while later. He took her still trembling body in his arms and held her. Things happened to people all the time, Dosha told herself, and she was fortunate. No harm had come to her because she had been frightened and come awake in time.

As grim as Socorro was, Captain Montero was more so. He immediately called and roused men to scour the house to check for more tarantulas. In the meantime, he held Dosha.

"It's late," she told him. "You shouldn't have been called. Spiders are a fact of life and I was lucky."

"Who else is there to call?" he asked gently. "My son is away and he expects me to take care of you. Do you feel a little better now?"

"Yes." Finally she said, "I'm usually far calmer than this in the face of trouble. What's wrong with me now?"

"You're far tenderer than usual," he counseled her. "I think you're taking it well. A tarantula can be hairy death and we all know it's possible. I'll ask Estela to fix you some hyssop tea and you can get some sleep."

She shook her head. "No. I think I want to sit up the rest of the night." And she began to think then. Had she heard a soft knock on the door when she was in the bathtub? And who was it? She would ask Estela if she knew, and it came unbidden. Again she saw in her mind's eye Marta skulking down the corridor. Why did the two connect in her thoughts? She would talk with Christian about this when he returned.

As Dosha, Socorro and Captain Montero waited for Estela to bring the hyssop tea, Captain Montero questioned Dosha gently and went over the horror again.

He stroked his chin. "Of course tarantulas are not native to Puerto, but we have many visitors now and some might bring in almost anything."

Dosha hesitated long moments, but finally she told him about seeing Marta near the end of the corridor the previous night. He nodded. "Keep an eye on her and so will I."

"I wish you had told me about her," Socorro muttered. "I've always wondered about that girl, but I wanted to be charitable. The spirits were not clear about her, so I agreed to let her come back. Perhaps it was a mistake, but that's for you to decide. You think then, Rafael, that *she* might have put the tarantula in Dosha's room?"

He thought a moment. "Anything is possible. It could

simply be a coincidence. But Dosha's thinking she heard a knock, seeing Marta going along the corridor at that hour of the morning one night recently. You've taught me, Socorro, never to brush away what's in our minds. This is so often our best protection; our hunches are our best policemen."

Pablo came then with the tea and a slice of lemon. Dosha thanked him and began to sip the tea.

"Is there anything you need to ask me, Captain?" Pablo asked. "I can get my wife if you wish to talk with us. Or with just me. I brought the tea because she felt there might be things you want to ask me."

Captain Montero mulled it over. "You've had exterminators here within recent months?"

"Just two months ago, señor. Señor Montero gave the order."

"I see. Pablo, would you say that Marta is happy here?"

Pablo laughed drily. "That one is happy nowhere. Hers is not the gift of happiness."

"Do you think she would do harm to someone?"

"Harm, *el capitán?* How do you mean this?"

The captain looked at Pablo narrowly, tried a different tact. "Does the girl have reason to be walking the halls shortly after midnight?"

Pablo looked startled. "No reason that I know of. She's a strange one. She has complained of not sleeping well. When she was here before when Señora Isabel...well, that is no matter." He looked at Dosha. "Have you or has Señor Montero seen her in the halls at some odd hour?"

Dosha nodded and told him about the incident. His eyes were sad as he told her, "I wish you had spoken of this. She was out of bounds. This is your home, not hers. If she wants to be out and about at night, she should have spoken with my wife or me, or asked your permission."

"You're right," Captain Montero said. "You're free to go

now, Pablo. Thank you for your help. Please be on your guard that nothing else untoward happens."

"Oh Señor, believe me, my wife and I will be." Then to Dosha, "Señora, we're so fortunate to be here with people like you and Señor Christian and Señora Socorro. We love our jobs and we'll do our best to see that all goes well from now on."

Captain Montero paced for a few minutes before he told Dosha, "I called my son. He'll be on very shortly."

The hyssop tea had quickly begun to take effect, but Dosha sat up straight. "You shouldn't have, *padre.*" Captain Montero smiled, pleased that she had begun to call him that term. Father.

"This is such a special meeting," Dosha explained. "And so much depends on it. With you and Socorro here, and Pablo and Estela, I've all the help I need. And Christian would've been home in the morning."

The captain looked at his watch. Eleven-thirty. "That choice is for him to make. He's my son and I know how I raised him. I certainly wouldn't want my bride to be alone at a frightening time like this."

"But it could've happened to anyone, anywhere."

"It happened here," Socorro said flatly. "We may be making, as Isaac used to say, mountains out of molehills, but that's a far safer way to live. But then the world has always been a dangerous place."

A half hour later, they heard the front door slam shut and Christian racing up the stairs calling Dosha's name. Captain Montero stepped out into the hall and told him where they were. He came in and came to her.

"Are you all right, my wife?"

"I am, sweetheart. I didn't want your father to call you. I had so much help. I didn't even want Socorro to call him."

"She did the right thing," Captain Montero said.

"Of course she did," Christian scoffed. "And my father did the right thing in calling me." He knelt by the chaise lounge she lay on and kissed her, took her hand. "You haven't answered my first question. Are you all right?"

"I am..." she had begun to say fine, but she wasn't fine. She hated insects with a passion, especially spiders. She had been bitten several times by the brown spiders so evident in Minden, and the bites had been painful. This spider bite might well have been fatal.

"I'll be all right in a little while," she told him. "But your meeting—it was so important to you."

He kissed her hand and his intense gaze held hers. "You're more important to me than anything in this world..."

"You want this job so much."

"I want you so much more. You're my wife and any moment now, if not already, you'll begin carrying our child. My darling, know that you come first, before any job, before anyone..."

She sat up then and put her arms around his neck. "I'm all right. I'm fine, now that you're here."

Captain Montero and Socorro looked at the couple and at each other and their smiles were wide and beatific. Both were remembering past loves and past happiness.

The two men Captain Montero had roused to search for spiders arrived and he went to let them in. The men first searched the couple's bedroom and declared they had found no more spiders. They put out heavy insecticide and moved on.

In the bedroom, Christian took Dosha in his arms.

"*Un momento,* love," she told him. "You haven't told me about the meeting. Did it go well?"

Christian's expression tensed. "Not as well as I'd hoped. The vice president who likes Francisco is holding out for him." He frowned now. "Ramon told me to keep my hopes high, but the vice president on Francisco's side may have stronger ties to the CEO than Ramon has. Then, remember the CEO was Francisco's father's friend."

Dosha's heart went out to him and she offered her body to him for solace.

Christian gasped with wonder as she drew him to her. "*Querida,*" he said huskily, "with you, I have everything in this world that matters most to me."

Chapter 14

"A night at Charcot del Plaza always cheers you up," Dosha told Christian in early August. "There's a samba contest and you love to samba."

Christian touched her face. "Stop worrying about me. I can take it. It's just not knowing, and that will soon be over. If all doesn't go in my favor, it won't be the end of the world. Not as long as I have you."

She leaned over and kissed him full on the mouth as they stood at the edge of Puerto's largest and most popular plaza. It was a Saturday night and many people had drawn together to simply celebrate living. Puerto was a town of parties. More people played musical instruments here than in any other part of the world and they liked an audience for their music.

Dosha thought she looked well in a pale blue silk crepe sheath with cutouts over the top of the bodice. The dress was molded to her narrow top and wide hips, and black patent strap sandals displayed her long legs to great advantage. "You're beautiful tonight, my love," Christian said softly as a tremor of delight ran through her.

She looked him over carefully, totally appreciating his lithe, virile body in the cream-colored sports shirt, the black slub silk pants and black knitted jerkin he wore. "And you are handsome." Then for just a moment Dosha put her hands over her ears and laughed. "It's loud early."

Christian placed his hands over her hands and drew her closer. His lips were little more than an inch from hers and his mint-flavored breath on her face excited her.

"Sugar sweet," she murmured.

"No, that's you. And I think our honeymoon is going to last forever."

"I won't complain."

At a chuckle, they turned to face a smiling Ramon and Pia. But Ramon's face grew somber as he said, "I want you to be very careful tonight, my friend. I'm informed that Señor Garcia, our CEO, will have a representative here. Suddenly things seem to have gone in favor of Francisco. I just learned this this afternoon. It's so important that you, as Americans say, keep your cool. If we've lost this one, there'll be other positions..."

His voice trailed off and he sighed. "But, of course, this is the position you've set your heart on. I won't give up yet and neither should you. Our CEO is a man who considers things long and carefully. He's fair-minded and you can be sure he'll do what he thinks is best. He's been good to both of us."

"That's true," Christian said. "Don't worry about me. As I just told Dosha, whatever happens, I'll be all right. After all, I have her."

Ramon laughed then and looked relieved. "I knew I could count on you. And listen, Christian, be especially nice to

Francisco tonight. Show the class you've always possessed in abundance. He's had just a little too much to drink and it's plain he has heard that things are going in his favor. We both know him to be a man whose head is turned by success and this will be no different. Take him in stride and be the man I know you are."

"Count on it," Christian said evenly.

"And now," Ramon said, "the first samba begins and who could resist it? I'll check with you two often tonight. And remember, there'll be other directorships that will please you, but I've not given up on this one."

Ramon and Pia moved away then to the smooth beat of the samba and Christian turned to Dosha, took her in his arms and moved out into the dancers. For long moments they both lost themselves in the sensuous music that was the heartbeat of human desire. Her hips moved smoothly a little away from his and his body performed the sensuous dance with an ease born of long, long practice. It was a dance he loved above all others.

The whole plaza resounded with the music that was all around them, with kazoos which were instruments fashioned of metal, and covered with papier-mâché in the shape of saxophones, trumpets, and other popular musical instruments. There were the real instruments, too, played by real musicians as the papier-mâché instruments were played by ardent amateurs. Heavenly guitars gave their players glorious melodies with their sensuous and sexy rhythms. And the famous kazoos held forth lustily, blown by strong lungs with years of practice.

Dosha thought that this was so much like La Carnaval, the festival in Puerto visited each year by people from all over the world. She had only been to one; it was something you didn't forget and she looked forward to coming back to the next festival. They would be living in D.C. then.

Two sambas played out and Dosha and Christian immersed themselves in the dance, the music and the camaraderie of those around them. Both were thoroughly breathless when they finished.

To give the crowd a much-needed rest, the musicians launched into the groups of raunchy songs that gleefully depicted politics and sexuality. These were tossed off with much eyeball rolling and thigh-slapping from the musicians and the crowd.

Christian laughed now. "I'm glad to see women join in this fun, especially the younger ones. Once only men dared respond. *Querida,* I'm glad the world is so much freer for women these days."

"And it's like you to want freedom for someone else. What can I say about you to let you know how much I love who you are?"

In answer, he leaned forward and kissed her lightly, then flicked his tongue in first one corner, then the other of her mouth. "I simply don't know what I've ever done to deserve a woman like you."

Francisco came to them then, smiling lustily. "Ah, my friends, it's a wondrous night, is it not?"

"It is that," Christian replied, taking note of the fact that Francisco had begun drinking early and was a little unsteady on his feet.

"I trust you're feeling well these days." Francisco grinned with his eyes half closed. "It's truly wonderful when things go your way, would you say?"

"Exactly what are you talking about?" Christian asked, careful to be on his best behavior with his cousin.

Francisco smiled narrowly. "I think you know what I'm talking about. Don't be too disappointed. The years have been kind to us both and perhaps they will be kind to you again as they are to me now."

Christian stood musing as the heat of anger filled him. The man acted as if he knew for certain that he had the position he and Christian so coveted. What had he learned? And when?

Antonia and Carmela came up to Christian and Dosha. Carmela's face lit up. "Oh my, you two look happy and, Dosha, that is a lovely dress."

"Thank you. I like both your dresses." And the two women did look well, with Carmela in off white and Antonia in the severe, but beautiful black she favored.

Carmela smiled then as she said, "I keep thinking I'll bring my girls down from the hills to enjoy such a gathering. They are a lively bunch and would like this. We have a couple of excellent dancers."

Antonia turned to her daughter, a look of mild exasperation on her face. "And what I wish is that you would go back to being the excellent dancer you were and move on with your life."

Carmela's level look at her mother showed irritation. "Mother, I'm doing what I most love doing, shepherding my girls. I have *been* married and it was wonderful, but I'm not ready to travel that road again."

A voice just behind them said, "And what road is that, my dear? But then I think I know. Do you mean the marriage road?"

"Francisco, you startled me, you naughty man. Must you sneak up on people like that? And why do you look so happy? What bank did you rob today?" Antonia laughed merrily at her joke and Francisco joined in, but Carmela was somber.

Francisco looked the ladies over carefully and seemed to desire them all equally, then his attention was riveted to Dosha for a moment. "The other two ladies I've known a long while, so I'm well used to their beauty, but I'm like a sultan gazing over his latest acquisition..."

"But my wife is not *your* acquisition," Christian cut in.

Francisco shrugged. "And so it is, but we deal in dreams here. I only mean to say that your wife is beautiful with a newly seen beauty and Carmela and Antonia are as beautiful as ever, but I'm used to them. Ah, I stumble. It's the wine and extreme happiness."

Antonia turned an inquiring glance on him. "And what makes you so happy?"

Francisco drew a deep breath. "I would say the culmination of a long-held dream. To win and win big at a game I've long played with a worthy adversary."

"Francisco," Antonia demanded. "Don't tease us. What is it you speak of?"

"Only tomorrow can I give you my news. You will be pleased, but not surprised. Am I not usually the winner, even when it's thought I've lost?"

Christian felt a ripple of sharper irritation, then the pain of an impending loss. He felt an emptiness in the pit of his belly. Francisco *knew* something. The man's eyes were shining and his body, even on the edge of drunkenness, held utter triumph. Dosha squeezed his hand tightly and he squeezed back.

Francisco's gaze went to Carmela then. "If it was marriage you talked of when I first came up, then I could offer you my hand. I've long admired you and with a certain position I'll need a hostess. Oh, I mean a future position, of course. I rattle on too much sometimes. I must not give away trade secrets."

Here Francisco lifted Carmela's hand and kissed it. "And your answer, my dear. Marrying me would link you to a family as illustrious as your own. Your father and mother hold me in high esteem..."

Antonia stood musing Francisco's question. She had not thought of Francisco for her daughter, but Carmela could do worse. But Carmela seemed interested in nothing other than those damned girls in that school in the hills. She was too young to be closeted like a nun. She would talk with her; the time for mourning her husband was over.

"Your answer, my dear?" Francisco said to Carmela.

Carmela smiled narrowly. "You're kind, old friend, and I appreciate your proposal even if it lacks romance, but I'm afraid my life is now set in concrete. I'm sure I'll die a widow long years from now with my girls paying me wonderful homage."

A rhumba began then and Francisco bowed low to Carmela who laughed and danced away with him.

"I'll see you two later," Antonia said. "I must find myself a partner. I'm very good at this dance."

On the dance floor, Dosha and Christian got into the gleeful spirit of the music. She enjoyed the rhumba almost as much as the samba and Christian was still teaching her all the fine points. Now he said, "Both dances begin in the brain. You have to love the music to respond. The basic rhythm is African in origin, further embellished in South America. Then the body must take over. Listen to the drumbeats and relax as it plays in your heart."

"I love this music," she said softly, "and I love being in your arms."

"I love holding you, *querida.* It's said that dancing is part of the art of love. That a woman who dances well will be good at making love. And you dance so well."

Dosha threw back her head, laughing. "And you, *novio,* have the honeyed tongue of a glorious lover."

Pia and Ramon danced close to them, then paused a moment as Ramon said urgently, "Señor Garcia is here tonight; he didn't send a representative after all. I wonder if he will make a public announcement about the position. He sometimes does such things. He has not attended one of these dances in a long while, but he used to come all the time. Ah, luckily for us, Francisco is not at his best tonight."

Christian nodded, thinking that Francisco didn't need to be at his best. He had the CEO on his side. Dosha saw the bothered expression on her husband's face and moved closer, as if to shield him with her body.

"Please, *querido,* it'll be all right. Remember you already have a very good position and as Ramon has said, there will be other openings." But she knew very well that certain positions come once in a lifetime, and Director of Cultural Affairs was one of these.

They were seated at a table on the sidelines, slightly winded from yet another strenuous rhumba. A pitcher of margaritas sat on the table before them and they still flexed their shoulders to another rhumba when Jaime Garcia, the CEO of Banc International came to them.

A medium height, balding man in his fifties with an attractive presence, he asked gravely, "May I join you?"

"Of course you may," Christian answered.

Christian introduced Dosha to his boss and the CEO rose and lifted her hand, kissed it. "I'm honored."

Christian called for another glass and the waiter brought it. Now all three sat sipping and Señor Garcia began at once. "You, of course, are wondering what my decision will be. It's a difficult one. Both you and Francisco are such brilliant men. I don't mind saying that you have more stability on your side. And it's plain to see that you are happily married."

Here Señor Garcia broke off and smiled at the couple. "And it's also plain that you are in love. I married late and I now know such a love." He leaned back in his chair and seemed to muse for a few moments. "I've known you and Francisco since you began with Banc International and I've watched you both grow. He drinks a bit too much and has no wife to stabilize him." He gave a short laugh. "But Francisco's father and I were old friends. That won't be the deciding factor for I'm a businessman first. You know how indebted I feel to your father for solving my uncle's murder."

The CEO's eyes were half closed in memory. "I see myself in Francisco. I, too, had no wife and I drank too much, but a woman saw the good in me and changed my life. Like you two, we love each other deeply. And like Francisco, I was lucky. I thrived at the bank in spite of myself and when the job as CEO became available I was married, settled, stable, ready. I'm asking that you understand if I choose Francisco."

"I'll understand," Christian said evenly.

"Because, of course, as I've said, there'll be other openings." He was silent for a moment before he turned his attention to Dosha. "I've heard from Ramon of the extensive plans you two had to work together to bring arts and culture to masses of people. I was impressed at the beginning; I still am. I've been thinking of other avenues that will let you utilize your dreams. Would you tell me more about what you wish to do, señora?"

And Dosha talked happily with all the passion she felt for the work Christian and she had planned. They would reach into every segment of society with scholarships and fellowships and grants for the best students. But others of lesser talent wouldn't be left out. They, too, would have help and sustenance. It was a formidable undertaking, they knew, but they felt they were up to the task.

When she had finished, she blushed and said, "Forgive me for going on and on, but..."

Señor Garcia laughed. "Plainly this is your passion, and I've enjoyed every minute of your talk. You have a lovely voice, señora. I wish now I had brought my wife to meet you, but one day soon I'll do just that."

They talked more about the mission of Banc International. "You see," the CEO explained, "we're not just a lucrative operation filled with hopes of making and handling the world's money. We pride ourselves on being a bank with a heart. In the end, we'll do much of the work the World Bank should be doing, and the position I had in mind for you is just the beginning."

Finally Jaime Garcia stroked his face and said, "Would you be willing to work with Francisco for a while, señora?"

"Work with him?" a startled Dosha responded. "What do you mean?"

"Just this. For a while until we can develop another position for your husband, you could assist Francisco, helping him with your ideas… Just until we could find and fund that new position."

Dosha shook her head slowly. "I'm not sure. I'm, of course, flattered that you want me for that position, but Francisco and I… I'll need to think about it."

Señor Garcia laughed shortly. "Forgive me. I think in a tunnel sometimes. I saw only the good that could come of it. You couldn't be too fond of Francisco." He turned to Christian. "You and Francisco are cousins, with the deep competitiveness some men have, and you're not friends. Still I'm grateful that you two have worked together as well as you have." He smiled as he looked at Dosha. "If you should change your mind and your husband concurs…"

Christian swallowed hard. The CEO had said "*had* in mind for you." So it was a fait accompli. He was *out*. Strange how he had held on doggedly until that remark.

Señor Garcia asked Dosha for the next samba and she graciously acquiesced. On the dance floor, she found him a talented dancer, but she watched Christian as he sat watching them and her heart hurt for him. But they had so much to be grateful for and who knew but what another position would be even better.

She danced the long set with Jaime Garcia, all the while

wanting to be back in Christian's arms and it was with a sigh of relief that she finally came back to him.

"We could leave early," she suggested as she placed her hand over his. A little distance away they saw the CEO talking with Francisco, who seemed to stand straighter.

"Let's stay a little longer," he said. "But just a little." He pressed her hand hard. "I'm feeling my blood run hot for you and there're things I intend to do to you that should make both of us happy. Ah, *querida,* if only you knew what you mean to me."

The air around them grew positively explosive then with wildly abandoned merriment and Christian murmured, "What a shame it would be to waste this joy. We'll dance and be happy, my love, and to hell with the disappointments life has to offer. I thank God for what we have."

And amidst the throngs of gyrating dancers and the raucous, yet beautiful music, they swayed and moved their bodies avidly, enjoying the music and their life.

That night at home they made love out on the balcony by their bedroom behind a high wall of open-topped awnings as they looked at a star-spangled night sky. This was what mattered, Christian thought, but it also swept his mind that there were other things that mattered too.

When they were sated, he stroked her gently as she stroked him and they talked for a long while about the lost job and inevitably about the deep love they shared.

In their bedroom they were fast asleep when the phone rang. Frowning, Christian picked it up as he glanced at the luminous dial. Two o'clock in the morning. Then he came abruptly wide awake. *Was Socorro ill?*

It was an ebullient Ramon. "You'll damn me, I am certain, for waking you, but you'll bless me when you hear what I've to say."

"I'm always happy to hear from you, my friend."

"You'll be happier. Señor Garcia called me a few minutes ago. He has spent the night thinking and he is charmed with Dosha. He told me that talking with her helped him to change his mind where he had been pretty settled on Francisco. He wants to see you in his office at 11:00 Monday morning. He will talk with you first, then later with Dosha, then with both of you. He told me to tell you that this time he won't vacillate. His mind is made up. You are the victor. Congratulations!"

With a whoop, Christian thanked him and hung up. He woke Dosha and told her the news. They hugged each other in bed, then got up and danced around the room without music. He turned on the stereo and found samba music and they danced wildly to that.

"It's a good thing we're apart from the rest of the house," he chortled. "People would think we're mad."

"Aren't we a little mad?" she asked him. "Happiness like this drives you a little crazy."

"The world is ours," he told her as he held her close, "but even without this new news, we hold all the happiness we've ever needed or ever will need."

Chapter 15

The meetings for Banc International began the next week. Dosha was surprised to find that she didn't feel nervous at all when she and Christian met with Ramon and Señor Garcia in Señor Garcia's luxurious conference room. Pia and Ramon were there.

Señor Garcia took Dosha's hand as they entered his suite. "You look lovely, my dear. You'll do our humble bank proud." Smiling, he turned to Christian, "And you, señor, are to be congratulated on choosing such a bride."

Dosha and Christian thanked him and they moved about the room admiring the paintings by Monet, Pissaro and Goya. There was one sculpture by Michelangelo. Dosha saw then why there would be a guard outside this door as well as in the hallways and in the lobby. Christian's eyes on his bride were warm and loving. He thought she rivaled any of the beauties in the paintings. She wore one of his favorite outfits of natural-colored silk which greatly flattered her superb figure. Francisco came in quietly, joined them.

"Ah Señor Salazar, I had hoped you would get here before we begin," Señor Garcia said softly, making it sound a bit like a reprimand.

Francisco smiled. "I was checking on the project we talked about, señor," Francisco answered easily.

At the curved and highly polished mahogany conference table, the six sat close together. A white-coated man came to serve the coffee, learned their preferences, poured, then put the heavy silver coffee service on the table. He brought an array of scones, doughnuts and pastries on silver platters, one with hot pastries that Dosha found delicious.

"If you would be kind enough to be our hostess," Señor Garcia told Dosha. Then he laughed. "Please don't see me as a male chauvinist. My lovely wife has trained me well enough. It's simply that I perform best with a woman's assistance. And speaking of assistance, I'll launch right in with our plans. I'm moving slowly because you two are in the honeymoon stage. We must move now, of course, because of our schedule, but I'm aware that you had a short honeymoon. As I've said, we'll make up for that early next year. But right now, I want you to have ample time for each other.

"I don't mind telling you that we'll all be very busy after the beginning of the year, but right now it's September and for the next few months we'll move slowly. First, we'll begin planning the whole operation from here in Puerto for Europe, for America and for Africa." He closed his eyes and leaned back. "I can see it now. Banc International's thrust into the arts. Culture for the masses. Music and art for the masses. It's a glorious dream and I intend to see it reach fruition. Certain elements of every society have always enjoyed the glory of art and music. It's our wish that it be available for all who want it to be. This is a wondrous undertaking."

Those in the room shared the dream and the camaraderie was warm and caring. Only Francisco seemed a little distant, but even he listened carefully. Dosha felt a sense of joy fill her as Señor Garcia talked. She thought she should pinch herself. Was she dreaming or really sitting here on the edge of something so magnificent? The CEO's presence assured her that she wasn't dreaming.

Suddenly Señor Garcia turned to Dosha. "Please tell us a bit about what you'd like to see done. Spare nothing. Price is no object as we plan. What would you like to see us do? Later there may be need to rein ourselves in, but here the sky will be the limit."

Christian's proud eyes were on his wife as she relaxed and began to talk.

She began softly. "I'd like to see us reach every possible soul we can to bring the arts and music to their world," she began. "From the outset, the inner cities would be completely included. It seems to me we have such an excellent chance to expand life as we know it to the masses so they might know what we in a different socioeconomic world take for granted..."

The CEO's eyes were narrowed and a smile played on his face. "*Sí, sí,*" he said. "Forgive me for interrupting you so soon, but I promise you full time to expound on your wishes. How would you begin? The first steps, please?"

Dosha thought a long moment. She had dreamed of this time. "You mean how would I begin in the inner cities?"

"*Sí.*"

She drew a deep breath, aware of Christian's eyes on her with ardent love. "I would immediately have our members set up meetings in the inner city communities. We would need to begin, of course, with leaders and community activists. They can be so helpful. We would interface with them, engage the media."

Señor Garcia nodded. "You explain this beautifully and I'm impressed. And then?"

"I'd suggest that we set up concerts in the inner city itself as well as city-wide concerts. I would try to put it all together in a cohesive whole. It seems to me we would work best that way."

Smiling, Señor Garcia clapped lightly as Dosha blushed. "I like this approach and I think it will work well. What do you think, Ramon?"

"I'm very impressed, but then Dosha, Christian, my wife and I have talked of this before."

"And you, Pia?"

"I think it's absolutely ideal."

Señor Garcia clasped his hands before him. "With you representing music and an excellent person I have in mind handling art, we can't fail. Christian and Ramon will handle the administrative side of this, so we're set. We'll have meetings with the art representative. He is Pedro Montez, the illustrious artist. Are you, by chance, familiar with his work?"

"I am," Dosha replied. "I admired his paintings and his sculptures when we visited the Prado in Madrid last spring. I'd be honored to work with such a man."

"And he'll be honored to work with you," Señor Garcia told her. He frowned then. "He was to be in this meeting, but his flight was delayed. Ramon will see that you meet him as soon as possible."

They talked a long while of Banc International and more plans for the future. Then Señor Garcia turned to Francisco. "Ah, Francisco," he said gently. "I realize it was a disappointment to you that you don't get your chance to handle the administrative side of music and art for the masses, but I'm fast pulling together something I think you will like. Please be patient."

"Of course, señor," Francisco replied. "I'm always honored to work for Banc International in whatever capacity."

The CEO looked at Francisco sharply. "Well said."

And Francisco sat thinking that the position Señor Garcia had in mind wouldn't suit him as well as this one did. He simply didn't have the depth of mind that would tell him that he competed brutally with Christian, his cousin, and would never be satisfied unless he could best him in every way.

They talked over two hours before the meeting ended and Christian and Dosha were shown to their luxurious adjoining offices at the other end of that floor. Señor Garcia even joined them there. He grinned at Christian. "Of course, as director you have the choice of offices. I myself prefer corner offices, but then I'm not on my honeymoon."

The CEO and Francisco left them then and Ramon turned to them, a wide grin on his face. "Ah, my friends, you finessed that meeting superbly. Rest assured that the CEO will back you in whatever you choose to do."

Ramon introduced them to their new secretary, a sedate older woman with a warm and winning smile. Maria Sanchez. "Please tell me what you want," she said, "and I'll see that you get it."

When Ramon and the secretary went out, Christian walked over and closed the door, tried the lock, then locked it, walked back to Dosha and stood a foot from her, looking at her lovingly as her heart raced. What did he have in mind? she wondered as she breathed too fast.

Christian chuckled and took her hand. "Don't worry, *querida*. I won't ravish you so soon, but heaven would forgive me if I did. You and I are going to love it here and we have a lot of work to do."

She breathed a little easier then, but she was also a little disappointed that he didn't give her a long, smothering kiss.

She would give him one, but she was skittish about where that kiss would take them. Better let well enough alone. Tonight she would prepare a dinner for him with wild rabbit stew and a dessert of American coconut-rice pudding he had come to love. And then? She giggled.

"Why do you laugh?" he asked.

She shook her head. "Plans that I have for you at home that will make you happy," she told him.

He looked at her closely. "You look secretive," he said. "Sexy and sensual and secretive. I think I'm in for a delightful surprise. Am I right?"

She nodded. "You couldn't be more right."

Dosha insisted that Christian take the corner office. She really preferred the adjoining one. Both offices had teakwood furniture and heavy glass and acrylic. Huge and small potted plants were everywhere and outsized aquariums graced both rooms. Floor to ceiling windows made the rooms brilliant with light if you wanted them that way.

Maria knocked and came into Dosha's office. "I just wanted to see if there are things you need. I tried to anticipate as best I could."

Dosha smiled at the pleasant woman. "You've done a good job, but you might want to check with my husband."

Maria's smile was broad. "I'll do that, señora. Oh, I'm delighted to be assigned to you for a little while until you can make your own choice."

Dosha nodded. "If everything works out, we'll give you every chance."

Maria blushed and her face was lovely. "Thank you, señora. That's kind of you. Yes, *gracias.*"

That afternoon, the CEO stopped by with Ramon and an attractive, redheaded man in tow. "Settling in all right? Don't hesitate to ask for what you want."

The CEO introduced the man as Pedro Montez. The tall, courtly man bowed to lift Dosha's hand and kissed it. Then he shook hands with Christian. "Señor, señora, I'm honored."

"No, Señor Montez, we are honored."

The CEO stroked his chin as he stood. "I'll call another meeting in a few days after I return from Switzerland."

Francisco came in then and the CEO introduced him to Pedro Montez. Francisco responded graciously, but he thought to himself: Damn my luck. I miss a chance to work closely with a man of Pedro Montez's stature, a man who is favorably compared to Goya. But oh, my cousin Christian, this play is not over yet. There are many scenes to come.

Chapter 16

The telephone rang that afternoon almost as soon as Dosha and Christian got home. It was a cheerful, giggling Caitlin who called.

"Did you get your package yet?" Caitlin asked.

"I haven't had a chance to check."

"Well, if it didn't get there today, it should tomorrow. We paid plenty to get it shipped express."

Dosha laughed. "Is it the love package you chicks told me about before we left?"

"You'd better believe it is. We opened it to make sure it was all there, then we added our own delicate treatment, wrote out advice on how you two should behave for maximum pleasure. We've all been there, done that. Girlfriend, we're giving you the benefit of the experience of all three of us—Raven, Viveca and I. Honey, you may never come down from the high this is going to send you on."

"Hey, you're making me overly eager. And this comes

from Tahiti? We're going to Tahiti on our delayed honeymoon next spring."

"I remember and I'm envious. Now you be sure you let us know how everything went."

"Oh, I'll be certain to do that."

"And, Dosh?"

"Yes, love?"

"Ah, you talk a lot when you call, about the Muñozes, especially Pia. Just remember *I* am your best friend, always. I love you."

"And I love you. You needn't worry that I'll ever forget that you're my best friend. We go back a long way. Pia's a doll, but she's not you."

"Atta girl. Now, Adam is here and he wants to tell you something. Don't let it upset you too much."

"What's this about?"

"He'll tell you. And everybody sends love. We all say to each other, 'When you talk with Dosh and Chris, give them our love.' And give Chris my love. Tell him I'll hit on him next time."

Dosha laughed. "It's not like he doesn't like it."

"One more thing. How's the job coming?"

"Splendidly. We don't have to go in except for meetings at the moment. We'll be back there in January, you know. I've got to call and talk with you about both our jobs and about a ball they have here in October, the *Baile de Isabel.* It's in honor of the wonderful late paragon Mrs. Montero," she said and sounded sarcastic.

"Listen, sweetie, you can hold your own with *any* paragon, and I'm dying to hear all about the ball and the jobs. Now Adam is looking at me hard, so I'll turn you over to him." She made a kissing sound into the phone.

Adam's deep voice sounded. "Sis?"

"Yes, my dear Bro. Caitlin said you've news for me."

"Yeah, and it may not be good. It's about Daryl."

She couldn't get the words out fast enough. "What *about* Daryl?"

"He may be headed your way."

"What! *Why?*"

Adam expelled a harsh breath. "Well, I'm not sure but the guy is going nuts. He came by my office this afternoon and asked what I thought of him going to Puerto de la Cruz. He said he's been there before. You there, Sis?"

"Yes, he told me that. It was before we got together."

"Well, he said he wants to apologize to you in person for any harm he has caused you. He said he feels badly about what he has done, but he's still adamant that he *did not* send the photograph. And I told you he took all the tests, but he still could be lying. He said he hasn't made up his mind, but to warn you that you're not to be surprised if you see him there. Lord, I *am* sorry. You don't need this grief."

"You're right, I don't, but I guess I'll have to roll with the punches. You know I appreciate your letting me know. You tried to dissuade him?"

"You bet I tried. I told him if he was really capable of caring for you, he'd let you alone, let you be happy. He grinned and said he might do that. He just hasn't made up his mind. Can you deal with this?"

"And anything else Mr. Stoner's putting down. I'm happy, Adam, the way I've never been before and I intend to stay that way."

"That's my girl. I told Stoner if he gave you trouble, I would crucify him. I'm glad Chris is making you happy. Is everything else going okay?"

"Superb. If I get any higher, I'll need jet fuel. I think you're more worried than I am. Now hold on. Chris told me next time you called, he wanted to ask you something."

Dosha put the phone hold button on and decided to go up

the stairs instead of calling up. Chris lay spread-eagled on the bed and he grinned when she opened the door. "Join me?"

She blew him a kiss. "Adam's on the line, sweetie."

She went into their kitchenette where she would prepare a meal of wild rabbit stew, sharp cheese and onion paella, mixed salad greens and the coconut-rice pudding with vanilla sauce dessert that was his favorite. Humming, she began to get the things together. She had made the stew and the paella the day before. Chris liked tossing the salad greens and he made a mean vinaigrette.

He kissed the back of her warm neck and nuzzled it. "I can't believe you are so good to me."

"Just returning small favors."

There was a knock on the door which Christian answered to find Pablo standing there with a big box beside him. "Señor, this package came for the señora a short while ago. I apologize for not bringing it up right away, but we were outside with chores. It's not heavy for so large a package."

Christian thanked him and picked up the box, took it into the bedroom and looked at the return label. Raven, Caitlin, Viveca. All three women's names were on it and a wide grin spread across Christian's face. Dosha had told him about this box and what the contents would be and he had eagerly anticipated it. He ran his tongue over his bottom lip and went to the kitchen for a knife to open the box.

"Did I hear Pablo's voice?"

"You did and he brought you a big box."

"Oh, yes, that's the box Cait mentioned."

His eyes on her were hot then and she drew a quick breath and looked down. She could feel heat flood her body and her knees felt weak. He saw the effect he had on her and it thrilled him. Good, because she had an even greater effect on him. He put his hand in his pants pocket, felt his erection.

"We could forget about dinner," he told her softly.

She drew a deep breath. "No, because this pudding is turning out just right and I don't want to spoil it. To me, loving you means feeding you well."

"Okay, we'll wait, but do you want to open the box?"

"Why don't *you* open it, *querido,* while I finish this?" She checked the baking pudding through the oven window. "We'll eat, put on some jazz, go to bed with the chickens and let nature take its course."

"I'm trying to help nature, you know."

"You do nature proud."

A little while later, the rabbit stew and the paella were slowly heating and the rice pudding was still in the oven when a second knock sounded. This time Dosha went to the door to find Marta standing there. She looked flushed and contrite. "Señora," she began, "forgive me for coming up without asking if I could see you, but Estela has been talking to me about what a fine person you are and that I should be proud to work here. I *am* proud and I want you to know that. You *are* a fine person."

Dosha didn't know what to make of it. "Why, thank you, Marta. You're very welcome here."

"Thank you. I know you told Estela you like chocolate milk, from the kind of syrup you don't find just anywhere. Today I went to a market near the Charcot del Plaza and I saw such a chocolate syrup and I bought some for you. It's a present. I would like to fix you some the way my mother fixed for me when I was a little girl."

Dosha relaxed then. The girl was coming around. "Thank you. I'd love that."

"Then I would bring it up tonight." Marta's eyes sparkled.

"Please not tonight. We have a very sweet dessert. Let's

save it for tomorrow night and I'll prepare myself for that delicious taste. I'll have no other sweets all day."

"Would you like whipped cream on it? I bought some."

"How thoughtful. I would *love* whipped cream. Why don't you keep the syrup down in the kitchen and I'll let you fix me the hot chocolate. You're very sweet."

Marta looked solemn then. "No, señora, *you* are sweet, and I beg you to forgive me."

Dosha patted the girl's shoulder. "Of course I forgive you." But the thought came to mind anyway that she and Marta would never be friends, just friendly. The way Dosha was with Antonia. Her eyes followed Marta as the girl turned and went down the hall and she continued thinking of Antonia. She had run into her on an errand in the Charcot del Plaza and the woman had been *so* friendly. They had talked of the *Baile de Isabel* and what they would wear. Somehow Dosha had not chosen to discuss her gown that D.C.'s fabulous dress designer Roland was making for her from the dress form he had of her.

Shaking her head she went back into the kitchen and sprang to full attention. Her rice pudding! But, no, it had three more minutes to go. With a sigh of relief, she waited, then took it out of the stove with her padded gloves and admired the delicate golden brown color of the rice crust. She had made the vanilla sauce earlier. A heavenly aroma of pure vanilla wafted across her nostrils as Christian came in.

"You're not going to believe your friends," he said merrily. Then, "Talk about your scrumptious desserts. Beautiful, and smells out of this world. Like its creator." Again he was at her back and he put his arms around her waist and nuzzled her neck. "Did I ever tell you how much I love you?"

"Oh, once in a while you say it. Not nearly enough."

He squeezed her. "Sweet little liar you are. I tell you

every chance I get. Come on, look at your goodies. If I get any harder, you could snap me in two."

This time she grinned. "Fat chance I'd have of snapping that thick wonder. Besides, I can only coddle it, stroke it, love it. I'm incapable of doing anything else."

He gave her a long kiss on her face, then ran his tongue down her neck as she shuddered. "What on earth is in that package?" she asked, laughing.

In a few minutes, she found out. There were two large bottles of pink liquid oil and when she handed one of them to him and he opened it, the fragrance was of peppermint. There was a note on the bottle label: *Safe to ingest.* She looked at him and rolled her eyes. Neither made a comment. She set both bottles on the dresser. Next was a short sheer black lace nightie and a black satin thong. Christian held it up saying, "My heart turneth over."

"Knowing you," she quipped, "I'm not surprised."

She laid the short list of instructions aside and took out a very soft, thick plastic sheet. Then shaking her head and smiling she begun to read the instructions.

Prepare to have the time of your life. Next exit to Paradise.
Turn on all the love juice at both your command.
Best if both are lying down flat.
Relax and let joy and contentment flood you.
Pour a little of this oil of wonder into the palm of your hand, each one of you, and lovingly rub on partner's body. Don't stop until you've covered his or her body.
Use your soft rose lighting.
Now kiss, caress, hug, cuddle, lick and probe your way to glory. That is an order!
Three friends who know about love

Dosha went into gales of laughter. "They're completely mad," she said.

Christian shook his head. "No, they couldn't be saner. I plan to comply. What about you?"

She looked at him archly. "What do you think? I have a few things to take care of to set this up. Let's bathe together before dinner and..."

"We may never get to dinner if we bathe together."

She playfully batted her long eyelashes at him. "I'll see that we do."

The late afternoon sun rays came into the windows and threw warm light onto their bodies in spite of air conditioning, and she set out to prepare for a night of ordered bliss. First, she called Socorro and told her they planned a romantic evening together, asked if she needed anything.

"Yes," Socorro said, laughing. "I need you two to have the best time imaginable. I love you both so much."

"And we love you. Now if you need anything..."

"I will not. Be happy and enjoy."

Next, Dosha left a request that Estela and Pablo take messages and leave them on the hall table. Then she decided to turn off her cell phone.

Chapter 17

The sun was beginning to set when Dosha and Christian sat in the sunken tub and lathered each other with scented bath gels. At first they splashed about like happy children, then became more grown up, quieter. He lathered and rinsed her breasts and suckled first one, then the other. "I can see where this is leading," he murmured.

She smiled. "I'm determined not until after dinner."

"Maybe a quick appetizer, full meal to come later."

"Um-m-m, complete with heady wine and rich dessert, but not now."

"If I begged you?"

"Wouldn't help."

"I know all your weak spots. You can't take it when I lick your breasts."

She drew a quick breath as he licked in circles around her nipples. Against her will, she told him. "Try me."

"What do you think I'm doing?"

"I'm loving it."

"I said you couldn't take it."

"I *am* taking it."

"And you're weakening. I can see it in your eyes. They're glazing over."

His rock-hard shaft was against her buttocks as he pulled her onto his lap and sharp fever suffused her. "Okay," she whispered, "you win." And he entered her syrupy wet, pulsing body and held back. He meant it to be a long time before he filled her with his seed.

To slow himself, he made conversation. "I think you're thickening a little around the waist. Could you be pregnant?"

Her head was on his shoulder and his warm wet skin felt good against her cheek. "You know I would tell you if I was."

His voice was low, husky. "I want a baby from you so badly. Son or daughter it doesn't matter. Any child from your body. Please give me one."

"You know I will, as soon as I can."

She was surprised to hear the raw passion in him then as he told her, "I've always wanted at least one child since I was little more than a child myself. I had such a wonderful childhood and I want to pass that on..."

"And Isabel was never pregnant?"

She wasn't prepared for his quick intake of breath or the harshness with which he spoke. "I don't want to talk about Isabel."

For a moment she felt completely cut off from him as his tone went cold. He had told her that Isabel betrayed him, but he had not said with whom. He had hinted that there was more than one lover. Her heart went out to him as she felt the sudden tenseness in him. She leaned back and plainly saw the hurt that lay on his face. She put her arms around him. "All right, we won't talk about her. I'll never mention her again if that's what you want."

"I am sorry..." He was back with her again.

"But it might help if you could make yourself talk about it."

"No!" Vehement and final. She found herself shaken. He buried his face in the valley of her wet breasts and began the slow, maddening licking that thrilled her so. Finally he raised his face. "One day perhaps I can talk about it. You're so sweet and patient and I appreciate your waiting. Let's wipe the past slate clean for right now and enjoy this night and follow your friends' orders."

She reached down into the tub and took a handful of water, splashed it over his scars and stroked them. "I always feel healed when you do that," he said. "You heal me in so many ways."

She kissed him full on the mouth and outlined his lips with her tongue thinking, *but I don't heal you enough because the hurt on your face was terrible a moment ago and in past times when you've mentioned Isabel. Oh, my love, if only I could take away the hurt. What on earth did she do to you?*

He withdrew from her body then and hugged her. "We had better climb out. We have dinner to get out of the way..."

"With my special rice pudding for you."

"I thank you, but I've even tastier things on my mind."

After drying each other, they walked very close together into the bedroom where she slipped into a pastel ombre silk caftan of rainbow colors and he donned a white tee shirt and close-fitting black Dockers she had bought him. They were naked under their clothes. Dinner was very good with the mixed salad greens and vinaigrette he had prepared. Their appetites were whetted by their hunger for each other.

"Leave the rice pudding on the warmer," he told her. "I'm pretty sure I'll want more later. This is inspired." He took her hand, brought her fingers to his lips one by one and smiled roguishly. "Your friends say we're to lick our way to glory."

"That's only one of the things they mention."

"I like the way you respond when I lick you. You slowly dissolve into me and I love the feeling when you do. Animals lick their young to soothe them and I know I'm soothed when you do that to me."

"Oh," she murmured, "I'm so thrilled when you lick me, I'm not sure whether I'm soothed or not. I guess I am, but thrills just take me over and I want to bind you, make sure I have you forever."

"You will always have me. I could never leave you."

She turned on rose lights that suffused the room and cast a lover's glow on their bodies. He put a Barry White album on the CD player and the deep resonance of the machine perfectly enhanced a master's music. Barry sighed and murmured and spoke his smoky words of love in harmony with its meaning and they were deeply aroused. The singer's moans struck sensitive chords in them. Dosha felt her blood run hot with passion and longing and desire that seemed to go into the marrow of her bones. Her fingers seemed awkward, clumsy, as they stripped their king-sized bed and spread the king-sized soft rose plastic sheet over it.

Coming to her, he quickly lifted the caftan over her head and gazed at her naked body, then stripped off his own clothes. She was torpid now and her eyes glazed over with hunger no mere food could fill. "Where do we start?" Dosha whispered.

"What do you want me to do first?"

"Just everything. I forgot my gown and thong they sent," she whispered.

"Some other time. Not now."

She sat on the edge of the bed and he got on his knees before her, bent his head to her core with his wildly flickering tongue going mad on her silken brown flesh until she clutched him, held his head in to her body. Her fingers laced through his hair and she shuddered as she murmured his name again and again. "I'm never going to let you go. Don't try to leave me because I won't let you..."

Christian smiled sleepily as he licked her belly, his tongue going into the indention. He loved turning her on like this even as his own body flamed with love and desire for her. He knew this woman well, was trusted by and trusted her implicitly. He worshipped her and never intended to let her go.

"Sweetheart, the oil," she said. She had put a bottle of the peppermint oil on the nightstand and he picked it up, poured some into his palm and rubbed it onto the other palm. And slowly he began to rub the oil onto her waiting body. He took special pains with her breasts, then went to her face and throat, arms. He stopped to kiss her breasts and suckle them again.

"Tastes good," he told her as he kissed her. "Damned good."

"I'll say it does. It's a good thing we have the plastic sheet under us. The bed would be a mess otherwise."

"It would be worth it. This stuff is light, like baby oil. It's just perfect."

"*You* are perfect."

"And you're not?"

Passion overwhelmed them both as he quickly spread the oil over the rest of her body, put the bottle aside and entered her, his shaft hard and throbbing. And he thought if Heaven got any better, he wasn't sure he could stand it.

"You didn't give me a chance to go over you."

"I couldn't wait longer. Your body calls to me and I have to come in."

"I'm glad you know that."

"There's so much that we feel and never have to say."

"Yes."

Fire flashed through her belly and her nether region and

her walls gripped him like a close-fitting glove. And he thought, he was big and he filled her, but those same walls would close around a smaller shaft and grip it just as well. Nature was quite a woman.

He pulled her long legs over his shoulder and worked her expertly in slow rhythm until she panted. "Yes, take it slow because I don't want this night to end. Could you make it last until dawn?"

"I don't want to exhaust you."

"I'll be energized. You do that to me."

"And you give me the energy of a god. *Querida,* how good you are to and for me."

She sat astride him then and leaned down toward him, the aureoles of her nipples pointed to him, her long hair framing her face. His shaft inside her swelled even more and was rockhard as she brought her face down to his. Her warm breath fanned his face and his breath was scalding hot as he worked her relentlessly. It seemed too soon to both of them that her walls began to grip him in orgasm, spasms of pure joy that caught and held for long moments, then relaxed in steady rhythm again and again. She was being flung onto sandy, sopping wet shores and the tide was washing over her in undulating waves of pure glory.

And he was like the king of some great kingdom. A woman's love did this to you, he thought, had done it to him. He had known the love of his parents and his grandparents, had thought he had found love with Isabel, only to be brutally shattered. Then when he had almost lost hope, his precious Dosha had come and given him life and hope and love. Passion. Desire. Everything that mattered. More than anything he wanted to fill her with his seed to make the child they both craved. And his very soul went out to her.

They slept then in each other's arms, but it was only for a short while. She came awake to find him poised on one elbow above her, lightly running his index finger across her brow.

"Thank you," he told her.

"Thank me for?"

"I dreamed about you, that we were making love again. I'll never get enough of you."

She smiled, wide awake now. "That goes double for me. Now I'll get busy giving you your just deserts."

She took the bottle from the night table and bit by bit rubbed the peppermint oil into his flesh, starting with his scalp. He lay back making purring noises as she kneaded him deeply, her fingers going into the muscle, then her lightly doubled fists.

"Lord, that feels good. You told me you took lessons in massage."

"Yes, Caitlin and I both did after I broke up with Daryl. Daryl and I never massaged each other."

"I'm glad, because I'm jealous of what you knew with other men before me."

"You needn't be. No one can hold a candle to you."

And Christian thought then he didn't know and he really did not care what other men had been in her life. He didn't care about being the first; he *meant* to be the last. He caught one of her hands when she had finished massaging him and held it tightly. Then he placed it on his shaft and she stroked it.

"Mr. Mojo," she said softly. "The magic Mr. Mojo."

"He loves you, you know."

"And I love him." She bent and kissed his shaft and fondled it and his heart pounded when he saw what she intended to do. And as she returned the favor he had given her earlier, he thought how much he loved her, how much power she had over him now. He wanted her, *needed* her with all his heart and this was never going to stop. All thoughts of anything or anybody else faded and there were only the two of them in this place and at this time.

Their kiss was long and ardent, with his tongue flashing into the sweet hollows of her mouth, then hers into his. When they drew apart, both laughed shakily.

"I have an idea," she said.

"Okay."

"I'll feed you more rice pudding. Are you game?"

"I'm starved. I may require a sandwich."

"Fine. We have plenty of rabbit stew left. Then there's something else."

"Okay."

"I want us to samba, naked."

He laughed throatily. "A *naked* samba. I like the idea."

"I bought music from La Carnaval. The best kazoo player in Puerto de la Cruz. This should be good."

"Yes, it will be. A brief respite from all this glory, then back again."

They put on terrycloth robes and went into the kitchen where they heated the wild rabbit stew and the rice pudding with its sauce. When they sat at the table, her cleavage made him smile with memory and anticipation. Half her thighs were bare. She put a foot in his lap and he pressed it against his shaft.

"Better let me eat," he growled. "This tabletop is not in my plans, but I could change that."

Their bodies glistened with the peppermint oil and the smell was heady. She thought then of him as husband and lover and of her friends. How lucky she was. The stew and the rice pudding seemed to taste twice as good to both of them as it had earlier. The house was quiet and she thought of Socorro and Isaac and the wondrous life they must have led. She thought, too, of Mel and Rispa, their love that had resulted in her and her sibs. But she thought most of her twin, Damien. Did loneliness now cut through him like a knife the way it had cut through her before Christian came?

"Honey, you're miles away from me." Christian's voice brought her back.

"Sorry." She pressed her foot onto his shaft again.

He caught her foot, squeezed it. "I'll say you are."

A little while later, she put on the CD with the excellent kazoo player and they shucked their robes and went into the vibrant, earthy movements of the samba. He was entranced as her hips undulated in wild abandon, leading him on, playing ancient games with him. His shaft was at full mast and she smiled at her own power to do this to him. He caught her close and held her for long moments, his hardness pressed tight against her.

"I meant us to dance a long time," she whispered.

His eyes were dreamy. "You do not, you know. The way you're throwing it at me says you want it now, wanted it when we began."

"You know me well." She put her slender feet on top of his and he danced them around the room in a new version of the samba. "This is the answer to how good can it get."

"Yes. It absolutely can't get any better."

The CD segued into an especially wild segment and she got off his feet and flung herself about in reckless abandon, hips rolling in slow motion, her eyes on him. He stood it for a few minutes, then caught her to him and massaged her as best he could.

"I'm going to take lessons in massage," he told her.

"Oh, good. I can see this happening all the time."

"You had better believe it." She noted that he spoke this time like an American and he didn't usually. He was taking on her American way of speaking. She was entering, no, *had* entered, his bloodstream.

"*Querida,* it's time for something else I want to do, something you like."

"On my knees?"

"On *our* knees."

He went to the CD player and put on a Luther Vandross record, came back to her. She had danced for him alone tonight, he thought, and the wildness of it had shaken him. Who was this woman in his arms? Isabel had been a wild woman, but he felt deeply that there was no comparison. Dosha's wildness was for him only. She abandoned herself entirely for him and he loved her for it.

Luther Vandross' silken, sexy, sensual voice poured over them as Christian got a bath sheet from the bathroom and brought it back, spread it on the floor and they both went to their knees. He entered her hotly pulsing walls from behind, slipping in easily, surrounded by fluid like heavy peach syrup and hot thick tissue. He could never get over the wonder of this feeling. He pressed all the way and felt as if he had gone past her womb and touched bottom. Pulling out a bit, he bent and kissed her back, tonguing the oil-covered flesh that tasted so good. And the gesture set fire to her body and her spirit.

Her body was very warm against his and his blazed with heat he couldn't believe. She deliberately gripped and released him for brief moments and he growled his satisfaction. He was completely in again. This was as far as he could go and as good as it got. But he wasn't sure if that was true because it was all so good. They were an expert team of lovers, doing what they did best. Her belly was on fire with him buried in her and she scorched him as he scorched her.

They took their time, savoring every moment. She was a ripe peach from summer's hottest harvest, he thought, and the thought filled her mind simply as *lover, give me all you've got.* She didn't have to say it, because in this, anyway, he could read her mind.

They were a long, blessed time and as Luther Vandross lured them on, she felt as if a siege of madness had taken her over and all in this world she wanted was more and more and more of him. And as lightning flashed through his body, he felt exalted, touching highest Heaven as he poured his seed into her body until he was spent and satisfied.

And beneath him, Dosha moved in steady rhythm until she felt him erupt and felt her own powerful orgasm that gradually shook her as limp as a rag doll. Then in quick succession two more. She trembled and went into spasms that gripped and relaxed, gripped and relaxed until she felt the same Heaven he knew. *Her friends had been right. This was their night of glory.*

In bed he held her, gently talked to her.

"Don't you want to fall asleep?" she murmured. "You worked so hard."

"*We* worked so hard. No, I don't want to fall asleep yet. I want to lie awake and go over this night, moment by moment. How different my life was before you came into it."

"And how different mine was. Christian, we have to be the luckiest people on earth."

It was much later that they slept, spoon fashion, and their dreams were warm and wonderful, prophetic of good things to come. Then she remembered Socorro's earlier warnings that they were to be very careful. They had enemies who meant to hurt and perhaps destroy them.

And in the hills of Puerto, Francisco and Juan talked in a small restaurant.

"It is over two months now since you mailed the photograph to Dosha back in America. I think it is time for something else to happen. What is it, Juan?"

Juan thought a moment. "I told you about the tarantula in the señora's bedroom?"

"You did, and what are you getting at?"

"Just this, señor. I have wondered if it really was an accident. Tarantulas are not native to Puerto de la Cruz. Marta has confided to me that she hates the señora. She did not explain why, but she adored Señora Isabel. Could *she* have put the spider there?"

Francisco rubbed his chin as he chuckled. "Anything is possible. Of course that was a foolish act. It could have bitten anyone. But then I have always thought Marta foolish."

"She can perhaps be useful to us."

"I suppose, but I do not like trafficking with fools."

"She told me she admires you."

Francisco perked up. "She did, did she? Perhaps she is smarter than she seems. At any rate, I am fomenting a plan to get even with my cousin. I will not need your help with this, but I have other more diabolical plans that may hurt and even kill him. Are you with me, for more money than you dream?"

Juan's head jerked up sharply. "*Sí,* señor. Simply tell me what it is that you want done and I will be sure to carry it through."

Chapter 18

Two days later an express letter came from D.C. The return address on the label said The Three Sirens and Dosha threw back her head, laughing. Opening the flat cardboard container, she pulled out Caitlin's light blue stationery, opened the envelope and read.

> We don't expect to hear from you for a week or so.
> You'll be resting from all that glory.
> The three sirens

Dosha passed the letter to Christian, who laughed delightedly. His eyes crinkled as he commented, "Who's resting?"

They had come from nearly a day spent on the Charcot del Plaza, had had dinner, seen a movie and were just getting in. The day before, another express package had come from Roland with sketches for her gown for the

Baile de Isabel. Now she found she wanted to study it again.

Upstairs in their bedroom, she undressed and slipped on pale green lounging pajamas with a gold chain belt that accented her small waistline and wide hips. Christian whistled lustily. Going to the closet, she pulled out the sketch and showed it to him again.

"Do you really like it?" she asked.

"It's beautiful and you'll look like a queen in it."

She propped the sketch on a straight chair and studied it some more. Roland had included a large swatch of the silk fabric in an ivory shade that would set off the superb teardrop pearl pendant Socorro had given her. The gown would be a masterpiece of drapes and folds that would reveal her magnificent breasts and flatter her tawny brown skin. Looking at his wife and the sketches, Christian closed his eyes. He was, he thought, going to have plenty to be jealous of the night of the ball.

By the time Christian could get into something more comfortable, Marta had come to announce that Señora Antonia wished to talk with her. Dosha looked at Christian. Antonia was the last person she wanted to see just now. Christian hugged her. "Maybe she won't stay long. I'm surprised, because Antonia is a stickler for etiquette and Puerto natives usually give notice that they will visit. It's not as if she is a close friend."

Antonia sprang to her feet when they came into the living room. "I must ask that you forgive me," she said. A large, flat package lay on the sofa beside her and she quickly withdrew a large sketch from the cardboard. "I simply wanted you both to see the sketch of my ball gown." She thrust it at them and laughed. "It's black, my signature color, but in glorious satin. The designer is Parisian, of course, and I shall go there for a final fitting." Dosha thought Antonia looked as proud as any peacock as she put her hands to her skimpy bosom. "Only my emeralds will do this justice."

"It's certainly beautiful," Dosha felt obliged to say, and Christian agreed with her.

Antonia looked closely at Dosha. "And *your* gown, my dear? Has your American designer sent you no sketches?"

Dosha shook her head and lied with a straight face. "We've worked together for so long that he can read my mind and..."

"But certainly you must know the color and the fabric."

Dosha was amused at the anxiety that Antonia showed. She shook her head. "He always surprises me and I let him. I've never been less than immensely pleased at whatever he creates."

Antonia looked disappointed. And she thought, I was so certain that she would have something to show when I showed her my sketch. Then she was petulant, thinking, Americans are strange, American women anyway. Imagine just turning oneself over to a dress designer. Certainly she, Antonia, wouldn't dream of doing that.

Antonia refused their offer of drinks and/or snacks. She talked a little while of the coming ball. "My daughter is a real problem," she told them. "She has chosen some mousy pink thing to wear to the ball. Of course, she is young and quite lovely, so almost anything she puts on looks well. I swear that young woman's life is in the hills with those girls she teaches. She misses her late husband dreadfully and I'm beginning to believe she will never recover from his death."

Antonia was thoughtful for a moment. "Of course, Francisco is very fond of her. He always has been." She shot a sly look at Dosha. "He is also fond of you, my dear. Francisco is a man who simply likes women and they like him. I keep telling him that he really should marry if he wants to get the position he wants at the bank. Do you not think so, Christian?"

"It's his choice," Christian answered evenly.

It wasn't long before Antonia began to get up. "I really must rush. My husband is to be home for dinner and he may bring someone with him. Please say you will show me sketches of your gown when you get them, will you?"

"I may not get any. Roland may simply surprise me," Dosha said again. "He has done that before."

"Oh I could never... Again, I apologize for coming without warning, but I get so wrapped up in the ball plans. I'm chair-lady, you know. Each year it must be perfect. My sister and I were not close, and she was quite a bit younger. I still miss her." She glanced obliquely at Christian's scowl, then fell silent.

Later, in their bedroom Christian turned to Dosha. "Encore for a couple of nights back?" He laughed when he said it.

"But we've had an encore."

He shook his head. "Not all of it."

"Let's wait a bit to go through the whole thing. The plaza has left me exhausted. All that walking and that horror movie."

"Then Antonia's visit," he said drily.

"*Especially* Antonia's visit. Remember what she once said to me, that a man must have a woman to entertain his guests and warm his bed."

Christian laughed. "You entertain my guests beautifully, even Antonia. And you set my bed on fire."

Dosha swatted him with a small pillow.

"Come to bed," he said, "and burn me some more."

"You're insatiable," she teased him.

"And I have a partner who likes me that way."

They listened to the soothing rhythm of Borodin's *Nocturne* and he stroked her feet and ankles. A knock sounded and Dosha answered the door to find Marta standing there, an anxious look on her face. "Señora, may I still bring you the chocolate milk?"

"Ah, yes, I would really enjoy and appreciate that."

When Dosha went back to Christian, he told her, "It looks like you've won Marta over. One small hurdle we have passed. I was going to suggest that we send her home if she had not changed."

Socorro called then. "How *are* you, my dear?" Socorro asked.

"Oh, I feel wonderful." They talked about the day she and Christian had spent. Finally Socorro said, "I hate having to tell you this, but I'm seeing darkness again and a vision of envy. I can't tell whether it's man or woman, just that it's there. I know you're being careful, you and Christian, for the clouds and the darkness are over him, too. I wish I either knew the whole story or didn't have this gift at all. It's maddening. Let me read the Tarot for you tomorrow, will you?"

"Of course. I'll come up right after breakfast."

"And I'll look for you. Good night, love, and sleep well."

When Marta brought the milk and Dosha tasted it, she licked her lips and told Christian, "It's too bad you're allergic to chocolate. This is great."

He grinned. "I can bear my allergies, as long as I'm not allergic to you, and that will never be."

Marta had chosen an especially lovely and large china cup to put the chocolate in and the fluffy whipped cream was delicious as Dosha tasted it from her finger before stirring it in. Chocolate always helped her to sleep.

In her apartment, Socorro was restless. What was wrong with her? she wondered. She had borne these strange feelings—the foreknowledge, the visions—all her life. Why was this so different? And she knew it was because she loved

Christian and Dosha so much and these new feelings swirled around them. She prayed hard then for God's blessing and for her gift to be clearer. At least she could warn them and they could stay on guard.

She climbed into bed, but sleep would not come. Why did she keep wanting to go to them, to *be* with them? As if she by her presence could protect them from all harm.

Dosha woke around midnight with nightmarish pains cutting into her stomach. She sat up and shook Christian, who immediately came wide awake.

"Something is terribly wrong," she panted. "Maybe it's appendicitis."

Alarmed, he said, "Hold on, sweetheart. I'm taking you to the hospital. It's not far away."

Christian quickly called Pablo and told him what was going on. And Pablo told him, "Let me take you, señor. You are in no condition to drive."

So Christian sat on the back seat with Dosha in his arms and he suffered with her as the short trip seemed the longest he had ever known.

Christian found a Dr. Rios he knew on duty who quickly asked Christian Dosha's symptoms. The doctor examined her in an emergency room as she lay moaning piteously. Then the doctor sprang into action, hurriedly galvanized a small team and set to work. Some sixth sense told Christian that this was no ordinary attack.

Later when their actions had slowed, and Dosha was in a private room, Christian asked the doctor, "What *is* it, man?"

The doctor frowned. "I've called Dr. Delgado, my mentor. He is a world-renowned expert on poisons and I'm pretty sure that's what this is."

"Poison!" Christian could hardly get his breath.

The doctor nodded. "We've pumped her stomach and we

have the contents, so it will be easy to tell what it is when the lab opens. The particular poison I have in mind mimics a heart attack. It's a strange thing, Christian, but I worked in the rainforests of Brazil and there is a yellow lily that grows there. When the powder from it is ingested, the patient will die within five hours if no antidote is given. And even doctors believe it to be a heart attack.

"Fortunately, we have an antidote, thanks to the efforts of Dr. Delgado and myself. I've never seen these symptoms in Puerto before, but I became very familiar with it in the rainforests of Brazil. When Dr. Delgado arrives, we'll need to go over your wife's activities the last few hours up until now."

Christian licked dry lips and he thought with fury of Marta. "A maid brought her hot chocolate around nine o'clock," he told the doctor. "We had an early dinner."

The doctor shook his head. "Had she ingested the poison at dinner, she would be dead by now. There are other poisons, of course, but my guess is that it was the hot chocolate that carried this particular poison."

Christian had called his father and now Captain Montero came to them. Christian and the doctor explained what had happened and the captain stood frowning and stroking his chin.

"I've kept my eye on Marta since the tarantula," the captain muttered. "She is almost certainly the culprit. Who else? But is she fool enough to do something like this, knowing she would be a likely suspect? Lately she has been so warm and happy, Estela and Pablo tell me. They even thought she might have found a lover..." He frowned more deeply. "You may be sure I'll question her as soon as I can get to your house tonight. This is unconscionable."

He hugged his son, looked in on Dosha whom he loved as dearly as he loved his son. Christian was with him and

Christian's heart turned over. Dosha looked so helpless lying there, so completely vulnerable. He was sick with rage at the cretin who had done this to her.

Dr. Delgado came in a short time, briefly examined Dosha whose stomach had been pumped and who lay exhausted by her ordeal.

"It will help if you hold her hand," he said to Christian. "Talk to her. If God is with us, she will pull through this, but she'll be very weak for a couple of days." His face was grim then. "Later this morning when the lab is open we'll run the tests. Dr. Rios has told you that he's familiar with what this poison might be. If it's not the yellow lily, then I know not only about that poison but about most of the other poisons in the world. God has sent me to you."

"And I'm profoundly grateful," Christian told him.

Christian was somber then. "I'll go to my wife now."

In the room, he took a chair by Dosha's bed and stroked her limp hand, kissed it, held it to his face. And he sat thinking that Marta was Isabel's protégée, Isabel who plundered his life even from her grave.

A seemingly sleepy Marta faced Captain Montero as they sat in the kitchen of Christian and Dosha's house. The captain had roused Socorro, who said she had hardly slept at all.

"I knew you'd want to know about this," he had told her, "so come along and listen."

Socorro had told Captain Montero how worried she had been with the dark visions coming in on her and he had nodded. "Your telling her helped. She might have died in her sleep had she not been aware that something was likely to happen. She was on the alert and I believe that saved her."

Tears now ran down Socorro's face as she glared at Marta. "Cretin," she muttered under her breath, but found no word bad enough to say. Estela and Pablo both looked frightened. What kind of monster had lived so close to them? they both wondered.

Captain Montero prepared to feint with the sullen Marta, throw her off guard with suddenness. His look at her was deceptively bland.

"You put the poison in the hot chocolate you brought the señora?"

He was surprised to have her answer, "*Sí,* señor."

Captain Montero's voice went hard, cold. "You admit it then? What *was* the poison you gave her?"

Marta shrugged. "It comes from South America and it should have killed her in her sleep. That is all I know."

The captain was beside himself. "What in hell do you mean, it should have killed her? What has she done to you, save being kind, that you would want to kill her?"

Marta's eyes narrowed to slits and she fairly spat the words. "I *hate* her. She has tried to take Señora Isabel's place and no one can do that. The señora was an angel, beyond all others."

The captain's voice was scathing. "That's your opinion only, and I consider it worthless, as I consider *you* worthless."

The captain thought to himself that he was losing it. He wasn't following the best rules of interrogation. He was getting inside her head all right, but he was badgering her and this wasn't the time for that. He needed all the information he could get. He forced himself to be calmer. Drawing a deep breath, he asked the girl, "Who put you up to this? Who are your partners in this? And don't lie. I'll know if you lie."

He and Socorro noted that Marta seemed very frightened then, but she quickly regained her composure. "I'm the only one," she declared in a loud, hoarse voice. "The new señora does not belong in this house with my mistress's painting still on the wall. To me, it's still Señora Isabel's house."

"Isabel is *dead!*" the captain thundered. "And you won't bring her back by trying to kill someone whose shoes you are not fit to kiss."

Marta seemed almost not to have heard him. "The new señora, she is not dead, then?"

"You're damned right she is not dead and she is not going to die."

"Pity." Marta's eyes glittered.

The captain leaned forward. "Tonight I'll put you under arrest and later on this day you'll go to the detention home for juveniles. God, how I wish you were eighteen so you could truly pay for your crime..."

Marta's shoulders slumped. The voice was flat, distant. "It does not matter what you do to me. Señora Isabel is dead. My life was over when she died. I love her so."

"You are *sick,*" the captain said flatly. "I'm going to have you examined and carted to a mental hospital."

"I said it does not matter. My heart died with her."

"Your very *soul* is dead!" the captain thundered again.

For a brief moment, Marta's eyes met Socorro's and the old woman saw the triumph in the girl's eyes and asked God to forgive her, Socorro, for wanting so badly to strangle her.

The captain leaned back then, breathing easier. He was a cat with a mouse in his paws. "And you say there was no one else involved in this? You are very friendly with Francisco. Did he put you up to this?"

Marta did a quick take, then laughed harshly. "He is half in love with the señora. He certainly wouldn't hurt her." And she smiled inwardly. Her secret was safe. He wasn't even close.

The captain leaned forward, saying to Estela, "Pack her bags. Tonight she will spend the rest of the night in jail after

I interrogate her further. Tomorrow she'll be with those who are as mad as she is."

"*Sí,*" Estela said quickly and went to do his bidding.

Chapter 19

It was two days before Dosha was allowed to receive visitors except Christian and by then she felt better than doctors had expected her to.

"You had a close call," the doctor told her again. "I don't want you stressed in any way."

Christian had filled her room with wild orchids and he sat by her bedside with a beautifully wrapped package in his lap. His smile warmed her heart as she asked him, "What's in there?"

"A gift I was saving for later, but I want you to have it now." He handed the package to her, saying, "Open it."

She slowly undid the wrappings and lifted out a navy jeweler's leather box. Snapping it open she gasped to find a pair of ivory drop pearl earrings to match the pendant Socorro had given her. "Exquisite," she breathed. "Give me a deep kiss. The orchids were enough."

He kissed her hands first, then gave her the deep kiss she

craved. "Nothing is enough. *Querida,* I was so scared." And even now his eyes on her were frightened that she could be taken away from him so soon, without warning. And he said a silent prayer of thanks that she had been spared. Her arms around his neck pulled him hard against her, thrilling to his touch.

After a while she said, "I was frightened, too. I was out for so long a time and everything was cold and dark. Dying must be like that when you don't want to go."

He placed a finger to her lips. "Don't talk about dying. We're both going to live a very long time and be very happy the way we've been."

She nodded. "Socorro prophesied that we would have moments of bliss and moments of trouble. Marta is an enemy. I wonder how many more we have. Francisco?"

"He's not *your* enemy, my darling, just mine. Actually, I think he likes you more than I want him to."

"I feel sorry for him. He has no one who really matters to him, or that's the way it seems."

Christian frowned. "I don't want to talk about Francisco. Your pity is wasted on him."

She nodded. "I expect you're right. How is Socorro?"

"She sends her love and of course she would be here if she were not recovering from that wretched cold. She and I both selected the earrings. She was so excited over them."

"Be sure to tell her I love them."

Captain Montero came in then, sat down and told them about Marta and what had happened to her. Dosha's face blanched. She hated being hated and it shocked her.

"You're looking surprisingly well," the captain told her.

"Thank you. What will happen to Marta?"

"She will go to a juvenile detention center and I believe their doctors will find that she is at least partially insane."

His expression hardened. He considered Dosha too fragile just then to know the full venom Marta had spewed.

But the captain did say, "I favor my theory that Francisco is very likely behind this. He likes Dosha, but he would do anything to hurt you, my son, and what better way to hurt you than by destroying the woman you love so dearly."

Dosha and Christian were both silent.

Captain Montero looked around. "I've ordered flowers sent, but I see my son has already done you the honor."

"Thank you. I can never have too many flowers. Aren't these beautiful?"

"They are. If I know my son, the lover, they remind you both of some magnificent moments."

Dosha blushed then and her eyes nearly closed with delicious memory of their night at the waterfall. "They do," she said softly.

Christian was still there when Antonia came bearing a big basket of fruit and nuts. "Ah, you don't look sick at all. You look like your usual attractive self." Her face went somber. "Of course I heard what happened and I'm so sorry. I feel responsible, because it was I who recommended to you, Christian, that you take the girl under your roof again. Something I bitterly regret. How could she do such a thing?"

"How indeed?" Christian responded drily. "The final decision was ours and no one could know."

"It's a shame Socorro didn't foresee this." Antonia's face bore a small degree of malicious triumph. She didn't think much of the old woman's prophecies or her much-vaunted gift.

Dosha shook her head. "But she did foretell dark things to happen. No one except God truly knows the future and no wise one even pretends to. And Socorro is oh so wise."

Antonia shrugged. "If you say so. Listen, my dear, Carmela would have come, but one of her girls had her appendix removed and she set up an infection. You know how she is about those girls. A regular mother hen. Why can't she have children of her own?"

"It's her choice," Christian said quietly.

And Antonia grumbled, "In the meantime, I'm totally without grandchildren." She stood up. "At least you'll be well for the ball. I must rush away to some of my husband's business."

After Antonia had left, Christian asked the nurse for a knife and a small plate, peeled and quartered a delectable Anjou pear and sampled a slice.

"This is for you, of course. I didn't ask if you wanted it. You look a bit hungry to me."

She grinned. "Not for the pear."

His eyes on her got dreamy. "Are you hungry for me, as I'm for you?"

"*Querido,* I'm starved for you. Last night was torment."

"Tomorrow you go home and to my arms. I may just devour you."

Before she could answer, Pedro Montez, Pia and Ramon and Francisco came into the room. They stood around her bed, congratulating her on looking so well and bearing gifts of fruit, flowers and other small items.

Pia flung her arms around Dosha and tears filled her eyes. "I've been so worried. And yes, I've been furious. We called often. I made some of the walnut fudge you like so much. We called and asked the nurse and she said you can eat almost anything now. Enjoy, my love. You've been through hell."

Ramon kissed her cheek and the CEO's face was very grave as he offered his sympathy as he squeezed her hand. "But ah, now, all the old verve is back and I'm looking forward to meeting with you two again."

Pedro Montez was his usual ebullient self. "I've missed you," he told Dosha. "Our infrequent meetings have become a part of my life and I look forward to having them resume."

Only Francisco was nearly silent, but he finally said, "I'm glad you pulled through. I thought so highly of Marta. I never dreamed she could do something like this." But his manner was detached and both Dosha and Christian wondered what he was really thinking.

Like Antonia, the group didn't stay long and after they left, a call came from Dosha's family, beginning with Mel. Christian had told them about the poisoning from the beginning and they had wanted and intended to come to her, but by the second day, the doctor had said she would recover and be fine, so there was no need for them to come.

Now Mel asked, "How are you, baby?" His voice was hoarse with emotion.

"I'm really fine now, Dad. I go home tomorrow. They keep you in hospitals longer here in Puerto than in the States."

Rispa was on another line and she cut in. "We want to see you so bad. My arms just hurt with wanting to hold you. First, the damned photograph, then the tarantula. Are you safe there?"

Dosha sighed. "Are any of us truly safe anywhere? Mom, the photograph was sent from somewhere in the States and we may never know who did it..."

On the conference call line, Adam cut in. "I'm always going to believe Stoner did it. Oh listen, Sis, did anybody tell you you got a letter from him to mom's and dad's address?"

Dosha nodded. "Mom mentioned it. She said she was sending it and you wanted to open it. You certainly may if you wish."

"Oh, hell," Adam said, "I ruled out letter bombs, etc. and decided to let it go on. You'll probably get it today."

"Enough. Enough," Caitlin's throaty voice cut in. "I just want to tell you how much I love you, as if you didn't know. And Marty is standing here, the bully, trying to take the phone away…"

Marty's rich voice was music to her ears. "I'm so sorry about what you've been through, love. Hang in there and you're either coming home for a spell or we're coming there. We love you too much to wait until January to see you again…."

They were all so warm and wonderful, Dosha thought. And they were her family, her beloved family. "Where on earth is Damien?" she asked.

"He's going to call separately. Have you talked with him?" Rispa asked.

"Yesterday. He was worried because I was still a little weak, but today I'm really fine."

Rispa hesitated. "You're not just putting on a big front, are you? Poisoning is a vicious act. The shock alone is enough to knock you out."

"You're right, Mom, but I'm not putting on any kind of a front. I really am fine."

She talked with Raven and was told that Viveca and Carey and their baby were in New York on a brief trip. They sent their love and they would call soon. Like her family, they had been shocked beyond words.

Christian talked with the family, too, and he mused that it was always like talking with his own family. When the conversation was over, a warm glow had settled on both Dosha and Christian.

They had hardly begun a new conversation and he peeled a sugar-sweet temple orange for her when Pablo came in with the express letter from Daryl. She asked Christian to open it and his eyes held a worried expression. "Are you sure you are up to this?"

"With you by my side, I'm up to anything."

The letter was surprisingly brief.

Dear Dosha,
You'll be glad to get this letter because it will mean the end of what must have been torment for you. I'm getting married at the end of the month. I'm not sure I can ever love again the way I loved you, but I'll tell you this, it's with a far saner love. I'm sorry for the pain I caused you, but it's over now.

I didn't send the photograph, but I can see why everyone believes I did and I'm sorry you had to go through this.

More than anyone, you deserve happiness. Live your life without any more trouble from me.

Someone who will always love you,
Daryl

Dosha passed the letter to Christian, who duly read it and put it back in the envelope.

"I don't blame any man for having a hard time giving you up," he told her, "but you're mine now and God help any man who doesn't realize that."

"You aren't a jealous man?"

"I am, you know. I hope I'm not a fool about it like Stoner, but I can't take the thought of losing you."

"And you never will," she said softly. "I'll always be a part of you." She smiled a little then, remembering Damien's song for them. *"All this and ecstasy, if love is good to me."*

Chapter 20

It was cooler than usual a few days later when the CEO called another meeting at the Puerto headquarters of Banc International. In a small, more intimate conference room, the CEO presided with his usual aplomb. After a hearty breakfast of orange juice, creamed beef and eggs with scrumptious English muffins, they were all ready to begin. The CEO, Christian and Dosha, Ramon and Pia, Pedro Montez and Francisco.

Glancing around her, Dosha observed that Francisco looked different. She had seen him hung over many times, but this time his expression seemed far away and he looked—how could she describe it otherwise?—evil. He looked like pictures of assassins she had seen with the faint smile and the reddish halo that bespoke a mind mired in savage fury. The CEO was talking to Dosha.

"You're your usual gracious and charming self," he told her. "I have a beautiful woman at home and two of the most beautiful women on my staff. And I speak of a vivid inner beauty of all three of you ladies."

He stopped, smiling broadly, and looked at Christian, then Ramon. "And you, señors, are to be congratulated on your choice of mates."

Dosha laughed and both women thanked him. Then Dosha said, "Please don't forget to congratulate us on our choice of husbands. They're the best."

The CEO laughed. "Spoken like a true wife. This meeting will be brief." He nodded to Dosha. "In response to my request that you give me a good all-inclusive idea for our cultural campaign when the time comes for Puerto, you said you have what you feel is a good one.

"As you are aware, I'll be leaving today for a time in Switzerland, so this meeting is to see you again and give you my blessings. The infrequent meetings will continue under the leadership of both Christian and Ramon. Now, señora, your ideas, please."

Dosha cleared her throat and was surprised to find herself a bit nervous. She believed so deeply in this.

"It's just this," she began, "that we sponsor a music and arts festival here in Puerto at the beginning of the campaign for Puerto. We're flooded with visitors from all over the world and they will take back the news of our plans. I'm in contact with a number of artists and musicians who can be called on and will respond well. I've already contacted many of them."

Pausing, she indicated a sheaf of papers lying on the table. "I've drawn up specific steps I suggest we take to ensure the success of this venture." Her eyes sparkled and she had the attention of the others as she outlined a few of these steps.

The CEO held up his hand. "You may stop there, my dear. I am, indeed, impressed, as I see your fellow members are."

He asked for comments and got them until at the end he looked at Francisco. "Well, Francisco, what say you?"

Francisco expelled a harsh breath. "Señor, I'm sorry, but I'm still in the process of thinking this over. I suppose it's a good idea. I do have others, but I haven't yet formulated them to my satisfaction."

The CEO looked at him narrowly and his voice sounded sharp. "But you *will* shortly?"

Francisco nodded. "Shortly."

The CEO continued. "As you all know, I'm a hands-on man and there are few like me. I delegate responsibility wherever possible, but I want to know the nuts and bolts of my operation and the people involved. We have a high level of tolerance for human failure, but the one thing we don't tolerate is a low level of interest and participation."

It seemed to the rest of them that he spoke of Francisco alone.

Christian, Ramon and Pia were all complimentary and Pedro Montez waxed poetic. "My coworker is not only a vision," he said, "she is a visionary. I offer you my congratulations and I'll enjoy working with you on this. I, too, have many friends who are artists and musicians and I can assure you they will give their utmost."

The CEO glanced at his watch. "There's nothing left for me to say except that this is my baby, as Americans say. And I'm copying a leaf from Ramon's book in frequently quoting the Americans I so deeply admire. I expect great things of all of you. This project should be in full swing by or before three years from now and it will be the talk of the artistic world. Please don't fail me."

At home late that afternoon, it had grown even cooler, unusual for Puerto, and the sky was hazed dark gray. They would eat late and Socorro proposed that she read Christian and Dosha's fortune. They agreed and Socorro thought that in fact she was skittish. Her mind seemed a jumble of thoughts and emotions and clouded visions. Perhaps their presence would help her clear it.

Socorro chose to read in her apartment where she felt she did her best work. Dosha would come first.

With Christian and Dosha seated on a love seat, Socorro had Christian set up a card table in front of them and took a padded chair opposite them.

"You look happy, both of you," Socorro said slowly, "and I'm glad, for this makes me happy, too." She drew a deep breath. "Right now I'll put the Tarot aside and read from the regular deck and a little later what is called the Wheel of Fortune." Smiling, Socorro chose a card at random and thought that that card and its background resembled Dosha with her glowing brown skin and off-black hair. Yes, she was a queen among women.

Running her tongue over her lower lip, Socorro had Dosha cut the cards into three packs with her left hand, known as the devil's hand. After each cut she turned the pack with the bottom card face up. First, a ten of hearts. Ah, Socorro thought, a lover of love, from the spiritual to the erotic.

Dosha's skin cooled when the second pack revealed the ace of spades and she laughed shakily. "The death card," she said slowly. "At my very first reading I turned up the death card."

Christian reached over and took her hand, squeezed it. Socorro passed a hand over her brow. "My dear, please do as I do and see it as merely another card. There's always death in this world and perhaps this time it foretells mine. I long so to be with Isaac sometimes. Turn over the other pack."

And the last pack was a seven of diamonds and Socorro

nodded. "As far as I'm concerned, that completely negates the power of the so-called death card. You're an artist and you are powerful and strong."

One minute Socorro read the cards and announced that she would now read from what is known as the Wheel of Fortune. But the words had barely left her lips when her eyes began to close and she seemed in another world, as Francisco had seemed in another world in the meeting that morning.

"What is it, Abuela?" Christian was concerned.

Socorro nodded. "Just bear with me a moment. Something is coming to me, something very powerful, much of it clear and I must feel and see it. Let us be very quiet."

And they followed her counsel and sat silent as they watched Socorro begin to communicate with her spirits and try to divine their meaning. Socorro's skin looked ghostly pale and Dosha was alarmed lest she was sick or dying. Dosha whispered to Christian, "Will she be all right?"

He nodded and whispered back. "I've seen her in this state before. She'll be fine afterward."

Christian held Dosha's hand tightly for a moment or two, then stroked her arm and hand as Dosha tensed. She couldn't help but think of the death card. Socorro had prophesied Isabel's death. Would she *say* if she foresaw Dosha's death? Dosha couldn't shake a sense of dread and a foreboding of something terrible about to happen. She had been through two ordeals lately: the tarantula and the poison. And before that the photograph of herself dead in a wedding gown.

Long minutes passed before Christian finally whispered, "She's coming out of it." And indeed Socorro was breathing more deeply with her body returning to its normal stance.

Socorro held up her hand and shook her head and they correctly interpreted the gestures to mean that they shouldn't talk just then.

After a while Socorro began to speak slowly. "I've not had

a great vision like that in a long while. Small ones, yes, but this was monstrous. I saw a young girl dying, but I don't know who or where.

"I saw a very angry man lash out, then simply dissolve as if the earth had swallowed him without a trace."

Socorro paused for a very long time before she continued. "God sends me visions. I'm only his vessel and this time the vision is very dark and dangerous. People I know myself to love are in this vision and there is death and destruction all around them. I was crying wretched tears I couldn't stop. A vale of tears."

Socorro's voice was a little shaky. "One thing I saw beyond all others was a more evil presence than I've ever known before. I couldn't tell if it was male or female, just that the malevolence transcends, as I said, all that I've known—and I've known much evil."

Socorro dug an embroidered handkerchief from her sweater pocket and passed it over her brow.

At a soft knock on the door, Captain Montero came in, his face somber. He greeted the couple and touched Socorro's shoulder. "Are you all right?"

"I am," she replied. "I've just had a vision and it has left me nearly drained."

"I've news that is stunning," the captain said. "Would you rather I told Christian and Dosha and they can tell you later when you're up to it?"

"No," Soccoro said sharply. "I'm up to anything, just a little tired. What is your news?"

The captain cleared his throat. "Marta drank lye and killed herself a couple of hours ago. They couldn't save her. The head of the facility that held her called me a short while ago with the news."

Socorro's shoulders slumped. "I saw it," she murmured, "but I didn't know who."

Christian had lived with his abuela's visions and her prophecies all his life and he was used to them. Dosha sat transfixed. Socorro had said she saw a young girl dying and Marta was dead. She had said evil and destruction were all around people she loved. Dosha? Christian? And when would this evil come to pass?

The four people in the room knelt and prayed for Marta's soul.

Later, when Captain Montero had gone, Dosha and Christian kissed Socorro good-night and went downstairs hand in hand.

"I need to play my new composition," Dosha told him. "And I need you with me."

Seated at the grand piano, she slid effortlessly into the pianissimo or soft strains of her concerto. It was her "Waterfall by Moonlight," and Christian closed his eyes and lived that honeymoon night again. He felt her naked body in thrall to his own, her mint breath on his face.

Christian thought as crescendos climbed in the air that he loved this woman with a passion that unsettled him even as it filled his heart with wonder. Yes, he thought, love healed, but love could also hurt.

Marta had been part and parcel of his life with Isabel. He knew now, when it was too late, he never should have let her return.

Chapter 21

"My dear, you are queen of the world!"

Dosha, Christian and Socorro came into the ballroom for the *Baile de Isabel,* which Antonia had declared she intended to be the most glorious of all. Francisco bowed low, lifted Dosha's hand and kissed it. He looked at Christian saying, "I envy you."

Dosha thanked him with no special smile and they would have moved on, but Francisco detained them with his conversation. Antonia always chose him as a close friend to help her plan the ball and he was in his element. Even so, it showed to Dosha and Christian that he had been drinking, but he still held it well. He threw his arms wide.

"Have we not done ourselves proud tonight?" Francisco was like a clucking mother hen. The ballroom was fabulous. Held at the ritziest marble hall in Puerto, the crystal chandeliers sparkled and the hardwood floors were polished to perfection. Soft rose lights flooded the floor area and lent color to the atmosphere. Potted palms lined the room and masses of lush multicolored orchids had been flown in from South America.

The faint odor of expensive perfumes blended in the air as merrymakers poured in. Five bands would play tonight and just then one of the smallest of them held sway with soft, romantic music.

Francisco looked around and smiled widely. "Ah, the women of Puerto are magical creatures, and you lead them all."

Christian put his arm around Dosha, drawing her close. He didn't especially like the court that Francisco was paying to his wife. "May I have this dance?" Christian asked her and she had put out her hand to go into his arms when Antonia came up.

"My dears," she greeted them before her eyes went over Dosha's gown and she smiled a bit. "Yours is a nice dress, but you might have done better with my French designer. The dress will do nicely though."

"Thank you," Dosha said. "I like it."

"And I *love* it," Christian said gallantly.

Antonia laughed. "Of course you love it. And it's your duty as a husband to say so whether you do or not."

Dosha smiled, knowing that she looked especially well with happiness in her heart and Roland's grand design on her body. The soft ivory silk exactly fit with Socorro's pearl pendant and the matching pearl drop earrings. Her tawny and silken brown skin had never looked softer nor lovelier. Christian's heart swelled with pride as he looked at her and he grinned inside thinking of what would happen after the ball when they got home.

Antonia's gown was black satin, worn with emeralds that would have done royalty proud. But tonight, Dosha thought Antonia's skin looked sallow and she looked less than happy.

Socorro was soon surrounded with friends and admirers. Splendidly dressed in ruby silk crepe with Austrian crystal jewelry and an Austrian crystal tiara, she glowed with the happiness of seeing so many of her friends again. Francisco held out his hand.

"Your friends devoured you the minute you walked in the door, but now I have a chance to ask you for this dance, you wondrous, ageless creature."

Socorro smiled widely and said to Dosha, "There are no more flirts left on earth like a Puerto man," as she danced off with Francisco.

Christian looked at the way the ivory silk draped and crossed over Dosha's breasts and he longed to take them out, play with and suckle them. His eyes were dreamy and she threw back her head laughing, pretty much knowing what was on his mind.

They danced then with slow, gliding motions and he whispered to her. "After the ball, should we have a naked samba again? Should we dance that one more often?"

She nodded. "I don't know if my heart could take it. *Querido,* I'm so happy. At least for a while everything has gone well." She crossed her fingers on his shoulder. "When we near a table or the door, I'll knock on wood."

To Dosha the world was once again a wonderful place to live. She was sorry that Marta had died, but she shuddered at what she, Dosha, would have had to endure in anxiety if Marta had lived. People escaped from mental hospitals and Marta had been a wily one. Yes, that and Daryl's letter that relinquished what he felt was his hold on her. And Christian wasn't distant at times anymore. Life and love were good to her.

Snuggling close to Christian, she told him. "I wish my whole family could be here. Of course, Marty's known it all and Caitlin has visited, but this ball is the talk of the season. Tonight I'm not jealous of Isabel and you at all."

He shook her slightly. "Never have you at any time needed to be jealous of me. I belong to you as completely as a man can belong to a woman."

Carmela danced near them with her partner that Dosha and Christian didn't know. Dosha smiled when she thought of Antonia dismissively saying that Carmela had selected some little pink nothing of a dress. But the young woman looked spectacularly well in what she had chosen, a low cut, backless gown in peach pink worn with expensive gold jewelry.

Now Carmela said, "Your dress is beautiful and you are beautiful in it."

Dosha complimented Carmela on her dress and turned as Pia and Ramon danced close to them.

Pia looked lovely in draped silk aquamarine jersey with diamonds. Ramon in the black tuxedo that was the monolithical attire of the men was the ideal foil for his wife's splendor.

"You're going to be the belle of the ball," Pia told Dosha.

"Oh," Dosha said, "I don't know about that. You're really lovely tonight."

"The CEO called to say that he couldn't stay very long, but he would make an appearance," Ramon told them and Dosha and Christian nodded.

Dosha glanced at Christian in his tuxedo. She thought he looked so handsome with the garnet carnation adding the only touch of color. He wore the heavy chunk gold cufflinks he loved that she had given him.

"What's the occasion?" he had asked her when she made him the gift.

"Love is always the occasion with me where you're concerned. I saw them while shopping with Pia and I thought they look as if they belong on my lover."

And that had begun a round of hugs and kisses and rough

play that ended with them in bed, a tangle of arms and legs, and now the memory made her smile.

Pia and Ramon danced away and Dosha noted Socorro still dancing with Francisco who seemed as taken as with a far younger woman.

Antonia flitted about, in her element, thinking this was one of the nicest balls ever. Isabel would have been delirious. She had loved fun and gaiety. But Antonia wasn't particularly happy. She just hoped that Francisco wouldn't get too drunk tonight. He didn't always hold his liquor well and he could be a mean drunk. Since the position he wanted had gone to Christian, he had been almost morbidly unhappy. It was almost as if he didn't already have a really good position.

Antonia hoped too that her husband didn't get too drunk tonight. He usually held his liquor well, but he got morose, withdrawn when he drank far too much. And she told herself that her husband was rich, not bad looking and she had the power and the status she had always craved. She was a lucky woman.

Antonia went to a microphone by the red velvet curtain and asked for attention. When the room was quiet, with a flourish she had the guard draw back the drape. A portrait of Isabel in a fabulous black ball gown held forth.

A murmur of excitement swept the room.

"My friends," Antonia said, "I felt it only fitting that we pay homage to a woman, my beloved sister, who did so much for Puerto. She is a legend and will be loved forever. She can never be forgotten. Please dance and be merry in her honor. The queen is dead! Long live Queen Isabel!"

A hush fell on the crowd and Antonia walked over to Dosha and Christian who faced her with choked fury. "How *could* you?"

Antonia smiled sweetly. "I know you will never forget her and no one can take her place."

Heatedly Christian told her, " I love Dosha more than I ever loved Isabel."

Antonia shrugged. "If you say so."

Socorro came to them, said to Antonia, "I would not have thought even you could be so cruel."

The ball didn't really get underway until eleven or so, and it always ended promptly at two because revelers had to be up early for church services. The CEO walked around the room, noting the merrymakers. He had an important announcement to make and he wanted to keep his eye on Francisco who he suspected wasn't going to take his announcement very well. The man was known to rely on liquor to pull him through. Francisco paid court to many women, but he seemed to keep coming back to Dosha, and the CEO knew that wasn't going over too well with Christian.

The CEO paused at Christian's side as Dosha danced with Francisco. "Please simply be the gentleman you always are tonight," he said. "It's plain that Francisco has imbibed too heavily. I may speak with him. I'm sure Ramon has cautioned you to be on guard." The CEO frowned. "I had expected him to take your promotion in a more mature fashion."

Christian half closed his eyes, looking at his wife and Francisco on the dance floor. "It's all right, I assure you. My wife is not especially fond of Francisco, but we talked with Ramon and decided to simply give him his lead tonight."

The CEO nodded. "I'll make the announcement after this dance. If Francisco is going to get completely drunk, he'll do it then. Good luck."

The dance ended and Francisco brought Dosha back and bowed low. "You have the prize of prizes in this lady," he told Christian.

"I'm fully aware of that," Christian responded.

Then the CEO was onstage at the microphone. "My friends, we're revelers tonight with little time or patience for business, but I have news that will add to your enjoyment. A wonderful couple, Señor and Señora Christian Montero—the wife is Dosha—will head Banc International's Cultural Affairs Division and we're indeed lucky to have them at the helm.

"Puerto is very much on the map as a place to visit, but this will put us on the cultural map, as we should be."

He went on to talk briefly of the work that would be done and how the people of Puerto would be involved. And he ended saying, "Of course Señor Montero is a native of Puerto and we all know and admire him. Both partners are one of a kind and I thank God they are with us because they are beyond compare. Now please give this couple a lusty hand."

The room rocked then with applause and some took up the cry of "Montero! Montero!"

Christian's eyes seemed to be drawn to Francisco as Christian gripped Dosha's hand tightly. Francisco visibly wilted before he got a grip on himself, bowed low to a nearby woman and moved onto the dance floor.

Dosha and Christian danced then to a lively rhumba. Their happiness drew the attention of others and people stopped them to offer congratulations. Socorro danced close to them with a handsome, middle-aged partner. She tapped Christian on the shoulder. "I have always been proud of you," she said, "but this is a night of particular pride."

She danced on with her smiling partner and Captain Montero walked over. He had brought a female acquaintance both Dosha and Christian knew. They both congratulated the couple and Captain Montero kissed his son's cheek. "You've always done me proud and this is no different."

No dance in Puerto was complete without the risqué songs

that mocked sex and politics. Tonight Dosha couldn't help laughing at them.

"They remind me of La Carnaval," Christian said. "And I look forward to that rowdy time."

"Um-m, we were here last year," Dosha responded.

A new and larger band had taken over and their music was sweetly romantic. Christian held Dosha against him and felt her luscious body thrum with love and desire and he was impatient now for the dancing at the ball to end and their own private dancing to begin. Closing his eyes he phantasized their naked samba and it sent flames racing through him.

From the corner of his eye during the next dance, Christian saw his father dance with his grandmother and the old girl moved superbly in a rhumba. She really was ageless, he thought, and he remembered her fondly as a much younger woman too.

Pedro Montez paid court to Dosha, complimenting her on her dress and her presence. "You remind me so much of my lovely wife who will be moving here when our latest baby is born. You both are blessed with being creatures nature has bestowed her best worldly goods upon."

Pedro was one of a few men that women loved and men liked. Christian often thought that he would be jealous of Dosha with another man, but not with Pedro. They all worked superbly well together.

Champagne had flowed the entire night, with hors d'oeuvres. Now the main food was laid out on long tables covered with snowy white damask, with gleaming silver and china, and sparkling crystal. Dosha shook her head at the delectable array of food. Roast pig, racks of lamb, roast fowl and roast beef, juicy meat pies with flaky crusts. There were cooked and carved raw vegetables and melt-in-your mouth rolls and pastries.

Dosha had to smile at the fact that there were ten varieties of paella here, from the sausage-filled that she favored to the absolutely plain, with only mild seasoning.

Walking to other tables, they took in the array of beautiful cakes and pies, tarts and cookies and kegs of ice cream. "Those desserts make me cringe," Dosha told Christian. "I foresee a pound of fat for every bite. And I already have more than my share."

"And," Christian said, grinning, "what is it your McDonald's says? 'I'm loving it'? Forget Antonia."

"You are one smooth operator."

They sat at a table and ate with Socorro, Captain Montero and his date, with Ramon and Pia and Pedro Montez. "Food simply tastes better when we're surrounded by good company," Socorro said and they all agreed.

Antonia came by, monitoring the crowd. "Are you enjoying yourselves?" she asked this group and they said they were.

"Oh," Antonia cried, "I do think this is the best of the balls ever." She nodded to Dosha. "Is it possible you bring luck to us?"

"Could be," Dosha said noncommittally.

They all had exquisite wine of their choice and sat back to let their food begin to digest. The glow of being with good friends was on them and, except for Christian and Dosha, they hated the thought of the night ending.

The CEO and his wife watched and discussed Francisco who seemed to sway more with each half hour. The CEO turned to his wife. "Perhaps it would be wise to speak with Francisco, suggest that he go home before he disgraces himself in some fashion."

His wife looked at him gravely. "It's such a grand ball and from what you tell me he's sorely hurt, so I would suggest you be kind to him. It will pass. These things always do."

Francisco saw Jaime Garcia and his wife and waved at them. They simply nodded in return. One thing, Francisco thought, Señor Garcia had always been largely on his side. As a friend of Francisco's late father, he had taken him under his wing after a fashion. He knew that in his younger days, Señor Garcia had drunk too much and been something of a roué, but he had settled down long before he was Francisco's age. No, Francisco thought now, the old boy would understand what he was going to do now. And he would never know what he planned to do undercover. He held his partner, a married woman he knew well, tighter. What was there about married women that intrigued him so?

Dosha and Christian changed partners with the CEO and his wife and Dosha found she liked dancing with him. The band that played had made the CD that Christian and she had danced to their night of the naked samba.

"You're an exquisite dancer," Señor Garcia said. "You and Christian complement each other in every way."

Then it almost seemed like fate when Christian claimed her for the next dance. The particular tune was the one they had begun their naked samba with.

And something like magic was in their blood as they smoothly undulated and wove with the vividly sensuous music. They were back in that night, steaming with passion and completely in love.

In a little while, they came out of their trance to find themselves surrounded by people who watched them, cheered them on. Throwing back his head with laughter, Christian hugged her and stopped.

"Marvelous!" the crowd murmured with merriment rippling through.

With a flourish, Christian bowed and thanked them.

Another band that played glorious sambas now took over and Francisco made a beeline for Dosha and Christian. "Would you please do a lonely man the honor?" he said to Dosha, and to Christian, "I'll return her safe and sound."

Christian glanced at his watch. It was now one o'clock and Francisco actually seemed to have straightened up a bit. Still reluctantly, Christian agreed to the dance as Dosha looked at him a bit apprehensively. She wasn't eager to dance with Francisco because she disliked men who drank too much.

There was one thing she had to give him, Dosha thought once they were on the dance floor. Next to Christian, he was the best samba dancer she knew. He flung himself into the dance with passion and his moves were graceful, fluid and powerful. He guided her with exquisite precision. Like Christian, he danced with his heart.

She had had a little too much wine and champagne and it was going to her head, so she didn't notice when Francisco began to gyrate more suggestively, nor when he moved her somewhat away from the other dancers.

She moved almost as expertly as he did and her mind was on the night ahead so that she took on the patina of love and desire and he felt it was driving him crazy. He envied the attention she and Christian had drawn with their samba. He, Francisco, was known as the best samba dancer in Puerto. That attention should have gone to him and Dosha. And he realized that he had actually planned it that way, but Christian had gotten there first again. So near and yet so far. But no, she was here and in his arms—*and it was time.*

Catching her suddenly to him in a powerful grip, he placed one hand behind her head and swiftly brought her mouth to his in a bruising kiss as she fought to right herself. His punishing mouth was on hers as his tongue tried to force her totally resisting teeth open. And he held on even as she kicked his shin, hampered by the folds of her ballgown. To Dosha, the hated kiss seemed endless.

Then vividly purposeful hands tore Francisco away from her and spun him backward as Christian cursed him between his teeth. Christian swung, but Francisco ducked and by then friendly arms bound Christian, not to protect Francisco who everyone felt deserved the blow, but to salvage the wondrous ball.

Francisco bowed low with a mocking smile. "I'm very sorry," he said to Christian with mock humility. "I found myself overcome by the music and the lady. *I was only the moth to her candle flame.*"

Chapter 22

Once Francisco stood surrounded by his few friends, Christian glowered at him, not trusting himself to speak. Dosha put her arms around her husband. "He's not worth your trouble, my love. Let's go on with the ball."

At the first sign of a fracas, Captain Montero had hurried over. His bulky body stood by his son. He said to Francisco, "You've had too much to drink and I think it best you leave."

"No," Francisco said. "I lost my head. I'll drink lots of black coffee. I'm a fool for a beautiful woman."

"You are a fool, period," the captain grated. "Go and get the coffee."

The merrymakers had grown a bit subdued. Of course, many of them thought, *something* happened every year. The atmosphere was too much like La Carnaval for things *not* to happen. Too much liquor. Old grudges. Flirtations were rife and Francisco wasn't the first man to be flattened for dallying with another man's wife. The bad feelings between the two cousins had existed all their lives, it seemed, but stopped just short of displayed hostility.

The band swept into soothing music. Ramon's eyes on Christian were sad. "It's of no importance," he said. "This is Puerto de la Cruz after all and people will understand."

"We're leaving," Christian said abruptly. He turned to Dosha, took her arm. She was alarmed because his face bore a savage anger she had not seen there before and she thought it might be a good thing if they got out of there. At home, they could talk about this.

The CEO came over, frowning. "I saw the whole thing," he told Christian, "and I'm sorry, but this type of thing has happened before. I can understand your anger and I assure you I *will* call Francisco to account. He'll go home, so you're free to stay and enjoy the rest of the night as best you can."

Christian shook his head. "No, we must leave, but I thank you for your concern. It means a lot to me."

Socorro had stood by, silent, her tender gaze on her grandson. She could have throttled Francisco. Christian couldn't help giving her a bitter smile. "Come, Abuela," he said, "and we'll go home. I'm sorry your ball was spoiled."

Socorro shook her head. "Yes, let us go. It has been a good ball and I've enjoyed myself, but Francisco showed his true colors, and that might not be a bad thing."

Outside, the night air cooled them and the heat of passion dimmed a little as the three of them began the trek home.

Back in the ballroom, Francisco found the trouble had cleared his head a bit and triumph filled his heart until the CEO came to him, his face like a thundercloud.

"You fool," the CEO said indignantly. "You've shamefully disrespected a coworker's wife and thus him. Francisco, because your father was my friend I've stood by you, forgiven you every wrong. I saw myself in you in your flagrant indiscretions, but this is unforgivable and I'll deal with you later.

"Go home now and examine your behavior, because unless it changes, you will be in deep trouble. Banc International does not tolerate the intolerable. Go home immediately and I'll call you early in the morning before I leave for Switzerland. The bank is not necessarily where you will work forever. Do I make myself clear?"

Francisco swallowed hard. He had made a great many mistakes and it simply had not occurred to him that the CEO would ever turn against him, no matter what. Now he saw the fire in the man's eyes and it frightened him. Banc International was his, Francisco's, life. He nodded.

"I understand, sir, and I'm very sorry. I lost my head. I had too much to drink and the lady is enchanting, you must admit..."

"Enough!" the CEO roared. "I'll accept no excuses and I don't wish to talk about it further at this point. Go now!"

And Francisco slunk away like a whipped cur, but out on the sidewalk he smiled to himself. Too bad what must happen to her. That kiss had been heady, the lips like strong, sweet wine. Exaltation shot through his body. Christian had been enraged, hurt, dishonored, and that was all that mattered. The CEO would not fire him, he didn't think, but he wasn't sure. He got into his Porsche and began to feel dizzy. He would have to be careful driving home.

Christian, Dosha and Socorro didn't talk all the way home and once there, Socorro pressed Christian's arm, kissed his cheek and went to her apartment.

In their room, as they stood, Dosha put her arms around Christian's neck and hugged him tightly. She couldn't help noticing that he wasn't wholly responsive. "It's all right, *querido,*" she said softly. "Francisco is a fool and a clown. He has never known what you have and he's envious."

But she drew away a bit and saw the bitter, faraway look in his eyes again. "Can you talk about this?" she asked.

He shook his head. "The time for talking was over long ago."

She hugged him again, feeling the heat of his body and she wanted him, craved him inside her. He always said she healed his every hurt. Could this one be so different? "Come to bed," she told him.

"No." He pushed her away gently and, yielding, she went and sat on the bed, as he began to pace like a caged animal.

"Let me fix you some hyssop tea. It'll help you to sleep. Or valerian tea? You've got to relax. It was a small thing..."

"No!" he said vehemently. "It wasn't a small thing. It's a thing that has lasted throughout my life, and will it *never* be over?"

She drew a slow breath. "Do you think I was flirting with Francisco? That I led him on?"

He shook his head. "I've never known you to flirt other than a little and that never bothered me. There are things you don't understand...."

"Then *help* me to understand. Talk with me, please."

He stopped pacing abruptly. "I'm going out."

She froze. "Out? At this hour?"

"Yes. I'll drive around a bit and clear my mind."

She got up and went to him. "You're in no condition to drive, *querido,* and you know it. *Please* come to bed, or we'll sit up all night and talk this through."

"The time for talking is over, *was* over long ago."

"What do you mean?"

But he was silent. He kissed her cheek and started across the floor.

She followed him, resigned. "At least let me walk with you to the garage door. Oh, *querido*. Tell me you won't hurt yourself in some foolish accident. I want to help you. Please let me help you. Please come back to me very soon... Promise."

The set expression on his face frightened her and his eyes looked hollow as he nodded and told her. "I'll come back to you soon and you're not to worry."

She pulled her ace emotional card. "This morning, I intend to take an early pregnancy test. If I'm pregnant, how will I feel if you're a mangled wreck on the highway?"

"I said I'll be back to you and I mean it. Come on and go with me to the garage if it will help you feel better. I'll be here to hold you if you're pregnant. You know I'd never let you down."

But you are letting me down, her heart screamed. What is it that hurts you so much worse than anything you've ever told me?

Each step was torment to her until they reached the garage door in the kitchen where he unbolted the lock, then put his hand on the knob as tears flooded her eyes. He turned, drew her to him hard, and suddenly kissed her, a ravaging kiss that left her breathless. Then he said, "Goodbye for just a little while."

And he was gone. She stood listening to the car motor start and purr, then he was out of the garage and gone. Her knees were weak with fear as she sat at the kitchen table. A sleepy Estela came to the door.

"Señora, I thought I heard someone. What is wrong?"

Dosha wiped her face with the back of her hand. "Thank you, but it's nothing. Go back to bed. I'll be fine."

And the woman looked at Dosha narrowly, but turned back, wanting to help and feeling helpless.

The phone was ringing when Dosha got back to their bedroom and it was Socorro.

"Are you all right?" Socorro asked.

"Yes. More or less."

Socorro hesitated for a moment. "I was standing at my window looking at the moonlight and I saw Christian's car pull out of the driveway. Can you tell me what's going on? I know how upset he is..."

It was Dosha's turn to hesitate. "He wouldn't talk about it. He paced terribly, then said he had to go out, collect his thoughts. Socorro, I'm so worried about him. He's in no condition to drive."

"You're right. *Querida,* let me come down and we'll talk about this. I'll tell you some things about Christian and it might ease your mind a bit. Lord, this has been a night."

In a few minutes, Dosha had seated Socorro on the chaise lounge and she sat in a big overstuffed chair nearby. They discussed the ball for a little while before Socorro said, "Francisco is a beast. I've always known it. His envy of Christian knows no bounds and he would do anything to hurt him. Still, because he is family, we've always tried to maintain appearances of sorts."

Dosha nodded. "Christian seemed unbearably hurt by what Francisco did tonight. I think people understand Francisco and it wasn't really that important."

"It *is* important, my dear—to Christian. In Puerto, when a man disrespects another man's wife, there is frequently bloodshed. We're a passionate people. Francisco surely understands that."

"I started to slap him. I was befuddled and by the time I could pull myself together, Christian had him in his grip."

"My grandson is fit and he has always been a fighter."

"Was my behavior unseemly in any manner, Socorro?"

Socorro's smile was tender. "No, my dear. You're incapable of unseemly behavior. It's Francisco's fault entirely. The stress between Christian and Francisco began when they were children. Francisco lost his mother at an even earlier age than Christian lost his. Isaac, Rafael and I were there to take up the slack for Christian. Francisco's grandparents were all dead and his father paid little attention to him. Then his father died.

"He was a mean child, sly and ruthless. We tried to include him in family gatherings, but in his teens, he stopped coming around. He made disparaging remarks from time to time about my part-African and part-Gypsy heritage and about Christian being mestizo. He takes an inordinate pride in his Castilian background, but it seems to do him little good."

For a full minute Socorro fell silent, then continued. "I will, as they say, cut to the chase. Francisco dated Isabel for a while, but he really didn't seem interested until Christian fell in love with her. Then he couldn't pay her enough attention. But then, he was only one of Isabel's many admirers. Gossip sprang up around her like wild clover. Were there lovers? Or weren't there lovers? She always swore to Christian that it was all a lie, that she loved only him.

"Christian was a mere youth when he fell in love with her and she was three years older. She was fascinated by his interest in bullfighting and she encouraged him, to our dismay. Then he was badly injured and we thought he would die, but he survived with the terrible scars. Later, he begged her to marry him and she did. She took him through hell. Christian has talked of fathering and raising children since he was a child himself, but Isabel wanted no children and he was hurt.

"His father begged him to divorce Isabel, but he loved her. He finished at the university at the head of his class and went into banking where he did well from the beginning. Francisco finished the university, too, and went into the same bank—Banc International—and he also did well.

"Isabel came from a privileged family with little money.

Her older sister, Antonia, married very well and Isabel drove Christian to get ahead and was never satisfied. She was a restless woman who got involved in the social life of the city and, in truth, she did many good deeds, won people over. At her death, her friends were devastated. Antonia set up the *Baile de Isabel* and it has been a resounding success."

For moments Socorro was silent again before she continued. "I've never understood the change in Christian after she died. The way she treated him, how could he love her? But he was sad beyond belief and we again feared for his life and his sanity. Then he met you when you came to visit your brother and the rest, as they say, is history. My dear, I thank God for you every day. You saved my grandson's life."

She stopped then and peered closely at Dosha who sat with tears in her eyes for what Christian had suffered.

"If he'd only talk, to me, to someone," Dosha said.

Socorro shook her head. "He's a reticent man. He always has been. There's so much about his life with Isabel I don't understand. I only know that he was bitterly hurt and he carries the pain deep inside. Keep trying to get him to talk with you because talk with someone you trust is a great healer."

"I will."

"And now, I'll go back and leave you to go over your thoughts and your feelings. Be kind to him when he returns. No matter what, in the end, Christian keeps a level head and he *will* return to you safe and sound."

Later, Captain Montero called and was alarmed when Dosha told him about Christian's leaving. "I'll look and I'll have men look for his car over the city," he said. "I wish you had called me earlier."

She was numb with anxiety and despair when she heard Christian's car come into the driveway and the garage. Tears of thankfulness filled her eyes. She sat, hardly breathing, when he turned the knob and her eyes lingered on him. The digital clock registered 4:30 a.m. He had been gone over two hours. He paused on the threshold. She wanted to go to him, but she couldn't move. Had he really come back as he said he would or was this a dream?

"Why aren't you in bed, *querida?* You need sleep."

"We both need sleep."

She got up then and went to him. "Chris, we have to talk. We simply *have* to talk."

"What is there to say?"

Stung, she turned from him, went and sat on the bed. "It's not a marriage when the people involved don't share their feelings. Something is eating you alive and I can't stand by and see it happen."

She had not known she would say it. "We hope to have a child, but I can't let a child of mine be born into this situation. I'm going to ask for a brief leave of absence and I'll go home to decide what I must do." Her eyes beseeched him. "You know how much I love you, but I can't take this anymore."

He came to her then and dropped to his knees beside her. "No," he said, "please don't leave me now." He buried his face in her lap and his tears wet the thin fabric of her gown as he put his arms around her and gripped her hips. "*Querida,* you can't leave. I *cannot* let you leave. I'll talk as best I can."

She leaned forward, stroking his shoulders, her fingers in his hair. "And I'll listen."

He sat with his face in her lap for a very long while, then he got up and took off his tuxedo jacket and flung it onto a chair, then sat on the bed beside her. "It hurts so damned much."

"I know and I'm with you."

He was still silent long minutes before he began. "I've told you some about my marriage to Isabel, but the part that tore me to pieces was when she finally admitted one affair—" He went silent again and his breath was ragged.

"An affair with Francisco?" she bluntly asked him.

"Yes, with Francisco. She said she would let him alone, that she realized she loved only me. She said she was sorry and begged me to forgive her."

His shoulders hunched then and she put her arms around him, shielding him from the pain. "She said she would try to give me a child and she swore she would be faithful…"

She simply waited. Then he said, "Her father begged me not to divorce her. I tried to do as he wished because he was dying and he had been my friend."

He sighed deeply then. "Dear God, I was numb. She was the first and only woman I had ever loved and I saw no hope of any future without her. I was willing to forgive her anything, but I couldn't lose her. Can you understand that?"

"I can."

"Except for my mother's death and the bullfighting injury, my life had been largely free of pain and it wasn't a thing I could handle well."

"None of us can. Do you *still* love Isabel?" she asked him, miserable at the thought.

He scoffed. "*Querida,* you can ask me that knowing how I love *you?*"

"It can be an old love that has never ended. I don't think you *want* to love her, but perhaps you still do."

"No, I don't love her. I'm sure of that…."

"There is more," she told him.

"Yes, there is more, but I go mad with pain when I think about it and I *cannot* talk about it. I beg you to please understand that there will come a time in the near future when I can and will tell you the sordid rest and may God save my soul. They say that God forgives even a mortal sin and mine is a mortal sin, believe me."

She was alarmed then. Isabel had died in a car accident in the hills. Had he been with her? Had he set it up or *had* it set up? My Lord, who was this man she had married? And her every instinct said he was a wonderful man she loved beyond all else. And he was incapable of doing this thing he couldn't forgive himself for after all these years.

"All right, we'll talk about the rest later. Thank you for telling me what you have." She stroked his back in long, slow movements. "Come to bed."

He sat on the bed beside her and suddenly took her in his arms in a savage, ruthless embrace that left her breathless. "Dear God, I love you so," he whispered. "I want to lose myself in your body, forget the torment I've known so long and find myself again and again in you, as I always have."

She slowly undressed him, unbuttoning his shirt with eager, awkward fingers, then slid off his pants and his underwear until his beautiful, naked body filled her eyes. His scars had never seemed so appealing. He slowly stripped her gown over her head and feasted on the luscious, creamy brown flesh that he loved so.

His every move was tenderly savage then as he took her with wildly abandoned hunger. "Do you know how much I want a baby from you?" he asked her.

"I know and I'll give you one if it's humanly possible."

He nuzzled her neck and shoulder. "But if it's not possible, I'll still love you almost more than I can bear. Just please don't ever leave me."

She spread her fingers across the back of his head and brought his mouth hard onto hers. Then she relinquished him and whispered, "I'll never leave you. Never."

Chapter 23

The next morning Christian slept heavily as Dosha came awake in the darkened room. She stretched and smiled at his arm flung out towards her and the badly rumpled bedclothes. It had been a night of wild passion before they were satiated and had gone to sleep in each other's arms.

Then she remembered the ball and Francisco and the hated kiss. Remembered Christian's rage and finally, what they had talked about at long last. The hurt on his face still lingered in her mind and her heart still hurt for him and what he had been through. She felt bound to him now with bands of emotional steel.

He came awake as she propped herself on an elbow and gazed down at him.

"You do strange things to me," he told her. "I think you have a magic wand."

"No more than you do to me." She touched his penis and grinned. "And you really do have a magic wand."

Pleased, he laughed.

"What time is it?"

"Ten o'clock. We haven't had enough sleep and I apologize for waking you up, but we can sleep again later."

"You wanted me to talk with you. You always have and I think it's helped a little. But there is more, *querida,* and it's worse. You are a forgiving soul and God is forgiving, but it seems I can't forgive myself." His face had grown somber.

"When will you talk about this thing you can't forgive yourself for?"

"As soon as I can. Please be patient. I now need a kiss so deep I drown in it."

She bent toward him. "How does this do for starters?"

Her tender lips fastened on his and her tongue outlined his lips, went into the corners and licked them. His breath was surprisingly fresh as she probed his mouth. He was so sweet and she…

His cell phone rang and he groaned a little as he answered it. Yes, last night had given him all he needed, but only for a little while.

"Christian?" It was Ramon.

"Uh-huh. Christian."

"How are you this morning?"

Christian thought a moment. He had deliberately kept himself from reflecting on the previous night.

"I'm doing fine. Well, maybe not fine, but reasonably well."

"You certainly handled yourself like the gentleman you are."

"I struck at a man. That is hardly being a gentleman."

"Under *extreme* provocation. Believe me, Francisco had it coming. I wanted to hit him myself."

Christian laughed drily. "Good things sometimes come from the bad," he said, thinking of finally being able to tell

Dosha much of what had gone on between him and Isabel. But he thought now that there was the worst part, the part that tormented him so. In time…

"Speaking of Francisco," Ramon said, "I'm to meet with him around one today and we'll go over his slim portion of our plans for the cultural affairs group. I wanted to talk with him about a couple of new ideas I have so he can think about them and give me some feedback when I see him. He's not answering his phone and I guess he's sleeping his foolhardiness off."

"No doubt."

"Is Dosha all right? She seemed to take it well."

"She's fine. She takes most things well."

"She's your claim to heaven. Well, Francisco will be contrite, full of remorse—or he will pretend to be."

"It doesn't matter. Of course, I'm still angry, but it's an old anger as well as new. I'll simply have to learn to deal with it."

He had no sooner hung up than Dosha's cell phone rang and Socorro's lively voice was on the line. "I didn't want to call you too early, but I'm full of spectacular energy this morning. I'm beginning to cook and I want you and Christian and Rafael to come for a scrumptious brunch."

Dosha laughed and wriggled her toes. "This sounds too good to be true. I was wondering what I would fix for breakfast. What time do you want us to come?"

"Oh, around twelve or so. I have to call Rafael. I hope he's not on some case or other. He's always so busy. Next time, I'll invite the woman he escorted to the ball. They seem to be fond of each other. She's brand new to him, I think."

"Yes, we just met her. He deserves someone nice and she certainly seems to be the ticket."

Christian looked at her drolly when she told him about the invitation. "I was going to bring you coffee in bed," he told her, "in gratitude."

She threw back her head laughing. "And here I was thinking the same thing about bringing you coffee in bed." She grinned a bit. "In gratitude."

She picked up his hand and looked at it. "If I had read your fortune, I would tell you you deserve the world and you're going to get it."

The brunch was a success from the minute Christian and Dosha walked in the door to find Captain Montero already there. He had brought a big bouquet of red tulips that Socorro had placed in a crystal vase. He looked at Dosha and Christian closely.

"Well, you two seem none the worse for last night's shenanigans."

"We're fine," Christian assured him.

Dosha and Socorro laughed at the fact that they both had on coral lounging pajamas and Captain Montero complimented them. "Beauty has no age limits," he said gallantly.

Dosha thanked him as Christian's eyes met hers and Socorro said gravely. "Your compliments are one of the things that made my daughter such a happy woman. Thank you, Rafael."

The food was melt-in-your mouth good and as they ate, they didn't discuss the ball. Instead they talked of the past, of Magdalena, Christian's late mother and Socorro's daughter, and of Isaac, his late grandfather and Socorro's late husband. They talked of the challenges and the glory of being biracial in the world and in Puerto. And they talked of Banc International and the roles Christian and Dosha played in the newly forming Cultural Affairs Division.

Just then Rafael's cell phone rang and he answered it. Ramon's agitated voice came through, "*El capitán,* there has been a murder here and I need your presence."

"Slow down, man," Captain Montero said. "Tell me what this is about. *Who* has been murdered?"

All in the room sprang to attention. "I had better begin at the beginning. I was to meet with Francisco at one. I called to get some things straight and there was no answer. Thinking he was sleeping off last night's drunk, at one o'clock I simply came over. I have a key and I let myself in. The lights were on in his study and I went in…"

"Yes, go on."

Ramon's voice was tight with horror. "He was slumped over his desk. His safe was open. And he was dead. His upper body was drenched in his blood. I checked for a pulse and there was none. I'm calling you."

"*Dios mío!*" Captain Montero exclaimed.

Captain Montero hurriedly told them what had happened and began to gather his things. Dosha looked at Christian with stricken eyes. He glanced away. He had gone out, she thought, and come back later. He had been sick with rage at Francisco. Now his face was calm, impassive.

Captain Montero placed his hand on the side of his son's shoulder. "Is there something you wish to tell me?"

For a moment Christian looked perplexed. "Tell you?" Then it struck him. "You will come back when your investigation is well underway. We'll talk then," Christian said.

Captain Montero took the time to kiss each one of them goodbye and he left. Christian was on his third cup of coffee and he thought it had never tasted better. He wondered who had killed Francisco?

Dosha and Christian looked at each other. Her face was haunted with fear. She had been so afraid his leftover rage from Isabel and this fresh rage would drive him to hurt himself. He had been cold and unlike himself when he had left last night.

He looked at Dosha and Socorro and said simply, "I did *not* kill him." Each woman breathed a sigh of relief, believing him implicitly.

Socorro sat for a long while with her eyes on the distance. "The spirits are with me more and more," she finally said. "They are trying to tell me things I must know to save those I love. I saw that same malevolent face twisted with rage, a face that was neither man nor woman, but simply the very face of hate. My God, that rage, that viciousness, as if it would destroy a world. I saw that form in the shadows before the tarantula, the poisoning, Marta's death."

Socorro was silent for a while before she said, "I've seen that face often lately and now Francisco is dead—murdered by a hand like the one I've only imagined. There's a black hood and a cloak largely hiding that face and completely hiding those hands."

And her voice rose as she wailed. "Oh pray, as we've never prayed before, for this wretched fiend will keep destroying as it tried to destroy you, destroyed Marta and Francisco. He may have been evil, but he deserved life. And this wretch who haunts my visions destroys the good as well as the evil."

When Captain Montero arrived at Francisco's house, his men were putting up crime bands and a team of homicide workers headed by a sergeant was already inside. Ramon rushed forward wringing his hands. "*Dios*, but I'm glad you are here. It was horrible finding him."

Captain Montero quieted Ramon as best he could and asked him to go into a smaller room while he discussed the investigation. Then he turned to the team. A little later with the lead sergeant in command, flash bulbs from the photographer went off constantly. The crime analyst took notes and the fingerprint man dusted for fingerprints. The captain went to Ramon who mopped his brow.

Ramon repeated what he had told Christian on the phone, that he had called earlier and gotten no answer, felt that

Francisco was sleeping. Later he had let himself in with his key. Now he further elaborated on his earlier conversation. "I found him sitting at his desk, his body turned sideways and blood was all down the front of him, from his chest down. I checked for a pulse, but his eyes had rolled back in his head and I knew he was dead."

Ramon had smears of blood on his hands and a spot on his face. The captain listened carefully, jotting down notes as he did so. "I'll ask the sergeant to have the crime analyst check your DNA," the captain said, "and later we'll fingerprint you. You've suffered a shock and you should get rest. When we're through with you, call your wife and ask her to pick you up. Get some rest. I'll need to talk with you further in my office Monday."

Ramon nodded. Captain Montero summoned the analyst who took rapid notes and the captain walked around monitoring the scene. Francisco's house was old and large. Montero had been there to parties many times. As furious as he was with Francisco for his behavior at the ball, he reflected that the tight-knit community wouldn't be the same without him. To ask who had done this was to fly in the face of reality. There were so many who could have done it. It wasn't well known, but Francisco was an avid gambler and not a very good one. He had once been deeply in debt to a gambling outfit in Torremolinos and Monaco was a favorite hangout.

Captain Montero knew that Francisco's father had left him a tidy inheritance and his position at the bank paid well. But gambling often emptied the heaviest bank accounts.

The captain shook his head. Francisco's enemies were legendary. Police knew from intelligence that gambling kingpins' goons were often after him. He played fast and loose with other men's wives and Puerto men were jealous and hotheaded. Lately gossip held that he and an older woman were having an affair.

It was easier, the captain thought, to decide who had not killed Francisco than who had. The man had led a profligate life, but a charmed one. No harm had ever come to him before this.

Then he stood stock still. After the first hours, he had simply stopped thinking about the night before and what he had seen. When he had finished talking with Dosha, he had gotten up and immediately gone out looking for his son. He had thought of the places he might have gone and had driven to Francisco's house. Christian's car had been parked down the street and Christian had been pacing in the streetlights in front of Francisco's.

Francisco's house was one of three on the block. There was a large park across the way. Captain Montero had sat in his car, breathing heavily, watching Christian as he paced. At times Christian lingered near the gate as if he would open it. Or had he opened it, gone in and come out? And the captain had told himself, if he makes a move to go in—if he hasn't already—then I'll go to him, stop him. Grimly he wished again that Dosha had called him earlier.

And it seemed much later that Christian stopped pacing, walked down the street, got into his car and drove off. The captain had followed him at a discreet distance until Christian pulled into his driveway and into his garage. The captain had stayed in his car, half sick with apprehension and watched the lights in Christian's and Dosha's bedroom. He hurt for his son's pain and all the old torment of Isabel's infidelities and mistreatment came back. Christian had gone through hell. Now he deserved happiness.

Captain Montero damned Francisco for his foul deed at the ball as he started his car and drove off. Did his son somehow sense his father's presence on the scene at Francisco's house tonight? And what had he planned to do? The captain drew a deep breath. Had Christian been inside and slain Francisco before he was pacing outside like a man who has done some dark deed and is sick with remorse?

It seemed a very long time before the sergeant came to him. Ramon had left with Pia. "Señor, it's done," the sergeant said. "The shots seem to be in the chest region to the heart. Whoever did it wanted him dead."

The captain nodded and said nothing as they set about sealing off the house. The body was taken to the morgue and a policeman was posted at the scene to keep unwelcome visitors away.

In his office in the very late afternoon, Captain Montero sat going over his notes. No gun had been found. He wondered if the killer was a man or a woman. Christian was the only suspect he knew of now, but he was certain others would turn up.

A young policeman came to his door, stuck his head in. "*El capitán,* there is a couple outside who insist that they talk with you. They say it's about the murder."

The captain sat bolt upright. "Send them in and hold my calls," Montero said.

The couple was middle aged and handsome, very well dressed. The man cleared his throat and said, "My wife and I felt we had to come. You see, we were at the ball last night and we live in the neighborhood with the señor who was killed..."

"*Sí. Sí,*" Captain Montero said impatiently.

"Well, we stayed almost until the ball was over and coming home we drove slowly because we wanted to continue enjoying the night... We live in the third house on the block."

Get on with it, man, the captain thought grumpily. Do you have a story to tell or don't you?

"Well, señor, as we drove along, we saw a man leave Señor Salazar's front door. He came down the walk, turned and stared at the house a long time. He paced up and down on the sidewalk in front of the house. *Dios,* it was weird. He was like a man possessed.

"My wife asked me if I thought the man was in trouble and I said he seemed agitated, very angry. We watched him for over fifteen minutes. Finally, another car passed along and parked ahead of us, maybe a half block away. Señor, we recognized your son, Christian, under the streetlight and we wondered because we had witnessed what happened at the ball last night. We're sorry it happened. Now we learn that Francisco is dead—murdered."

"That is all too true."

"Have you any idea who did it?"

The captain shook his head. "Not yet."

"I pray it wasn't your son," the woman said. "It's a terrible thing to disrespect a woman and her husband the way Francisco did."

Captain Montero looked at the couple long and levelly. "Thank you for coming in."

Juan let himself in the back door and found Estela and Pablo sitting at the kitchen table. *"Buenos días,"* Juan greeted them, certain they knew by now about Francisco. Working for many socially prominent people, Juan usually got news long before others.

"You heard about Señor Francisco?" Pablo asked.

Juan nodded. "I heard and I passed by his house. Too bad. He was a nice man."

The two people made no comment as Juan got himself a shot of tequila and sat down.

"You drink too much," Estela told him.

Juan grinned crookedly. "It eases the pain."

Pablo shrugged. "More bad things happen to some than others. Let's talk about something pleasant. Life goes on."

Juan looked at them obliquely. He was grateful to them for helping him get settled in Puerto years ago. He had, however, kept his own counsel and they didn't dream how well he knew Francisco. He was glad no one knew because he might be considered a suspect in the murder.

"You are quiet tonight," Pablo said. "Like you lost your best friend."

Juan wished they wouldn't talk and that he had not come. He was sick with disappointment. Francisco had often given him nice sums of money and had promised him much more.

The ball was hardly over when Juan heard about the kiss. He had slapped his thigh and laughed. What a delightful scoundrel Francisco was, he had thought, and now he mourned the loss of the money Francisco would have paid him.

Chapter 24

"Who do *you* think killed Francisco?" Dosha asked her husband.

Dosha and Christian stood by the bay windows in the living room looking at a huge Drago tree in the back yard.

Christian shook his head. "I have no theories, no suspects. Francisco antagonized so many people. It could've been almost anyone."

Dosha shuddered and rubbed her arms that were peppered with goosebumps.

As the telephone rang, she said, "That's probably Ramon and Pia saying they are on their way over here."

"Probably."

But it was Antonia, and her usually strident voice was hushed. "I apologize for not calling earlier, but I've had a beastly headache all day and my beloved husband has left things in disarray for me to straighten out." She paused for a moment. "I also want to apologize for my friend Francisco's behavior last night. Actually he has a heart of gold, but the manners of a satyr…"

"You've not heard then?"

"There is not much I haven't heard, but I've been closeted all day with this monster headache. What did I miss?"

"Francisco was murdered this morning after he left the ball."

Antonia screamed into the phone. *"What?"*

"Yes."

"Do police know who did it?"

"I don't believe so."

"I think I would faint if I were not sitting down. My poor, poor friend. But then, I never expected him to die in his own bed," Antonia said and hung up.

Dosha turned to Christian. "Come and sit with me in the sunroom with your head in my lap." Christian nodded. "Sounds good."

Once on the sofa with his head in her lap, he told her quietly, "I went there to kill him, you know. I got as far as his door and I even raised my hand to ring his bell, but your face rose before me, begging me not to do this thing. And I thought about the baby we may have. Socorro. My father. My friends. And suddenly my life seemed very rich and full.

"The thing I can't forgive myself for was and *is* still there and it would haunt anyone with half a soul, but talking with you helped. I know that now. You always said it would."

"If only you could bring yourself to talk about the rest."

He nodded. "Tonight when we're alone, I'll try. It's not only my scars you've healed, but my spirit is healing."

And Dosha's spirits lifted. Whatever lay on his conscience, he had to forgive himself, had to for the sake of the child they hoped to have and for their marriage. Had she actually said to him that she would leave him? She knew now she never could.

The door chimes sounded and Estela led Pia and Ramon back. Pia carried a gaily wrapped package. "Wild plum preserves," she explained. "Ramon raved over them, so I thought I'd share with you two." She set the package on a table.

Then Pia was somber. "Have you listened to the evening news?"

Christian shook his head. "We turned off TV all day. The radio. We've only listened to music."

"It's just as well," Ramon said. "Francisco's death is the news. Every channel. Do you have any idea who did it?"

"No," Christian said. "No idea at all."

"You know," Pia suddenly said, "all the way over I kept wishing I could hear you play Chopin's Nocturne in E Minor. Would you play it for us?"

"Of course."

They went into the living room and Dosha sat down at the piano and then slowly began to play. This was one of her favorite pieces and Christian often asked her to play it for him.

The music calmed and soothed them all and finally, when she had finished, they applauded her.

"That was so beautiful," Pia said. "Could we please hear your newest composition, the one about the waterfall?"

"'Moonlight and the Waterfall,'" Dosha told them and began the eerily similar sounds of rushing water cascading down a hill.

"Dear Lord, that is beyond beauty," Christian said. He closed his eyes and all the anxiety and torment left him for the next minutes as his beloved put her heart and soul into her music. Their honeymoon and the time at the waterfall filled him and he could feel her tender flesh pressed against his. He remembered other times when she had played for him alone.

They were back on the sun porch when his father and another policeman came in. Montero didn't waste time. "My son," he said gravely. "I've come to arrest you for the murder of Francisco Salazar."

Christian felt as if the breath had been knocked out of him. "I didn't kill Francisco," was all he could manage.

His father's voice was formal. "There is a couple who will testify that they saw you in front of the house around the time Francisco was killed. You were at the door as if you were coming out. Then they saw you pacing back and forth in front of the house."

"I don't deny that, but it does not add up to my killing him."

His father continued. "After I called Dosha, I went to Francisco's house and I, too, saw you there."

"Then you must have seen me leave."

"I did. But whether you left before or after he was slain, I don't know." And he repeated, "I now arrest you for the murder of Francisco Salazar."

Socorro's voice sounded from the doorway. "Rafael, do you not know your own son? If you don't, I do. Christian could never do this thing. He couldn't kill."

Rafael Montero half closed his eyes. "Christian *is* my son, but I've worked with human torment nearly all my life. And I know as much as I know anything that *all* humans are capable of murder. At any given time, a man or a woman is capable of, will do *any* foul deed."

"No. Please God, no!" Socorro moaned.

The captain's eyes on Socorro were kind. "You know how this must hurt me, but it has to be. The law is above me, above my son and a man has been murdered."

Socorro said, "Please give him time to clear himself. And he *can* clear himself. If he had done this thing, I would know it and my heart and the spirits tell me he is innocent."

"I'm sorry," Captain Montero said.

"I'm going with him," Dosha said.

The captain nodded. "You may ride with us in the police car." He looked at Socorro. "But not you, Socorro. Only one can go."

Socorro turned then and fled the room. There were prayers on her mind and in her heart. And the spirits called to her to talk with them.

At the police station, Dosha sat in a waiting room while Christian was booked and fingerprinted and photographed. She was cold and numb and she tried to look ahead to a brighter time. Like Socorro, she believed in Christian's innocence, had to believe in it or lose her grip on sanity.

Finally, her father-in-law came to her. "He wants to talk with you," he said. "I can allow you twenty minutes. We don't have sufficient evidence to hold him indefinitely, but we *can* hold him for four days. I only pray that by that time, something or someone will have been able to clear him."

Christian sat on the side of his bunk bed, alone in his cell. He tried to smile as she walked in, but couldn't. She went to him and he stood up. Their kiss was impassioned, drowning in need.

Gently he disengaged her arms from his neck and he told her, "*Querida,* I said I would try to tell you the thing that torments me so. Sit on the bed with me."

And Dosha sat, little aware of the guard pacing slowly outside the cell. Christian cleared his throat and began.

"The night Isabel ran off the rain-slicked road—and died, she came to me. She had spent the previous days in a villa Antonia owned, to be away from me, she said.

"It was raining when she came and she said that being pregnant, she shouldn't be out in weather like this. I was stunned. She hadn't mentioned being pregnant. Francisco was out of town. Her father had died and she now wanted the divorce as soon as possible. She said she would marry Francisco and they would move away. Again, I asked her to reconsider. I felt as if my heart had been torn out of me.

"Isabel could be cruel and she was cruel that night. No, she said, she didn't love me, had never loved me. She had lied to me. She had always wanted Francisco and now she had him. I raged at her that Francisco belonged to *all* women and would never belong to one. I think I got through to her because she looked stricken.

"She was very defiant. 'Francisco and I belong together,' she said. 'You and I never have. I didn't want your baby, but I *want* his. Figure that one out for yourself.'

"I knew then that she loved him, that she had loved him all the time she was married to me and I went mad, I think. The child I wanted. All the pain she had caused me washed over me and I wanted to kill them both.

"'Then *go* with him' I yelled at her. 'And may God damn you both.'

"Reality closed in on us then and we realized it had begun to storm. She asked if she could stay until it had eased up, or the night if it didn't. And I refused her, drove her away. She was going to the hills, I guess back to Antonia's cottage or to Francisco's when she ran off the road. I should have taken pity on her, but I was beyond pity. She died on that road as surely as if I had killed her."

"But you were *hurt*—unbearably hurt. Surely you can see that," Dosha cried.

"All I can see is that I wanted them both dead for what they had done to me. My heart was crushed and savage with hate. I felt I had strange power that night, like Socorro. I could bend the world to my will. Destroy if I wanted to. I wanted her dead, and it has always seemed to me I killed her. And now him."

Dosha shook her head. "I hope talking about this with me clears your mind. You can't keep torturing yourself."

The time was up then and both were crying bitter tears when they parted.

As he had said he would, Captain Montero sent her home in a police car and all the way she thought, she had to call her brother, Marty, when she got home.

That night the dream came early. In a meadow she held a darling baby in her arms and Christian stood by looking at them fondly. Her heart nearly burst with love for their child and she was happier than she had ever been.

Then suddenly a black cloud enveloped them and in the darkness the baby was snatched from her. She looked to the heavens, unbelieving, and Christian swore helplessly. Then she was crying, crying bitter, wretched tears, like Socorro's vale of tears.

She woke up panting and couldn't sleep for the rest of the night.

Chapter 25

Next morning Dosha came groggily awake after only a few hours of sleep. At first she was numb, her mind a blank, then the previous afternoon came flooding back to her. Christian was in jail for the murder of Francisco. She groaned for a moment, then buried her face in her pillow.

She had called Marty and he couldn't get a flight out until the next day for any price. He had been astonished about Christian and of course he knew Francisco. "You hold up, you hear," he told her. "When you were in the hospital, Caitlin and I would've come, but you were out of the woods so quickly. Now the twins have mild flu and I'll be coming alone. Caitlin sends love. Give Chris my best and let him know I know he couldn't have done this thing."

Just then she was aware of a queasiness in her stomach that was growing worse. Dear God, she couldn't be sick now when Christian needed her. Flu was going around here too. She quickly threw her legs over the side of the bed and ran to the bathroom. Inside, she knelt in front of the toilet bowl and gave up all the food in her stomach in one big retch.

Once finished, she began to laugh a little with tears in her eyes. She had carefully monitored her sister-in-law, Caitlin's, pregnancy and it had begun something like this.

Standing up, she got her early pregnancy test kit from the medicine cabinet and with shaking fingers went through the procedure. Her eyes went wide. *It was positive!* Of course, she would need a blood test to make certain, but if it was true, then Christian would have something to be happy about. She would tell no one until the blood test confirmed it.

Going into her kitchenette, she got orange juice and made herself a soft-boiled egg and toast. She could barely wait until nine o'clock when she would call her doctor's office and arrange for a visit.

Two hours later, dressed and waiting for Pia who would go with her to the doctor's, Dosha couldn't remember a time when she had been so nervous. The same doctor who had seen Caitlin when she was pregnant in Puerto was Dosha's doctor and he was cordial. The lab was in the same building and he would put through a rush request.

Time seemed to go both swiftly and in slow motion. Just as she was about to leave, the phone rang and it was Captain Montero.

"I wanted you to know that your CEO is here at the police station and he's talking with Christian. I had to ask that an exception be made to a shorter visiting period today because Christian talked with you yesterday after he was arrested. I don't have to tell you that this job is as political as it's bureaucratic. The CEO is one of our powerhouses, and he wanted you to know he will call you when he has finished talking with Christian.

"Dosha, I love you like a daughter and I couldn't have chosen a finer wife for my son."

The lump in Dosha's throat made it hard for her to talk. "And I couldn't have chosen a better father-in-law."

On the way to the doctor's office, Pia was delighted, but a little apprehensive about a possible false pregnancy. "Well, we'll put that one to bed in a little while," she said. "What's the news about Christian?"

"His father says Christian is holding up well. The CEO is visiting him this morning and will call me. We're so lucky to have him as our boss."

"*Sí.* We *are* lucky."

A little while later the test was complete and the doctor put an arm around Dosha's shoulders. "First, I'm so sorry about Christian. Any fool would know he couldn't do this thing. If I'm to judge by the glow on your face, I would say your dreams are about to be realized, but glows, as we know, can mislead us. Call me early this afternoon for your test results."

"Thank you," Dosha said.

"Give Christian my best regards and when he's home—as I'm certain he *will* be—come back to see me again. We'll talk about babies and the care of you and your baby." And he chuckled, "Not to mention the hapless father."

They were on their way home when Dosha wanted to stop to pick up a box of the candy that Christian favored. They were inside the candy shop and a worker was gift-wrapping the package when Dosha's cell phone rang. To her delight, it was the CEO.

"My dear, I'll not ask how you are because I can imagine how you are. I've talked with Christian and I want to assure you that we at Banc International will do everything in our power to get to the bottom of this.

"At any rate, we'll hire the best lawyers available and we'll also get the best private investigators. You might be surprised to find out what they can uncover. Christian is in good spirits and that's always helpful. I've come to love him like a son since I've worked with him and we'll leave no stone unturned. With Francisco I did my best, but I couldn't reach that part of him that lived away from the laws of God and mankind."

He cleared his throat and his voice was hoarse. "Francisco's father was my friend and I feel I failed them both, but only God can judge."

"You did your best," she said simply. "No one could ask for more."

He sighed. "You're right, of course. I'm being remiss. I need to know how *you* are holding up."

"I have to be there for my husband."

"As we're there for you. My wife sends her love."

"Thank you. I don't have to tell you that your kindness and concern at a time like this means so much."

"Everything that we *can* do, we *will* do. Captain Montero tells me that your brother is having difficulty getting a fast flight. I can remedy that. Please call him and tell him one of our corporate jets will pick him up this afternoon."

Dosha couldn't help crying as she thanked him profusely. And she thought, with people like this behind him, with Socorro's, Captain Montero's and her love behind him, there was no way could Christian kill Francisco. But Christian was Puerto to the bone and Puerto men took the honor of their women seriously.

She told herself that Christian had traveled widely, had lived abroad and was cosmopolitan. However, when it came to matters of the heart, the inner heart was likely to win. And what if Christian *had* gone inside to talk with Francisco and Francisco had further insulted her? She didn't want to think about Christian's answer and the possible consequences.

* * *

The call came from the doctor's office around two-thirty that afternoon. The pregnancy test was positive. "Come in as soon as possible and talk with me about prenatal care," the doctor said. Her cries of joy brought Estela from the kitchen.

The doctor's pleasure was infectious. "Congratulations to you and Christian and may this be the beginning of a large and happy family."

She thanked him, quickly told a beaming Estela and Pablo the news and went racing up to Socorro who sat down with her hand spread over her heart.

"Oh, my *dear,* a baby in the family. Not since Christian have I had that pleasure. Have you told him?" Getting up she hugged Dosha tightly for a few minutes.

"No, I see him briefly this afternoon and I wanted to wait, to make sure."

"A wise move. Give him my love. Tell him I expect him home any minute now."

Dosha smiled and placed a hand on her stomach. "Little one," she said softly, "you are coming into a family that wants you so much."

Later that day, Dosha found Christian in surprisingly good spirits. She went to him, hugged him and they kissed, oblivious to three other couples in the visiting room. She whispered in his ear, "How does it feel to be a father?"

He held her a little away from him, his eyes blazing happily. "What do you mean?"

"What do you think I mean?" She placed his hand on her stomach. "It'll be a while before your baby moves, but use your imagination as I'm doing, Daddy."

Chapter 26

"Marty! Thank God you're here!"

It was 1:00 p.m. Dosha and Marty hugged each other with fervor. His heart hurt for her; her happiness at her pregnancy couldn't erase the pain of Christian's troubles.

Immediately he asked her, "When will I be able to see Christian?"

"Not until this afternoon at two. That's visiting hour."

He nodded. "How's he taking this?"

"He's trying to hold on. He's happy about the baby."

"Yeah. We're all happy about the baby. Are you okay? No, let me rephrase that. Do you think you can hold on?"

"Yes, I think so. Have you eaten? I can fix you whatever you'd like for lunch."

He shook his head. "On the private jet, we had a feast for brunch."

His luggage that was delivered with him sat on the floor nearby and she glanced at it. "Can you stay a while?"

"You see the big bag? It'll hold me for four or five days, then I've to go back, but if you and Chris need me, I can return and stay a while."

"Good. Come let me take you to Socorro and I'll help you unpack your things."

"You'll do no such thing. I'll have my bags unpacked in a jiffy. Caitlin has trained me well. She sends you all kinds of love and she'll come, too, a little later. Lord, Sis, I just can't believe this."

"Neither can we. Would you like to lie down a while?"

"I'm too jumpy. After we see Chris, I'd like to go down to the Charcot del Plaza just to look around and pretend that things are still the way they were when I lived here. Sis, Chris and I were a pair, both having trouble big time with cheating women, crying in our beer, our hearts torn up."

She smiled a bit. "Now look at you. You've both got women who worship you..."

"And whom we worship." He looked thoughtful. "Sometimes we just have to look past the present, but I want to know more about you."

They sat in his room and talked about the tarantula, the poisoning, Marta's death and Francisco.

Marty's sanguine face was calm. "I can't say I ever liked Francisco. I knew he was envious of my buddy and things were never right between them. But Francisco pretended otherwise. He asked for an invitation to your wedding and got it. After he met you, Christian was so happy, he would have given anybody anything they wanted from him. You've made him happy. That's for certain."

"And he has made me happy." She mentioned the portrait he had painted of Isabel that hung in the living room alcove.

"I guess that's one of my best."

"Chris offered to move it to the museum, but I wouldn't

let him. I hardly see the woman when I look at that painting. It's your painting it I see."

He nodded. "You always were one of my biggest fans. Sis, can you tell me a little more about what happened the night of the ball?"

She told him hesitantly, reluctantly reliving the whole sorry mess. Christian's fury at the kiss. The things he had told her about himself and Isabel. The vivid love they had made. When she paused, he said, "I remember so well the hell Isabel put him through. It seems the whole city knew about Francisco and her, but Christian didn't believe it in the beginning. He loved her so."

Only then did she tell him that Christian had gone out, had stayed out a while, that his father and others had seen him at the front door of Francisco's house and seen him pacing up and down in front of the house.

He abruptly stopped her. "You know his state of mind. Do you think he killed Francisco?"

She didn't answer immediately. Then she said, "He's always gone away from me to places I couldn't reach in his heart and mind. I know he still suffers. We talked the night of the ball, but he couldn't tell me everything. Then the day they arrested him, he told me. He keeps feeling guilty." She told him what Christian had told her in jail. Marty's eyes were sad as he said, "Poor guy."

She came back to the earlier thread of their conversation. "Do I think Christian killed Francisco? Marty, how can I know? He was beside himself with rage when he left here that night. You know Puerto and how a man regards the honor of his woman..."

"Yeah, I do know. But I know, too, that Puerto can be lighthearted, fun loving and overlook much. The hostile thing between Christian and Francisco was very old, and Christian was always hurt about it. Finally, he *did* believe what he heard about Isabel and Francisco and it shattered him. Then, too, he wanted children and Isabel refused to give them to him. That hurt..."

She looked at him steadily. "I don't want to believe he killed Francisco and I don't think I do believe he did. I know he didn't mean to, but a human being has a breaking point, Marty, and I think Chris was at his. Let's talk more about this later. Socorro will want to see you."

In Socorro's apartment a little later, she and Marty embraced. "If only you could have come back at a happier time," Socorro said.

"I'll return later, when Chris is free," he said. "I'll host a party on the Charcot del Plaza and how we'll dance, you and I."

"No one dances like you," she told him, "and I'll look forward to that time. You will see Christian this afternoon?"

"First possible time. You *are* taking care of yourself? At times like this, only God can take us through."

"You are right. The spirits tell me that there is more trouble ahead, much more that will burden our hearts and make us all sad. But tonight I saw a rainbow in my vision, beautiful and from God, so there will be an end to this. But when, dear Lord, when?"

Socorro blinked back tears. "I'm sure Dosha has asked, but is there anything you would like to eat? A little wine perhaps. I still keep your favorite wines here." She smiled at Dosha. "I used to call Marty and Chris my boys and I spoiled them shamefully."

"Later I'd like some of the wine," Marty said, "but not now. I'll just stay and talk with you two and restlessly await the time when I can see Chris."

Dosha looked thoughtful. "There is one thing we need to do, set up an impromptu conference call with the family. They'll want to know everything. After that, we can leave."

* * *

They managed to get Mel and Rispa on the conference line. Adam was at his office, Damien was available, and they all told Dosha how much they loved her. Dosha's two sisters-in-law were at work.

"How's Christian?" Adam asked. "Anything new?"

"No, nothing," Dosha said.

"From what you tell me, the evidence is weak, but strange things have happened with circumstantial evidence."

"You're right," Dosha said.

"I'll come if you need me," Adam said. "Any one of us will."

"You bet, baby," Mel and Rispa said as one.

"Right now," Dosha said forlornly, "there isn't anything anyone can do."

Chapter 27

Rafael Montero sat in his office with his feet propped on his desk. He had been a very busy man since Francisco Salazar's murder. No new evidence pointing to Christian's guilt had been found, but the first was damning enough. Christian had been seen by a reputable couple leaving the murdered man's house around the time Francisco had been killed.

Christian had said he went to Francisco's house in an enraged daze, found himself at the door with his hand raised to ring the doorbell and had gone back out to the walk where he paced for a while before getting into his car and going home.

Yes, Captain Montero thought, Christian's boss had provided the best the world had to offer in lawyers and it was likely that Christian would serve no time, but the gossip would always besmirch his good name, and his position at Banc International would be compromised.

"Captain." A young policeman knocked and came in. "I've more reports on the investigation you wanted me to pursue. The bank statements have come through for the past three to four years and they show a clear pattern. At the beginning of that time, Señor Salazar was frequently overdrawn and large checks were made out to a man we've found to own a gambling casino in the south of Spain.

"Then over three years ago, large deposits of money began to be made by the señor and they continue to be made. The last deposit was three weeks ago for one hundred thousand dollars."

The captain whistled and repeated the sum. "This was by check?"

"No. All transactions were by cash."

"I see. Did he continue to pay large sums of money to the gambling casino owner?"

"Yes. Three weeks ago also he made a payment of seventy thousand dollars. The señor, apparently, loved to gamble."

"Apparently."

"Sir, I continue to work on the other matters you assigned me. I told you I'm gathering information on the married woman the señor was involved with. Her husband had sworn to kill the señor, but he's been away in Germany for the past two weeks. He's to return shortly."

The captain nodded. "The minute he returns, have him brought in for questioning. Bring the woman in as soon as possible. Thank you and that will be all for now."

Montero glanced at his watch. Dosha and Marty should be arriving to visit about now. He leaned back. Ah, that was wonderful news about the coming baby. He would be a grandfather at last and the news was lifting Christian's heart. Socorro was overjoyed to find that she would at last be a great-grandmother. It was damnable that this murder had happened. He believed his son and believed it likely that the married woman's husband had slipped back into Puerto, done the killing, then left again. Another part of him said men had killed since the beginning of time and Christian was no different.

There were no longer any gambling debts for Francisco. He had paid them all. Who had paid *him* all that money? And for what?

Promptly at two o'clock Dosha and Marty stood up as Christian walked into the visiting room. Christian kissed Dosha hungrily then turned to Marty and the men hugged, both with tears in their eyes.

"You came," Christian said simply. "I had hoped you would."

"Yes. I told Dosha that when she was sick from the poison, she was out of the woods so fast we didn't come. Then when I heard about your misfortune, I tried to book the first flight out, but in the end, as you know, your CEO had me picked up by corporate jet. So here I am. You seem to be holding up well."

"It's knowing about the baby, I'm sure, but even before that, it's knowing that I'm innocent. I didn't *do* this thing..."

Marty nodded. "I know that in my deepest heart. Keep your hopes high. Somehow I just feel you'll be exonerated. How can it be otherwise?"

"I think you're right."

Dosha looked at Christian as hungrily as he looked at her. Then he smiled broadly. "How *are* you, *querida,* and how is the baby?"

"We're both doing well, I think. We're both waiting for you to come home."

He smiled a bit, then she told him, "*Queridò,* I brought you a newspaper. When I was here before, I told you about the articles and you wanted to see one. Today, there is a longer, more comprehensive article about the whole affair.

They wanted to interview me and I didn't think this was the time. If you'd rather not see it now..."

"Please leave it with me. I'll ask the guard if I may keep it. And thank you." He reached over and gripped her hand.

As the two men talked about Marty's family and Puerto when Marty had lived there, Dosha felt a flash of sadness. God couldn't be cruel enough to let Christian languish in prison for a murder he didn't commit, but God moved in mysterious ways.

The same young policeman came again to Captain Montero's door and knocked. This time the captain was in deep thought and he was gruff. He missed talking to his son and his heart was daily growing more troubled. "Come in," he said impatiently.

The young policeman seemed eager and anxious. "Sir, there is a couple here to see you. They say they have news about Señor Salazar's murder you will want to hear..."

"News about... Well, show them in."

The captain told himself not to get too hopeful. In cases like this people came out of the woodwork, crazy people, people looking for publicity, people wanting to settle old grudges. He stood as the couple came in, came from around the desk and shook hands with them.

When they were seated, he asked if they wanted coffee or some other beverage and both shook their heads. Both people were attractive. The young man hunched his shoulders. "Right now, captain, I'm not sure either one of us could hold a cup of coffee, our hands are trembling so. We're sorry it has taken us so long to come forward because we wanted to come the very day it happened. You see..." He stopped, frowning.

"Yes, go on."

"Marisa and I are in love and her mother thinks I'm not

a proper husband for her. I'm poor, but I don't intend that that will always be the case. She's twenty and I'm twenty-one and we *will* be married..."

The captain nodded, trying to hide his impatience. "I believe in love, and I congratulate you both."

The young man wet his lips. "We were in the park across the street from the murdered man's house." He blushed bright crimson. "After a tryst. We saw this man pull up a bit down the street and after a while get out of his car. He seemed to us a bit disoriented. He walked slowly to the gate, opened it and went to the door. But he was only there a minute before he turned and came back down the steps, and came out the gate, closed it and began to walk back and forth."

The captain leaned forward, his heart beating fast. Listen carefully, he told himself, then prayed, dear God, let this be what we need it to be. "This man didn't go into the house?" he prompted.

"No. Never. He paced maybe ten minutes on the sidewalk, then he went back to his car, got in and drove away. We were there an hour after that and he didn't come back. But captain, someone else *did* come after him."

The captain was electrified. Two pieces of good news. "Yes," he prompted again. "Can you give me a description of that person?"

"I can give you a description, but not a good one because the person wore a cloak and a hood—black or some dark color. That person walked up to the gate, opened it and walked to the door, let himself in and we never saw him come out."

"You couldn't tell if this was a man or a woman?"

"No, because the person was medium height and so covered up. Anyway, we saw the señor who was arrested and we think we know he didn't do it. We didn't come forward because then her mother would know about us meeting each other. Then, too, we're afraid. A person like the one in the cloak and the hood could be dangerous to us. We want to help, but is protection possible for us?"

"Yes, you will have police protection if you *are* willing to cooperate fully."

"Yes, we are. We've grieved over the thought of an innocent man being held for a murder we're sure he didn't commit. We were there until nearly five o'clock and no one other than those two people went near that house."

"How soon did the person in the cloak and hood come after the first person left?"

"About a half hour. In the meantime, we saw another couple get out of their car and go into their house. And a car parked down the street while the man was pacing and pulled off after he left." The captain nodded. That would have been his car.

"I cannot begin to tell you how thankful I am that you came forward. Your testimony will be immensely helpful."

"We're happy to do this," the young man said. "We know now that this man being held is your son and we're sorry for his troubles."

They stood then and the captain shook hands with them again. The captain blinked back tears and offered a prayer of gratitude. The scales were more than even now. The first couple had said they felt Christian *could* have come back later. This young couple had given a more likely scenario.

Leaning back in his chair, Rafael Montero stroked his chin and wondered if there were other witnesses who'd seen the cloaked figure. A figure bent on murder.

Chapter 28

Christian was free!

Puerto de la Cruz sang with the news. The first couple who had come to Captain Montero had come to the police station and said they had reconsidered. They simply could no longer say they had seen Christian coming out of Francisco's house. They had seen him outside the door and their imaginations had done the rest. They said they didn't want an innocent man punished for a murder he didn't commit.

So Captain Montero happily found himself back to square one in the investigation of Francisco's murder, but a terrible weight had been lifted from his shoulders. At least *Christian* hadn't done it. Now he stood in his son's house with friends who had come to wish Christian and Dosha well. News about Dosha's pregnancy had spread fast and there were added congratulations.

Marty was still there. He hugged his sister and his friend. "I'll do quick sketches of you two before I leave. And don't forget I'll finish the wedding portrait I'm doing of you from sketches and from you when you return to America. Only I'll have the beautiful, happy subject to work from." He took photos of them for the family back home.

"Now that's a painting I'd pay a king's ransom for," Christian said.

"And it all comes free. I'm sure it'll be one of my best."

Dosha, Christian and Marty had talked twice on conference calls with the Steele family back in Minden and D.C. and with Damien in Nashville.

Antonia was one of the first to hug Christian. "Ah, I knew you could never do such a thing." Huarto gave him a hearty hug.

Christian could only stand in his living room, smiling happily with Dosha by his side. He caught her hand and squeezed it. "Tell me I'm not dreaming," he said.

"You're home with me and this is no dream," she told him. "What you just went through was a nightmare."

In the midst of all the friends, they both breathed silent prayers of thanks as they had since he'd been free.

Pia and Ramon were overjoyed and stayed close by the side of their friends. Now Pia's face was giddy with delight. "We're both powerfully pregnant," she mused.

"And happy to be so," Dosha responded.

She saw Socorro winding her way over to them. Once there she grabbed her grandson in a bear hug and told him, "I don't think I'll let you two go to America in January. I never want you far away from me again."

They were interrupted by a woman news reporter asking questions. "Were you ever afraid you would be found guilty?"

Christian shook his head. "I was afraid of so many things, but I felt close to God through this ordeal. And my wife has been a wonderful person to have on my side, along with the rest of my family and my friends.

"The CEO of Banc International, my boss, has stood by me from the beginning and I'm more grateful than I can ever fully express..."

The reporters asked Christian to kiss Dosha and he did until she blushed and whispered to him, "We're not alone, *querido.*"

"But in my heart we are alone," he murmured.

Antonia came back to them. "Carmela sends her love," she said. "She never doubted for a minute that you would be free. Just now she is again caught up with one of her girls. A family crisis. Such devotion. It would be well spent on a child of her own. I was so happy when I was carrying her." She glanced at Pia. "Both of you will soon begin to know that joy, if you don't feel it already."

Dosha laughed. "I think I felt it even before I knew I was pregnant."

"Um-m, me, too," Pia said.

The food was catered by a group who had offered their services free. Now Christian said, "I'm going to the kitchen to tell Pablo and Estela to come out and enjoy the festivities. There are enough servers here to serve the servers. Those two don't need to work so hard."

The same musicians played now that had played at the *Baile de Isabel* and at La Carnaval, adding their joy to this occasion. Dosha couldn't stop a blush of pure joy as the fantasy of their dancing the naked samba raced through her mind.

Pedro Montez came to her. "I couldn't wish such happiness on a more worthy couple," he told her. Then he grinned. "I'll wait until Christian returns, then ask him if I may dance with you."

In the kitchen, Christian spoke with Estela and Pablo who took him up on his offer and thanked him profusely. On the way back to the group, Juan stopped him, his face somber.

"Señor," he said, "you've always treated me with the greatest respect and I've always appreciated it, but I've not always treated you with the same respect. Now, please accept my deepest apologies."

Christian looked at Juan, puzzled. "I've never noticed that you treated me with anything other than respect. I don't understand."

Juan nodded, sighing. "But you *will* understand. Sometime soon you *will* understand."

Juan moved away then and Christian stood looking after him, then he went back to those celebrating his freedom. By Dosha's side, he held up his hand for silence.

"My family and my friends," he said, "this is a happy time for me and for you. But in the midst of our joy and celebration, let's not lose sight of the fact that a man who lived among us has been cut down in his prime. He lies cold and silent where we are warm and laughing. So let's grieve even as we celebrate and thank God for our lives and our good fortune."

A long moment of silence followed Christian's short speech, then someone began to chant Christian's name. The love and the friendship in this room filled Dosha and Christian's heart. And Dosha thought now her life was everything she wanted it to be. She wasn't afraid any longer, only happy.

Chapter 29

As Dosha moved about in the lovely honeymoon cottage rooms of Cielito Linda, she reflected that life had settled down nicely. Christian was attending a series of meetings for directors of Banc International. The meetings would end tonight and they had decided to spend a week at the honeymoon cottages.

She hugged herself. Nothing else had happened in almost a month. Juan had confessed to Captain Montero that Francisco and he had sent the wedding photo of Dosha lying dead in a wedding gown. The captain had notified Adam, but they had decided against pressing charges.

It was 7:00 p.m. and after a long, leisurely bath sprinkled with French lavender, she had lain on the bed, naked, her soft, tender body alive with imagining Christian at her side. Now she had dressed in dusky rose silk lounging pajamas with a long leopard-print scarf at her waist and gold sandals. Shining gold hoops were in her ears and she wore a matching wide gold bracelet. Pregnancy made her skin glow and she simply looked forward to life.

She surveyed the round dining table in the dining area. Covered with padded rose damask, it was a perfect background for the excellent wedding gifts friends and relatives had given her. Royal Doulton china. Oneida silverware. Waterford crystal. Christian would be home around eight-thirty and they would have dinner. She thought about the meal she had prepared, beginning with shrimp paella and... She had to call Caitlin and just talk about female things. At a knock on the door, she frowned. Now who?

Going to the door, she found Carmela standing there. The woman looked terrible, she thought. What on earth was the matter? She was as pale as a ghost.

"May I come in?" Carmela's voice was hoarse, ragged.

"Yes, of course. Carmela, what's wrong?"

Carmela shook her head and she looked dazed. She carried her purse and a large tote. "May I use your bathroom?"

"Of course." Dosha told her where the bathroom was and Carmela went in.

Damn, Dosha thought, I expect she'll want to visit a while and I *did* want to talk with Caitlin. It didn't seem long before the door opened. Dosha was at the windows looking at the newly dark terrain. She and Christian had spent their honeymoon in this cottage and the waterfall wasn't far away. Carmela cleared her throat and Dosha turned as her breath nearly stopped and she froze.

Carmela stood before her garbed in a long black cloak and hood, her face a blazing white. "Sit down!" she commanded.

Refusing to be bullied, Dosha did some commanding of her own. "Carmela, what *is* this? What're you doing? And why are you looking at me like that?"

The shock had been so great that at first Dosha didn't see the small silver gun Carmela held.

"I'm not playing with you. *Sit down!*"

"All right, but you must tell me…" Dosha slowly lowered herself to the sofa.

"I'll tell you that you will never bear a child for Christian. The child you carry will be born in hell. Only *I* will bear Christian's child."

"What are you talking about and please put the gun away. What *is* wrong with you?"

Slowly Dosha's mind cleared and icy fingers traced along her spine. She was smothering in fear. *Carmela was mad. Carmela hated and was going to kill her.*

"There is nothing wrong with me that Christian's love won't cure."

"My husband Christian?" To her own ears, Dosha thought she sounded foolish. And it came to her in a flash. The young couple had seen someone in a long black cloak and hood let himself in Francisco's house and never come out. With horror she knew now that Carmela had killed Francisco and she was going to kill her, Dosha.

"He won't be your husband long."

Drawing a deep breath, Dosha said, "I'm expecting Christian any minute now."

Carmela shook her head and laughed scornfully. "I talked with Christian late this afternoon and he told me the meetings would end after eight. He will come home to find you dead and I'll console him later as I consoled him after Isabel's death. He was turning to me and he would've been mine if you hadn't come to Puerto.

"I've loved Christian since I was a girl, but like most men, his head is turned by *putas*." Whores. "Isabel was a *puta*. Certainly *you* are, with your fancy body and your come-hither eyes. Once you're dead, no one else will come along. He'll turn to me again, and *I* will bear his child. Oh, I've waited so long for this day."

Carmela gloated now. "Christian will come home expecting a night of romance and find a night of grief." Her laugh was soft and sinister. "But he won't grieve long, for *I* will console him. Oh, he considered me too young in the beginning, but I'm not too young now. My body cries for him."

Dosha began to get up. "No, Carmela, you *must* stop this. You're ill. Let me get help for you. I'll call your mother."

"Be still," Carmela raged. Her voice went octaves higher and she was loud and shrill where she had been quieter.

The phone rang and Carmela barked immediately. "Don't pick it up! I mean it!"

Oh, Lord, Dosha thought numbly, it was probably Christian on a break. Perhaps Caitlin. Christian was going to find her dead.

Carmela paced like a ferocious animal. "I want you to know the whole story before you die. I killed them all and I'm proud of it. *I am the angel of death.* I was close to Christian and we were falling in love before Isabel began to flaunt her wares at him. I confided in her that I was in love with him and she laughed at me. 'Just watch me take him from you,' she challenged me. And she *did* marry him. Men are such fools. I married Arturo because my father said I should be married and I'm a dutiful daughter.

"Arturo knew I didn't love him, but he made the best of it. Then Isabel told him that I was in love with Christian and he began to accuse me of still loving Christian which I did. How could I deny it? He accused me of sleeping with Christian. Of course I denied it, but he wanted a divorce. There has not been a divorce in our family for over two hundred years. So I had to poison him with the poison from the rainforests of Brazil, the yellow lily.

"The doctors all thought it was a heart attack, but Isabel suspected the truth. She had been at our house often and knew I got packages from Brazil. She knew I was interested in botany. She was too clever. A few months after Arturo died, she began to threaten to go to Captain Montero with her suspicions. She signed her own death warrant."

Carmela's eyes glittered.

"I had a run of pure luck. I was passing the house the night Isabel came out into the storm. I saw her face in the porch lights during a lull in the storm and knew she was torn up. You see, I knew all about Francisco and her. I told Christian, but he refused to believe me.

"Very well, so I followed her as she drove to the hills. Fate was kind. I had waited for a chance to kill her. I felt she was going to a cottage Francisco had there and I followed her and knew what had to be done. I crowded her off the road from the slick pavement down a steep embankment. She died in that accident, as I meant her to. Had I failed, I would have found another way. The fates have blessed me. They mean for me to have Christian. Then, too, I killed her to keep her from destroying him."

She had to make a move. Dosha struggled to find something to say. "You're a religious woman. You can't live with this. Don't add another killing to your sins."

"*Don't speak to me of sins, you strumpet.* He was mine and you stole him as Isabel stole him. After Isabel was dead, I took Marta under my wing. She was sent home and I visited her there. I was the one who asked that she be let back. Christian and Socorro agreed. And oh, she was my worshipful ally. With a little luck, she would have succeeded in killing you with the tarantula and when that failed, the yellow lily. But it didn't happen. You were damnably resistant.

"I visited Marta in the juvenile home and I convinced her that she couldn't go on, that death was the only answer. I took her the poison and she did my bidding."

Dosha closed her eyes against tears that ran hot and cold at once. To die at the hands of a madwoman. She didn't expect Christian before eight-thirty. No one else was to come by. She was trapped and as good as dead.

Carmela paused and looked at Dosha long and hard. "Killing you is going to be the sweetest of all. But first, about Francisco. Then I will almost be finished. Francisco knew about Isabel's death and Isabel had told him she felt certain I killed Arturo. He happened to be driving by on the nearly deserted country road where I forced Isabel's car off. He told me later he parked a little away and watched the whole thing. He blackmailed me not to go to Captain Montero and I paid him. I felt I had no choice. I didn't want to kill again."

"But Francisco got greedier and he was bleeding me dry. I inherited a lot of money on Arturo's death and I had money of my own, but at the rate Francisco was going, it wasn't going to last forever.

"Francisco is a family friend. He and my mother were especially close and of course, my mother and I aren't close. I took his key from her ring of keys and kept it and the night I killed him, everything worked perfectly. He was falling-down drunk and stumbled into his house. I parked on a side street and waited. I crouched down and saw Christian drive up, get out and go to the house. 'No, my darling, don't,' I cried to myself. 'I'll do it for you.'

"After Christian left, I put on my cloak and hood, went to Francisco's house and let myself in. He was sitting in his study at his desk when I walked in. He was still very drunk, but he sobered a bit when he saw me with the gun.

"'No, don't do it,'" was all he said, and I shot him four times directly in the heart. I had a silencer made to muffle the shots and he never tried to stop me. I waited to see if he was dead and when his eyes rolled back in his head, I went to his safe. I knew the combination and I took out stacks of money. I was taking back as much as I could. I left by the back way."

Carmela looked exultant then, proud of what she had done. Dosha couldn't help looking at the ravaged face of her tormentor who looked as if she were pursued by a thousand evil spirits.

"I'll give you a minute to pray for your wicked soul, then I'll kill you."

And Dosha prayed with all her heart for Christian, herself, her baby, and for Carmela. She sat transfixed with icy fear, wanting to place her hand over her abdomen with her growing child. Her mind was crystal clear.

"Stand up. *It is time!*"

It seemed to Dosha that there was some movement outside and she fought down a hysterical desire to laugh. That was wishful thinking on her part, she thought. She stood up on knees almost too weak and shaky to hold her. She had no tears; it was too late for tears. The minutes seemed endless and her whole body was covered with goosebumps and ice cold sweat.

Dosha's glance was drawn to her engagement and wedding rings and the jade ring Socorro had given her. Where was the luck it was supposed to bring her? Then she felt a calmness spread through her and knew that she would fight to the bitter end.

Carmela smiled a twisted little smile from hell. Dosha saw the other woman's muscles tighten and knew that she would pull the trigger. She had nothing to lose as she began to throw herself on the mad woman.

It happened all at once. There was a splintering sound and the door burst open as Christian and the manager rushed in.

"Drop the gun, Carmela!" Christian shouted. *"Now!"*

Carmela moved a step closer to Dosha, cried "No," and pressed the trigger.

Dosha felt the hounds of hell tearing at her flesh as she moved further over to protect her baby. But she quickly saw her blood-soaked pajamas. It seemed to her that she was hit directly in her abdomen, so there was no hope for her or the baby. As she fell, she heard another shot and thought that this meant the end for her. She had lived such a blessed life. She was only out a very little while, then in a precious few minutes, she began to regain consciousness and, opening her eyes, saw Christian's beloved face as he cradled her in his arms, his tears on her face. "*Querida, querida,*" he moaned. "Dear God, please stay with me."

It took a little while for the ambulance to come. Christian and the manager stanched the blood as best they could and they bathed Dosha's face with cool water. Christian's eyes on her body beheld everything he really wanted in this world. He barely looked at the other woman who lay dead on the floor.

Dosha's breath was labored, but she had to tell him, "I love you so much."

"And I love *you* so much. Oh, my darling wife." His tears fell on her and dimly she thought: this is Socorro's vision, her *vale of tears*. For they would all cry for her and her baby.

Blackness closed in like a warm, enveloping cloud as she felt herself falling into blessed oblivion.

Christian held her. The manager found a pillow for her head and cut and tore sheets to provide bandages as best they could.

No one of the three paid attention to the woman who lay nearby as her life ended in malice, darkness and frustration.

Chapter 30

She was healthy and she was happy, so Dosha came awake in the hospital far sooner than doctors expected her to. Christian sat by her bedside holding her hand, anxiously staring at her beloved face.

"Christian," she moaned softly.

"I'm here, baby," he murmured and kissed her hand. "Don't try to talk. Just rest."

She moved a bit, wondering at the swath of bandages around her midsection. "I was shot," she murmured. "Carmela shot me. She loved you, wanted to have a baby for you."

He leaned over and placed a finger to her lips. "Hush, *querida*. That's all behind us. Carmela shot herself in the head. She's dead."

"She loved you. She said she had always loved you."

"Carmela was mad. Please don't talk about it now."

"All right. How is my baby?"

The doctor came into the room as Dosha asked the question. "Our baby is fine," he said, "and you're a miracle itself. I predict that you'll be up and around and out of here in a very short while."

Christian watched in amazement as Dosha smiled a wide, beatific smile. And both their hearts expanded with wonder. She felt sorry for Carmela who had never known what she, Dosha, knew, and now never would.

It was that afternoon before Dosha was well enough to talk and to listen. "How did you get there in time?" she asked Christian.

It was the last thing Christian wanted to relive, but he had to tell her.

"The Cielito Linda manager saw Carmela earlier and felt she was acting strangely. He knows her very well, has been worried about her and confided in me a few days ago. I meant to mention it to you. This time she passed right by him, looked right through him and he said she seemed to him quite mad. He watched her as she went to our cottage and you let her in.

"He knows you are pregnant and he wanted to look out for you. He called me and told me what was going on. I excused myself from the meeting. I had said I'd have to answer calls because of your condition. I left immediately. Fortunately, the meeting had been moved to a location closer to the cottages because of a water main break.

"I saw the manager standing in front of our front door listening, and he beckoned to me frantically to hurry. In a flash I heard Carmela threaten to kill you and together we smashed the door in with our shoulders..."

"Did you know Carmela was in love with you?"

He drew a deep breath and was silent for a few moments. 'She told me once she was. She has never been mature enough for me. I stayed away from her without being churlish since our families were friendly. I know now Carmela always seemed strange to me, somehow marked with death and it always bothered me."

He paused a very long moment and his eyes were full of tears. "Thank heaven, my darling, we weren't too late."

She stroked his hand. "Don't cry, *querido*. I'm alive and our baby is safe. The nightmare is over for us, thank God. We go on from here with each other and our little one."

He grinned then. "Make that little *ones*, because I plan to have a world of fun making many children."